# THE DEAL

# THE DEAL

## JOE HUTSKO

A TOM DOHERTY ASSOCIATES BOOK

NEW YORK

Note to Reader

This is a work of fiction. All the characters, organizations, and events portrayed in this book are fictitious or are used fictitiously. Although aspects of the story told in this novel were inspired in some respects by actual events, those events have been completely fictionalized and this book is not intended to portray, and should not be read as portraying, actual events.

A Forge Book
Published by Tom Doherty Associates, Inc.
175 Fifth Avenue
New York, NY 10010

Forge® is a registered trademark of Tom Doherty Associates, Inc.

ISBN 0-312-86872-3

First Edition: January 1999

Printed in the United States of America

0  9  8  7  6  5  4  3  2  1

To the memory of my father

Stephen M. Hutsko

# THE DEAL

# PART I

The deal was in motion.

As he guided the BMW Z3 roadster onto Highway 280, Matthew Locke felt as though his mind were spinning as quickly as the wheels that propelled him forward.

Appraising his position, he quickly cut over to the fast lane. He briefly wondered why the traffic was so light, then shrugged it off. He had more important things to think about. Bright sunlight and warm air rushed through the open windows as he gained speed and set the cruise control at seventy miles per hour.

Then Matthew noticed the clock, and realized that, for the first time in as long as he could remember, he was two hours ahead of the nightly 280 rush. His workday had ended sooner than usual. There was nothing more for him to do except wait for tomorrow to come.

Still reeling from the confrontation, he took a few deep breaths and tried to relax. He wasn't recovering from the sort of unpleasant agitation brought on by fear. No, this was the sort of nervousness that comes from excitement. The useful, energetic kind. The

kind that Locke so fondly remembered feeling more than twenty years ago, those nights before facing a final exam he knew he would ace.

Admittedly, there was maybe the smallest tinge of anxiety mingled somewhere in all of that good nervous energy. While he was always ready for a good contest or debate, he had little tolerance for unreasonable opponents.

Like Peter Jones.

Matthew had tried one last time to compromise with the stubborn founder of Via Computer, Inc. Unfortunately, the outcome had yielded exactly what he'd expected.

Nothing.

Matthew did not want things to end this way. Not exactly, anyway. But there was no alternative. It was ridiculous. The conflict that he'd just left had been more like a vicious counseling session between a distressed married couple, instead of the calm, civil encounter you'd expect between the two most senior executives of one of the decade's most innovative companies.

Thinking back on it, he'd hoped that casually dropping in on Jones, unannounced, the way he used to, would make it possible for the two to simply talk out their differences, like reasonable men. But even as he'd set out on the short stroll between his building and Jones's, he began to have doubts.

Halfway there he stopped abruptly, right at the core of the Peter Jones legacy. He looked around and observed the sprawl of Spanish-style, single-story buildings, each painted white and topped with a red tile roof.

What Jones had started nearly a decade ago in his college dorm room had blossomed into the cluster of buildings spread all around Matthew. And even farther, to offices and factories throughout the world. And here he was, caught in the middle of it all, ready to turn Peter's world upside down.

The sun beat down on Matthew's wavy black hair. He was tall and lean and dressed in casual khaki slacks and a faded blue Polo shirt. For an instant he felt unusually out of place, an imposter.

It had to be done, Matthew reminded himself. Business was business, and that's what he knew best. It was why Jones had hired him in the first place. Keep that in mind, he thought as he straightened himself up and resumed his step along the gently curving sidewalk, making his way to what employees solemnly referred to as the Epicenter.

He reached Peter's building just as a small party of engineers was heading out for a break. Matthew held the door for them, nodding his greetings as they passed by, and went inside.

Peter's friendly secretary, Ben, cut short his phone conversation the moment he saw Matthew approaching. To be polite, Matthew asked if Peter was in. But before the secretary could respond, Peter's own voice answered from behind, "No."

Matthew turned just in time to see Peter's office door slam shut. He complimented Ben on his striking new haircut, then knocked gently on Peter's door.

"Nobody's home," Peter said from behind the closed door. "Please leave a message at the tone. Beep."

Matthew was not amused. He glanced at Ben, who merely shrugged. Matthew went inside, closing the door behind him.

Peter sat typing furiously on his keyboard, his back to Matthew. He'd been through this little routine with Peter too many times to count. He would wait.

The office was small and sparsely furnished, with a simple overstuffed sofa and industrial gray carpeting. Peter sat before his computer at an expansive Scandinavian table. He wore faded Calvin Klein jeans, a gray Armani A/X T-shirt, and Teva sandals. He hummed to himself as he typed away, pretending Matthew wasn't there.

"Nobody's home," Peter eventually repeated over the sound of his clicking keyboard.

It was astonishing, Matthew thought, how Peter had changed. How everything had changed.

The feeling of a troubled father-and-son relationship was stronger than ever. With no children of his own, Matthew had, in the course of their working together, come to care deeply for Peter. He would be lying to himself if he didn't acknowledge the fact that he put his own career first. But unlike former business relationships, this one had turned very personal, and pleasantly so. As the more mature of the two, it was his duty to be firm, to put things in order, even if it meant dealing harshly with the younger man. While Matthew wanted what was best for himself, he wanted what was best for Peter, too. Indeed, Peter's cooperation would benefit them both more than if they remained at odds. And that was what he had come here to communicate. Though whether he would get through to the customarily petulant young founder was another story.

Having waited a reasonable minute or two for Peter to finish up whatever he was typing, it was time to get down to business. Calmly, Matthew said Peter's name.

The room fell silent. With an elaborate sigh, Peter slumped his shoulders. Since Matthew, now sitting on the white muslin couch, obviously wasn't going away, he might as well deal with him. He turned around.

Matthew corrected himself. One thing certainly had not changed: Peter's eyes. A brilliant shade of blue, certain and sharp, they had earned Peter the nickname "Laser Gazer," which no one ever dared say to his face.

Matthew met the infamous gaze and was almost able to hold it before wavering. Two years in the younger man's company and he had never been able to completely hold Peter's stare for more

than a few beats. It was unsettling. And stupid, Matthew privately admonished. Christ, he was exhausted by these ego games. He cut to the chase.

"I'm not here to waste your time, Peter. Or mine. But I figure it's only fair to warn you about the board meeting. Unless you and I can come to some sort of agreement, right now, on how we're going to run the business, you'll leave me no choice but to propose some drastic changes tomorrow."

Peter simply sat there and went on drilling him with his look, unfazed by anything Matthew had said. Unwilling to play the stare-down game anymore, Matthew glanced at Peter's computer screen.

For some reason his curiosity about what Peter was working on got through to the younger man, who abruptly shifted in his chair, blocking Matthew's view. When he turned back around, the screen was dark.

He gave Matthew an insincere smile. "Hey, for once we agree on something. Yeah, there'll be some changes tomorrow, Matthew. You can count on that."

The gravity in Peter's tone went unnoticed. Matthew was instead considering what he'd briefly glimpsed on Peter's screen before he'd dimmed it. It appeared to be a drawing, with little connected boxes. Probably a sketch of a new system or peripheral design, Matthew guessed. His frustration flared anew. It was precisely the sort of thing Peter should be concentrating on—working up new designs—while letting Matthew worry about running the business.

"Anyway," Peter said. "I'm tired of talking." He flicked away a shock of bright blond hair from his brow. "I know all about your plan to suggest a reorganization, Matthew. What, you're surprised? Did you think I wouldn't find out? I know everything that goes on here." He made a disgusted noise. Then, to signal the end of the

discussion, he took a pen in hand and directed his attention to a blank legal pad. He began spiraling the pen around and around, from the middle of the page outward.

"Peter, listen to me. It's not too late. The reorganization is only one possibility. If you'd just hear me out. I don't think you realize the severity of things around here. How bad it's gotten. You have to face the facts."

Peter was unmoved. He started humming to himself as he spiraled the pen wider and wider.

"The board is pissed off about schedule slips. There's the battery problem. The budget overruns. The handwriting recognition? Christ. It's become fodder for Leno and Letterman. And with the weak sales—"

That got Peter Jones's attention. He leaped to his feet, rigid with anger.

"Look, Matthew, don't fucking come into my office and tell me how to run my company. You don't know the half of it. I've wasted way too much time with you. Just leave me alone now."

Matthew held his place. "Peter, please."

"Out. Now."

It was hopeless. Matthew could see there would be no getting through to Jones. "Okay, Peter. You win." He rose to leave.

The room was still and Peter stood there breathing hard, working his menacing gaze.

Matthew turned to the door, then paused. He looked at Peter but said nothing, held the stare until finally, for the first time in Matthew's career at Via, Peter relented.

"What now?"

"That's all I want to know, Peter. Just that. What. I don't want to argue. I just want to know what."

"What's what you want to know?"

"What went wrong, between us."

Matthew steeled himself for more flailing. However, Peter's reaction surprised him as his fury abruptly gave way to a sort of melancholy.

Unable to look at Locke anymore, Peter lowered himself onto the sofa and casually crossed one leg over the other, and held the pen bearing the Via logo by each end between his fingers. Emphatically, yet softly, he explained.

"I don't know why I get worked up. I guess it's because I wanted to believe things could work out. But they can't, Matthew. They won't. Because you don't understand. Don't get it. Oh, I think you've tried your best, but it's not first nature to you. You just don't comprehend the meaning of inventing products like Via's. Yes, you're comfortable with marketing and trends and statistics, I'll give you that. But in the long run, the products are all that really matter. That they are true to the visions that inspire them." He slipped the pen into his pocket, his eyes drifting across the room to rest on his docked At Hand PC Plus prototype, his latest invention. "My visions are my products."

And then Peter sat there for a few moments wearing a rapt, slightly smiling expression, departed to a place where everything was sharp and clear, where he could see things no one else could see.

The only thing Matthew saw was a man gone—off the deep end, perhaps. Talk about virtual reality, Matthew scoffed to himself. In his estimate, Peter had lost touch with Via's business reality a long time ago. And while they'd had their share of arguments in the past, Peter had never seemed quite so unhinged. So out of touch. It was sad, really. But at the same time, Matthew felt relieved. After witnessing Peter like this, in his strange far-off state, any doubts Mathew had about proceeding with his plan were long gone.

Peter blinked. He was back. He looked at Matthew with clear

eyes. In a tone that was at once condescending and perplexed, he said, "What is it that you see, Matthew?"

The car phone jingled, snapping Matthew back to the present—and sparing him the effort of an answer.

After Matthew Locke left his office, Peter Jones readjusted the brightness knob on his monitor and went back to work.

He moved the pointer to a series of connected rectangles, and highlighted the name inside the uppermost box. He pressed the Delete key. "Matthew Locke" disappeared. Peter frowned at the literalness of this small yet meaningful act, of deleting from his computer the man who had become a threat to its promising future.

He typed in his own name, and reworded the title below it. "Acting President and CEO." Beneath his new box were many others, each labeled with the corresponding division's vice president. Peter's name appeared beneath one of these lower boxes as well, as "Vice President, At Hand PC."

It was that simple. A click here, a little typing there, and voilà, a resolution to a problem that had gotten out of hand. But that didn't mean it felt good.

The man Peter hired two years ago to run the company's day-to-day business had failed. For all his management strength, Matthew did not fit into Via's culture the way Peter had hoped he would. Looking back, he distinctly recalled the moment when he first began to doubt Matthew's value. It was when Locke had casually asked Peter if he'd ever considered building a computer that would run PCSoft's popular PortaPC operating system. Peter had just stared at him, as though he were joking. And then, as if that suggestion were not enough, Locke had gone so far as to speculate on the feasibility of aligning Via with a potential heavy-hitter partner—perhaps the world's biggest computer company, International Computer Products.

How dare he propose Via abandon its founding vision of putting powerful personal computers into the hands of the individual, in favor of selling out the company to the hugely impersonal ICP and its uninspired line of products.

Ludicrous. And Peter had merely brushed it off as naive. Now he only wished he'd paid greater attention to Locke's intimation. No wonder their friendship—if that was what you could call it—had fallen apart. Until their disagreement, they had spent nearly every Saturday together, going for long walks or drives to discuss technology, culture, trends, product concepts. Then suddenly Matthew was no longer home on Saturdays when Peter would drop by. Peter had felt wounded. He'd become closer to Matthew than to any other male acquaintance he'd ever known. Or so he believed. However, when he thought about it, he realized that he'd been the one doing most of the talking when they were together. He'd foolishly confused true friendship with what was proving to be a sort of clandestine counterintelligence gathering, Matthew now poised to take everything he'd learned and use it against Peter. In truth, the two men were as different as night and day. Had he really believed they would work well together? That they enjoyed more than a business relationship? All right, maybe he was being a bit melodramatic, overly suspicious—or maybe he was just more hurt than he was willing to admit—but whatever the excuse, he knew he couldn't let his disappointment cloud his view. Via was his life, and to lose it would be a mockery, like being publicly executed, a fate far worse than losing the only real paternal friend he'd ever known.

With their "training" sessions no longer of interest to him, Peter had devoted himself fully to completing the At Hand PC Plus. Once it shipped, it would put to rest once and for all the criticism the original At Hand PC had received. The original At Hand was the result of three years of hard work and engineering magic. It was compact and thin and easy to transport, and its

battery lasted for days on a single charge. In its simplest configuration, the device was about the size of a slender hardback book, and almost as light. It fit easily into a briefcase, and worked as either a traditional notebook computer, or as a keyboardless "slate" device. Its built-in modem made it easy to access the Net, as well as to send and receive faxes. Users interacted with the At Hand by either drawing and jotting directly on its color active-matrix display, or by using the roomy keyboard and trackpad that gracefully slid out from the unit's underside. Despite its handwriting-recognition flaws, the At Hand's flexibility drew considerable praise. Back at the office, users had the option of turning it into a powerful desktop system by simply snapping on a variety of components. All the right accessories were in place. Expanded keyboards. Mice and trackballs. Monitors. Printers. Scanners. CD-ROM drives. Stereo speakers. Network connections. Every peripheral available for ordinary PCs.

Peter clicked the Print button. His laser printer hummed, and moments later the new company organization chart rolled out.

Nowhere in the drawing did Matthew Locke's name appear.

Matthew reached for his ringing car phone. Was it Peter? If so, he could turn around at the next exit and be back in no time. Though he had every intention of proceeding with his plan as it now stood, he would nevertheless give Peter until the last minute to see things his way.

"Peter?"

"Matthew, it's Eileen." His secretary. "I called Peter's office. Ben said you left ten minutes ago. What happened?"

"The usual. It's like talking to a brick wall," he said. "If I have any important—"

"You do. Two. Janice Lane called to say she's accepted the offer to coauthor your autobiography. She informed *Fortune* this after-

noon that she would be taking a leave of absence for the length of the project. I sent her the background reading you wanted her to catch up on. Second, Laurence Merrill. You were scheduled to go over tomorrow's meeting. She's in your office now, holding on the line." His secretary said good-bye, then put through Matthew's public relations chieftain.

"Hi, Matthew. I've prepared a short press release to send over the business wire after tomorrow's board meeting." She spoke quickly, considerate of his time. She read the brief statement, and his heart quickened as she read the last line.

"'Relinquishing his role as chairman, Via cofounder Peter Jones will stay on board as the company's leading visionary, focusing on advanced technologies and future product designs.' Does that work for you?"

"Sounds fine."

"If you'd like to conduct phone interviews with key press contacts, I'll need to know now so I can make arrangements."

"Pick the ones you think are best."

Before taking her call he'd been eager to be alone to review his plans—but now, he felt oddly unwilling to end their conversation. Something about her voice had a soothing effect. Her words, spoken so decisively and with such assurance, eased his anxiety.

"When this settles down, let's spend some time together to work on my strategy for the press. A mission statement, reflecting our new, more mature perspective."

Laurence gave a lighthearted laugh. "Boy, you never slow down. Always thinking one step ahead."

Her laughter caught him by surprise. Until now, Laurence Merrill had conducted herself in a strictly businesslike fashion. In light of the seriousness of the company's current state of affairs, her easy manner was a welcome breath of fresh air. He hadn't heard laughter, or laughed himself, in a long time.

"Just the nature of the business," he said. "Anyway, thanks, Lauri."

"You're welcome. And by the way, I'd never noticed the picture on your desk here of you and your wife in the Alps. It's lovely."

His buoyant mood took a sudden nosedive with the mention of his wife, Greta. It also reminded him that he was only minutes from home. And once there, he could forget getting any serious thinking done.

He thanked Laurence again, then snapped the phone back into its cradle and settled into the comfort of the car's sculpted leather seat.

Tomorrow's meeting. The press. The future. There was so much to think about. And there was nothing he enjoyed more than pondering every angle, every detail. He couldn't wait to get all of it down in the autobiography he'd agreed to write.

He'd confided to his editor the changes that were about to occur. She had been overjoyed—the new developments would make the book more compelling and dramatic for readers. Indeed, the way Matthew saw it, tomorrow's showstopper would go down in high-tech history as merely the first in a series of thrilling chapters chronicling Via's return to the forefront of the industry. It was all part of his divine plan.

He'd spent the last six months analyzing and plotting its current phase. All the pieces were in place. Dissolving the executive staff's confidence in Peter as a leader, while building its trust and gaining its loyalty for himself as company president and CEO, had been a delicate undertaking. The first part, to gain immediate support upon arriving at Via, had gone smoothly. He had quickly become a credible and qualified champion of Via's proprietary platform—a status he admitted he could not have attained without Peter's focused coaching and friendship.

Just a year ago a *Fortune* cover touted Peter and Matthew as "The Brains and Brawn of Silicon Valley." The jocular photo of

the pair was similar to that of a Hollywood buddy film promotion poster.

On the left stood Peter, wearing his customary jeans and an emerald cashmere V-necked sweater, the sleeves pushed to the elbow and his arms folded across his chest. Of slight build and tenuous stance, his physical composure was that of a lanky high school student. Yet his eyes revealed more. They were the eyes of a man wise beyond his years, whose mind operated at a cycles-per-second rate equal to ten brains (or so the story went). He was thirty-one at the time.

Matthew stood beside Peter with one arm hanging loosely over the younger man's shoulder. He wore khaki pants and a chambray work shirt with the sleeves, like Peter's, rolled to the elbow. His thick, dark hair was a stark contrast to the subtle but noticeable creases in his face, especially around the hazel eyes. He stared into the lens with the burning determination of a college graduate who, diploma fresh in hand, sprints eagerly toward the Challenge. He was forty-four.

Tensions began to surface around six months after the cover story hit newsstands, when the newly introduced At Hand PC met with only mild commercial success. Though the device's aggressive use of breakthrough technologies had won industrywide accolades for Peter and his team of engineers, buyers were dubious—and with good reason. The device's not-quite-ready-for-prime-time handwriting recognition drew harsh criticism for its inability to interpret anything but impeccable penmanship. Peter's well-publicized dream, of making the At Hand PC the hottest-selling portable computer for the masses, turned into a bitter irony as the device's notorious misspellings got nightly laughs on *The Tonight Show*. The At Hand snatched a paltry slice of the fastest-growing market in the computer business, while software giant PCSoft's portable operating system, PortaPC, running on devices offered

by the clone makers, steadily gobbled up the largest wedge of the pie. To make matters worse, there were few applications available for the At Hand when it was introduced, and those that developers had promised were late.

As sales showed no sign of picking up, the pressure on Peter's team intensified. Enhancements that would significantly improve the handwriting recognition, among other things, were behind schedule. With so many obstacles to overcome, Peter ran for cover, leaving Matthew to contend with Via's share-sensitive executives and board members. He assured them that Peter would come through with the promised improvements, and his methodical East Coast style had an interesting effect on the anxious principals: They believed him. Tomorrow he would test that confidence with an ultimatum.

In the solitude of his car, the plan seemed like the only natural solution to curing Via's stalled condition. Still, there was no guarantee that tomorrow's decision would swing in his favor. He reminded himself of his discussion with Laurence just minutes ago, the over-and-done-with tone of her voice as she'd read his statement on the other end of the line. He felt his spirits lift.

And he felt something else lift, too. His mind's eye fixed on the image of the young and attractive Laurence, her hand clasped around the telephone's handset, her words forging a new alliance between them. He pressed his palm to his groin. He knew when he'd interviewed her for the position that her attractiveness might become a distraction. A temptation. Only once had he seen a pair of hands as beautiful, and those were his wife's.

*Were.*

And thinking this, his daydream quickly petered out. He took the Woodside exit, then turned onto the rustic road that wound its way up to his home. He downshifted and navigated the steep, twisting grade. As if commiserating with the machinery that helped him get this far, he let out an exhausted sigh.

On either side of the road he passed enormous gates fronting the estates of Silicon Valley's most powerful executives—including Peter's mansion, which Matthew didn't bother to look at as he passed it. More than six months had gone by since he last visited Jones's home. And ever since Greta told him last year that Peter was no longer welcome in their home, Matthew and Peter spent less and less time together.

As much as Matthew hated to admit it, Greta had been correct. Had he ignored her, he might never have distanced himself far enough from Peter—out of his power of persuasion, as Greta liked to called it—to a place where he would realize his own power.

He made a mental note. When all of this was settled, he would do something especially nice for her. Unless of course she'd already taken care of herself.

Collecting a few technical reports to go over at home, Peter decided it wouldn't hurt to check on the status of a few last hurdles facing the At Hand PC Plus project team.

Ambling through the cubicle-filled office, he exchanged passing greetings with several of his favorite engineers. He worked his way to the rearmost corner office, occupied by John Dulin, and parked himself in a chair.

"How's it coming?"

"It's coming." John lifted his soldering iron and blew away a trail of smoke. "I think I've got this battery situation licked once and for all." Not one for idle chatter, the engineer returned his attention to the electronic components scattered about his worktable.

"Let's hope so." Peter glanced at the pile of batteries stacked beside an exposed At Hand Plus chassis. Each cell was charred with a caramel-colored resin. After the At Hand began shipping,

a few retailers reported that some units were overheating and smoking. It turned out that the At Hand's internal battery was situated too close to the charging unit. The operations department came up with a quick fix—a small insulated barrier that had to be squeezed into place by hand during the otherwise automated production process. As though the handwriting-recognition debacle weren't embarrassing enough, the press had had a field day with this latest unfortunate development. Joshua Ellis, a hack high-tech reporter with the *San Francisco Examiner*, broke the story with the headline "Via's Fiery Fumbled Fingers At Hand." Christ, Peter couldn't wait for the At Hand PC Plus to ship. He'd show them all.

Peter had the utmost faith in John Dulin, who had been with Via since the beginning. He was confident that John would fix the battery problem. The obvious solution would have been to install a small cooling fan inside the computer. However, Jones wouldn't permit it. He intended for the At Hand to be the world's most quiet and unobtrusive mainstream computer ever invented. Tech journals pointed out that it couldn't be done, that you *had to* cool the unit's hot-running processor with a microfan. Peter countered with his standard reply: "Anyone who says something can't be done only says so because they aren't smart enough to figure it out." Put to the challenge, Dulin, after two sleepless nights of sustaining himself on soda and popcorn, delivered, revealing a design that cooled the machine by natural convection.

Peter leaned over John's shoulder for a closer look. "I'd sure hate to see us go back to the drawing board on that sweet little battery charger." The engineer assured him that the problem would soon be history. Not entirely convinced, Peter stayed right where he was, hovering like a hawk.

Dulin stopped what he was doing and set down the soldering iron. He made an elaborate show of retrieving his portable CD

player and headphones from a nearby drawer. He looked at Peter with tired eyes. "How about a little faith here, huh?"

Jones raised his palms and grinned. "All right, all right. I'm outta here. I just wanted to make sure you were coming along okay, that's all." He left the engineer with his head bobbing through curling smoke trails.

These were the little triumphs that excited Peter. Achieving what others said was impossible. It was no secret that the engineers were the only people in the company for whom Peter felt genuine admiration and respect. And secretly, awe. They were the conveyors of his visions, the ones who turned his radical ideas into real products.

Making his way to the front of the building, he swung by the software testing lab. Inside, a dozen engineers each sat before a Plus prototype, putting the new system software enhancements through their paces. The group was oblivious of his presence as screens scrolled and flashed, styluses scribbled and tapped, speakers chirped, and printers cranked out performance results.

Satisfied that everything was going according to plan, Peter exited the building and hopped into his black Z3. His natural appreciation for all things elegant and functional had inspired him to make BMW the company car of choice for senior executives. They picked the model, and Via picked up the lease. The only rule—an unspoken one—was no one could pick the same model as Peter Jones. There had been a single exception, however, when Matthew had ordered a Z3 for himself. They weren't exactly alike: Locke had chosen silver and preferred to drive with the hardtop on, while Peter always zipped around with the top down. Nevertheless, the executive staff wondered how Peter would react. To everyone's surprise, Peter had been flattered. For a while, anyway, until things had fallen apart between them. Now he wondered if Matthew had chosen the car only to imply that he and Peter were

somehow equals. He'd thought they were, but sadly he'd been wrong.

He felt foolish now for having nearly lost control when Matthew had come by to try and talk things over. But at the same time, he didn't know how else to act or feel. He was ill-equipped for this sort of corporate maneuvering. All his adult life he had dealt squarely with his employees, his peers, his critics, and his competitors. Sure, business was war, but somehow Peter had always managed to play by his own idealistic rules. No one knew— or thought he knew—better than Peter what was right for Via. Until now. It wasn't fair.

Speeding down Orchard Avenue, he passed the large, modern three-story sales and marketing building, where Matthew and the other senior executives were stationed. Peter kept his office with the engineers, far from the ritzy corporate offices. Though his title was chairman, his paramount job was to create Via's computers. And to do that he belonged in the trenches, with his team. Especially now. The last place he wanted to sit was across the hall from Matthew Locke.

He zoomed out of the complex's main gate and headed for Highway 280. Waiting for the on-ramp traffic signal to change, he glanced in his rearview mirror at the Via logo glinting in the golden afternoon sunlight, atop the corporate building. The logo depicted an abstract highway lane stretching into a far-reaching, rainbow-hued horizon. He adored his company's name and logo. *Via: by way of, through.* Together, they epitomized everything he strove for in his life's work.

Accelerating onto the highway, he felt a small gush of pride as he stole one last look at the emblem. He'd paved a path that had put the world's most truly personal computers into so many hands, into so many lives. He enjoyed a good measure of self-satisfaction at this achievement, not to mention the riches that flowed to those who helped make Via the legendary company it was today.

And though he was uneasy thinking about tomorrow's dis-
agreeable business of ending the Via journey for one man who'd
lost his way, Peter could already sense the relief that would follow.
After tomorrow's meeting, he would be back in the driver's seat, on
his own.

As it turned out, Matthew Locke's estimate of his wife was right on the money. As usual, she'd already rewarded herself.

He found Greta in the living room, fussing over the largest crystal bowl he'd ever seen. She was facing away from him and didn't notice him coming in. He stood watching as she carefully inched the bowl this way and that on the waist-high black lacquered pedestal.

She wore designer jeans and an oversize saffron sweater that drooped past generous hips. Her hands were covered by a pair of delicate silk gloves, her copper hair pulled back in a medium ponytail that accentuated her look of concentration. He knew her so well. And by the looks of things, she was having her doubts, not quite sure she'd made the right decision.

He strolled into the room. "It certainly is striking."

She turned at the waist, careful not to let go of the bowl. Her knitted brow relaxed and her expression gave way to the mischievous smile that generally followed only her naughtiest, most extravagant purchases.

"Darling, I didn't hear you come in. You're home early." She leaned over and pecked his lips. She made one final adjustment to the bowl, then stepped over to the wall switch to turn up the overhead halogen lamp. The bowl twinkled and glittered, casting prismatic sparkles in every direction.

"I was in the city getting my hair done, and I just happened to stop by Gump's," Greta said, lifting a glass of white wine she'd started. The emporium was San Francisco's infamous toy store for the wealthy. "It's a James Houston original. Just look at that engraving, Matthew. That detail." She clucked her tongue in appreciation.

Matthew leaned in for a closer look at the half dozen salmon circling the bowl's rim. The illusion was impressive: The fishes stirred up a spray of tiny air bubbles in their struggle against an invisible current. He had to admit, the piece was breathtaking.

"I was going to wait until after tomorrow to show it to you, darling," Greta said. "But I know everything is going to work out just the way you planned it. Anyway, when I saw it I just had to have it. Such brilliance."

"How much brilliance?" he asked, with a quizzical grin.

"An absolute steal, Matthew. You wouldn't believe it if I told you." She raised her glass and toasted the bowl. "Now, let me fix you something to drink."

He decided not to press further. If it made her happy, then he didn't care what it cost. It was one of the give-and-take aspects of their marriage that he had come to accept. His money for her pleasure. It was the only way he knew how to satisfy her.

Her newest thing fit in nicely among the living room's other precious objects. The Hepplewhite antiques with their forged hearts, the Wyeth, the small but valuable collection of first editions. And, as always, vase after vase of fresh flowers, brightening each of the mansion's thirteen additional rooms, every one as carefully and exquisitely decorated as this one.

Matthew leaned in again to inspect one of the salmon more closely. He admired the way the creature labored majestically against a powerful, unseen force, compelled onward by an instinct to fulfill its obligation. It was that way in business, he reflected. The journey hard and strenuous, the instinct to always keep moving forward the same. Pure and simple.

He frowned at his choice of word, *simple,* and the sudden and undesirable effect it had on his mood. Once more his thoughts returned to Peter Jones. Like an unwelcome visitor, Peter's excited voice invaded his mind. *If you get simple beauty and naught else, you get the best thing God invents.* It was a quote from the poet Robert Browning, one Peter often recited during design meetings.

Matthew's self-confidence began to waver. Not completely, but enough to make him feel uneasy. Christ, how he couldn't wait for tomorrow to get here, and be done with it.

He straightened up and looked around the room. So much material worth. And all thanks to Via. A fact the press never let him forget. Practically every profile written about Via or Matthew carried the obligatory line or two describing his compensation package. The four-million-dollar salary. The stock options worth ten times that, give or take a few million. He was set for life. Yet this assurance no longer mattered the way it used to. There was more to it than the money, more than the position he currently held. Owing again to Peter, he, like the thousands of dedicated Via employees, had fallen under the young founder's Byronic spell. How Via, unlike any other high-tech company, really put people, the end users, first. How this charter developed the Via customer base into the most loyal in the business, if not the largest. To be at the top of so humane a company was an uncommon experience for Matthew, and it felt good. Special. Powerful. And staying in that esteemed position all depended on tomorrow, and what would follow over time. Tomorrow was everything. He positively be-

lieved his life depended on emerging victorious from tomorrow's board meeting. Otherwise...

Otherwise what? Would he die? He nearly laughed out loud at his own sense of melodrama. No, of course he wouldn't die. Not literally.

Yet when Greta returned, holding out his gin and tonic in one gloved hand, he wasn't so sure. In a way, a large part of him had died several years ago, after her accident. Sometimes when he looked at his wife's gloved hands he felt as though more of himself were falling away, bit by bit, until one day he would feel completely lost with her. On the whole, however, he had become adept at ignoring both, her hands and the intense feelings they stirred in him. Or no longer stirred. Sadly, they were one and the same.

Yet he was not a man without passion. His work at Via had become his real passion in life, his salvation, his means of giving and expressing himself in a way so unlike his former, material picture of success. In that past life, as he had lately come to think of it, his public image—one of Manhattan's industry movers and shakers, the successful, happily married business leader—was important to cultivate. But here, in California and at the freer-spirited Via, none of that seemed to matter. And that suited him fine. His calling had changed, and he had changed with it. Indeed, tomorrow was only the beginning.

Interpreting her husband's reflective expression as consent, she graced him with a warm smile, the devilish look gone now that they had passed the money part of her latest acquisition. He accepted the cocktail, tasted it, and planted a grateful kiss on her forehead.

Greta touched his arm. "Come take a load off."

He followed his wife to the brocade settee and sank into the soft cushions. He eased his head back and rested his eyes.

"Is everything all set, darling?"

He nodded.

"Good." Greta Locke took an appreciative sip of her wine. "I'm telling you, Matthew. I can't wait for you to be able to relax once this all settles down. It feels like you've been at this for ten years."

From her tone he knew there was more to her sympathy than just his own peace of mind. He also knew what he should say to include her in the future she envisioned. Instead, he said: "He says I don't know what I'm doing. That I don't have a clue. No guts, no vision." He opened his eyes. "Unless I'm completely overlooking something, I don't think he realizes what's going to go down to-morrow." Matthew looked at his wife.

"He deserves it."

Matthew shrugged, not wanting to cover the same well-worn ground again with her.

Greta loathed Peter. After their first dinner together, during the recruiting visit to get acquainted with Jones and the West Coast, she had complained about his conduct. How he would excitedly tug on her husband's arm when describing his computer things, or when Matthew's observations harmonized with Peter's own thoughts. And Matthew hadn't been much better back then, either. The countless evenings he would arrive home from work with Peter said this, Peter said that.

But the thing Greta despised most, Matthew knew, was what she had called their "play day." Every Saturday, like clockwork, Pe-ter would be at the door before she was out of bed, calling on Matthew. Off they would go, sometimes for the whole day. Matthew would return bursting with new ideas, retreating to his home office to make notes or search the Web for details on the subjects they'd discussed.

Until Greta had had enough. One morning, while Peter was waiting in the entrance hall for Matthew, she wondered aloud

from the top of the stairs when the last time was she'd spent a Saturday with her husband, just the two of them. After that Peter stopped coming to the front door. Instead, he took to waiting outside the gate. "Like a mongrel," Greta observed after reading an article about Peter Jones that revealed he was an orphan. Well, that explained everything, she told Matthew. Peter Jones saw him as a father figure, it was so obvious. That Matthew might see Peter as a son never really occurred to her.

When she commented one evening that his growing attachment to Peter was causing him to lose track of why he had come to Via in the first place, Matthew took offense. He countered that the time he spent with Peter was necessary if he ever wanted to realize the deal at its best. Greta sneered at that, pointing out that even she could see that Jones would never go for Matthew's plan, no matter how friendly they became. Matthew eventually agreed, yet he was resistant to adjust his fondness for the younger man.

So Greta made it easy: She forbade him to invite Peter into their home. How Matthew was to accomplish this without offending Peter was his problem. No more Saturdays. From now on, she demanded, he would spend Saturdays with her, even if it meant working in his home office all day. It was for his own good, she insisted.

And in the long run, Matthew reflected as he finished off his gin and tonic, she'd been right. Had Greta not intervened, he might never have brought up his transformation plan with Peter Jones. She had also been correct in how Peter would react to the suggestion. There was no chance in hell Peter would consider making Via's products more compatible with the competition's....

His wife's touch startled him back to the present.

"Poor darling. So tired." She brushed a wave of dark hair from his forehead. The fabric of her glove raised a chill on the

back of his neck. He moved her hand to the sofa cushion, patted it to keep it there. Then he set his empty glass on the coffee table and locked his hands behind his head.

"Did I mention the *Fortune* writer accepted the offer for the autobiography?"

"Terrific, Matthew. I think. Unless it's the one I'm thinking of. You interviewed so many candidates I've lost track. Not that man who kept calling day and night, is it? Which one was he? He was so horribly nerdy. Jonah something-or-other. Sort of seedy. And bitter, was how you put it, if I'm not mistaken."

"Joshua Ellis. Very bitter. And disreputable, I found out. And no. It's not him. It's the young woman. The one you said had suspicious eyes."

"Mmm, her. Well, she did look at everything so suspiciously. She did, Matthew."

"That's why she's a journalist, Gret. It's her job."

"There are going to be a lot of disappointed runners-up. You considered how many? Six or ten different writers?"

"Something like that." He shrugged. "Anyway, business is business. And they already know that, they're writers. My press chief said she'd contact them to say I've gone with someone else. Anyway, we won't get started with the interview sessions and actual writing for months. For now this *Fortune* writer will go over piles of background material, that sort of thing. Which is just as well. I mean, it's not as though I don't have enough to worry about. Maybe I said yes too soon to doing this book thing. You think?"

"Shhh, relax. Just take it easy, Matthew. You'll be fine after tomorrow's over, darling, I promise."

He smiled appreciatively and looked once more at the crystal bowl. A golden ray of setting sunlight cut into the object from the French paned windows overlooking the valley. The reflection was so brilliant it hurt his vision to contemplate it for more than a few

moments. He rested his eyes again and briefly considered what he could promise her in return.

Unable to think of anything new, he turned his thoughts once more to himself.

Arriving home, Peter was greeted by a vigorous piano sonata and a vibrant hum that rose and fell in perfect time with the music. He moved toward the pleasing medley, winding his way through the more or less empty mansion to the large sunny parlor in back.

Moving toward her he smelled the sweet fragrance of her long white-blond hair, brightened and warmed by the sunlight streaming in through the open windows beside her.

His shadow gave him away and she turned and greeted him with an appealing smile. Her cheeks were slightly flushed, her sapphire eyes lively.

He casually rested a hand on her shoulder, a simple expression of admiration for her talent. "That was wonderful. It's like this entire house comes alive when you play."

She turned a cheek to his hand and closed her eyes. He waited a moment before easing his hand away. He knew better than to touch her, to encourage her, yet somehow he hadn't kept himself in check.

She stood and stretched, a long and luxuriant reach, tanned shoulder blades showing through her flowery sundress. He took her seat and folded his hands together over one knee, turning his attention to the windows and expansive view of the verdant hills and distant Stanford campus. He spied the crown of Hoover Tower poking through the far-off treetops, and recalled his first encounter with this beautiful young woman, three weeks ago.

He'd had the honor of giving the commencement speech to the Stanford graduating class. At the reception that followed, she introduced herself. Her name was Ivy, and he was charmed at once

by her easy comfort with him. It usually went one way or another. Many were so impressed or intimidated by his reputation and wealth that it was impossible to get past all of that and into comfortable and interesting conversation. But on rare occasions, such as this one, new introductions were a pleasure, the meeting of two vigorous minds.

He took an instant liking to her when she described the speech and language interface she was developing for the At Hand, whose intuitive design, she all but gushed, had inspired her to begin the project in the first place. That touched him. He asked her where she saw the program eventually going, and she said she wasn't sure. She had no agenda for the summer, and had halfheartedly committed to a cross-country road trip with friends for lack of a more tempting course. Feeling a sudden compulsion to help, he offered her the opportunity to continue developing the speech and language component at his home office. She arrived the next day with a duffel bag, some books and clothes, a few Zip disks, and a backpack.

Peter regularly had houseguests. Most were students who, like Ivy, had taken him up on the generous offer to use his thoroughly equipped computer lab. While he never gave it much thought, he supposed his goodwill had something to do with being raised in an orphanage. Except for his work and his lover, Kate, when she was in town, his life was surprisingly spare. Though he needed a fair share of quiet time to think, he didn't enjoy being alone, and having bright young minds around kept things interesting. In exchange for the agreeable feeling of companionship the students added to his life, Peter had helped a number of them get a practical start in the business. In return for his hospitality, he asked only that they pick up after themselves and respect his private things. He allowed them to come and go for as long as they liked, and his doors were never locked. He left it to Alice, his

live-in maid and cook, to stay on top of the various artists-in-residence.

It was Alice who now appeared in the doorway, wiping her hands on her apron. She was a small, voluble Spanish woman who wore her black hair pulled into a tight bun. She graced him with an affectionate smile.

"Good evening, Mr. Petey." She turned to Ivy. "I finished preparing your meat and spices. You better start cooking if you want the flavor best."

Ivy thanked Alice, then took Peter's hands in her own. "I'm making you a special Mediterranean dish tonight. A little something for letting me crash out here with you."

"Great," Peter said. His voice sounded strange to him as he casually withdrew his hands and picked up some notes Ivy had been working on. He didn't have to look up to sense Alice's eyes on him. He knew what she was thinking. And he was thinking the same thing. It had happened a few times in the past, when his hospitality would take an unexpected, and occasionally unpleasant, turn. Once, a couple of young men had taken off with some computer equipment and a platinum pocket watch Kate had given him. And then there were the women.

If he'd learned anything from his experience with women guests, it was that it was best to keep his interest focused on their work, not them. But with any highly artistic person, the two were often difficult to separate. He glanced at diagrams and charts, yet didn't really see any of them. "Hey, it looks like your research is really coming along."

"Sure is," Ivy said with evident pride. She gave his hand a playful tug. "Come on. I'll give you a quick demo of the latest module before we eat dinner."

As she led him out of the parlor, Peter met Alice's concerned eyes. She was all too familiar with the course the woman's stay was

taking. He countered with an expression that he hoped passed for utter helplessness, and followed Ivy's lead just the same.

Staring at himself in the bathroom mirror, Matthew blew a long sigh. He couldn't remember the last time he'd felt like this, both exhausted and keyed up at the same time. Squeezing some toothpaste onto his toothbrush, he observed his wife in the reflection, through the partially open doorway. He turned on the faucet and continued to watch her as he brushed his teeth. She was seated at her vanity and taking in her own reflection, about to begin her nightly ritual.

The procedure held an ironic fascination for him—but only at moments such as this one, when he could behold the process unnoticed. What fascinated him most was the way she performed the entire routine without ever once looking directly at her hands. He wondered if that was what continued to draw his curiosity. The possibility of perhaps one day catching her looking at what she was doing. Really seeing. And maybe catching him as he caught her. Would it change anything? He couldn't say, either way. Which was the problem. Neither he nor she ever spoke about it. So he just kept watching and waiting, wondering each time if it would ever change. Tonight was no different.

Observing the back of her head, with its coppery hair piled neatly on top, he could tell by its tilt that she was inspecting her face. The faint, fine lines around her eyes, her lips. At the same time, he watched her hands go to work. Removing first one glove, then the other. Her right hand reaching for the crystal lotion dispenser. Pressing out a copious portion of the creamy substance. Drawing both hands together, methodically working the lotion between them. Firmly, assuredly. Until the drying friction slowed them down. And now the finish. Sliding open the top vanity drawer to retrieve a fresh set. White silk. Exclusively tailored to her specifi-

cation. The left momentarily at odds with the right. Until she had them on, everything in place, creating the illusion once more. A perfect pair of hands.

But a gloved pair, nevertheless. Matthew was unable to see past that fact. How could he, when it was so apparent? He snapped off the bathroom light.

Greta had climbed into bed, the sheet and blanket folded just below her breasts. "Well, well. Your business pajamas. I love those on you." They were Matthew's favorite pair. Light blue, pinpoint oxford cloth, the same material he preferred for his tailored shirts.

Matthew smiled uncertainly, unsure of her sincerity. Maybe it was just more of the same guilt, an unflattering reminder of his "all business" nature, both in and out of bed. He settled on top of the blanket, sealing her in on her side. He clamped his hands behind his head and stared at the ceiling, his mind working over the possibilities of tomorrow's meeting.

Greta turned on her side. "Darling, don't keep thinking about it. Try to relax." She stretched over him to turn off his bedside lamp, her breasts grazing his chin, then settled herself gently on his chest.

The valley shone into the room brightly through the row of windows beside the bed. Millions of orange and yellow dots of light, far in the distance, shimmering in the unusually balmy late spring night. They lay there in silence for a while.

Her voice was quiet when she finally spoke. "Matthew, I've been thinking. About what you do. How involved in it you are. And everyone else but me, it seems like. It's everywhere I turn. I just feel so left out."

For Christ's sake, he wasn't up for this conversation again. Especially not tonight.

"Greta—"

But before he could protest, she got the rest out. And what she had to say surprised him.

"Would you mind if I sit down with your computer tomorrow? Just for a bit. To try to write a letter or something?"

He was positively relieved. "Of course not. That would be fine. I'm happy to hear it. It's easy. Just click on the little Via roadway logo in the left corner to get started. Like I showed you that time, when I first brought it home. It's all there. The word processor. And the Web. Just be careful not to throw away any of my things. Better yet, why don't you create a folder for yourself. Call it Greta's Things or whatever you like. Your own little storage space."

"I don't know. You know I'm all thumbs with this computer stuff. I mean, I know its not going to bite me or anything. That it's just like you always say, an appliance."

"Just like I always say."

"Yes. Well, I'm sorry, Matthew, for not being more curious sooner. I guess I was always so interested in all the other things in our life that I never really paid attention to what you're so interested in."

"I've never expected you to become a nerd, darling. But I have to admit I'm pleased to hear this. It's never too late to learn, to try new things."

"No time like the present, and all that."

"You got it. So just do it, Gret."

She shook her head and laughed at her own anxiety. "You're right of course, Matthew. So all right already. I've waited long enough. I'll try, then. I'll learn."

"You do that." He kissed the top of her head.

"Now I'm excited. Thank you, darling."

She kissed his neck, eased her gloved hand down his torso. He sighed through his nostrils and closed his eyes.

But it was no use. He remained unresponsive.

He turned his head to look out at the shining valley, and patted her hand.

"Let's go to sleep."

>     >     >

Seated atop a stool at the console range, Peter watched with mild amusement as Ivy bustled about the kitchen. She left a mess in her wake, yet had the meal under control. A pot of fragrant lamb stew bubbled lazily on the stove. In the oven, two small pizzas baked away.

He'd taken pleasure in watching her roll out the dough and work it into small rounds. She'd topped each with an assortment of fresh vegetables and spices. He appreciated how she would suddenly stop talking to concentrate on the recipe, then pick up again where they'd left off. Although she had been his guest for nearly a month, this was the first opportunity he'd had to really get to know her.

Misunderstandings with female guests in the past cautioned him from getting too close, but she was so interesting, and her company was a welcome relief from the residual distress he'd felt after his afternoon with Matthew Locke. And from thinking too much about tomorrow's board meeting, which at the moment seemed a million miles away.

She stirred the stew with a wooden spoon, drawing out a taste to test the flavor. She frowned.

"Not quite there." She pointed the spoon at a row of spices out of her reach. "More cayenne."

He grabbed a small jar filled with yellow powder.

"That's curry. Next one over. Right."

He handed her the jar, watched her sprinkle a good measure of the spice into the stew. Her lively dinner preparations brought a rosiness to her face that, with her white-blond hair, made her look as though she'd spent the day at the beach. She wore tattered, oversize jeans cinched at the waist with a rainbow-pattern bandanna, an oversize white dress shirt with no bra. When he realized he was staring he thought of something to say.

"So you do this often? Cook up gourmet meals after a day of coding?"

That amused her. "Yeah, right. You kidding? I've spent the last semester holed up in a dorm room with a hot plate and instant noodles."

"You make it look so easy, like second nature."

She shrugged. "I don't know. It's simple. You just follow the directions. I guess I'm just a quick study." She held his gaze until a bell chimed. "Pizza's done." She grinned with evident pleasure, breaking their link.

Peter felt an irregular but not unpleasant stirring in his chest. Careful, he warned himself, watching as she slipped on an oven mitt and bent to retrieve the appetizer. He knew he should look away, yet he was unable to. Her baggy shirt shifted at the collar. Something about her neck caught his eye, but before he could give it a second thought his attention was drawn elsewhere. Her breasts, he observed, while not large, were ample enough to illustrate gravity. Reaching inside the oven she made a quick inhaling sound as a small burst of heated air struck her face and set dancing a few stray wisps of her fine hair. An instant later a delectable aroma wafted his way. He swallowed.

She shifted to one side, and he glimpsed her neck once more— and his throat tightened. Rising with the tray in one hand, she used the other to brush her hair out of her face, giving Peter the opportunity to fully see, just for an instant, the inside collar of her shirt.

Which wasn't her loose shirt at all, but his. He knew his own name when he saw it. And that's what he'd spied on her collar. No, his collar. The small identification label, put there by the dry cleaner, bearing his name. His heart stirred anew, not so agreeably this time.

Setting down the hot tray, Ivy smiled at him. Then frowned. "What is it?"

He was momentarily dumbfounded. He tried to form a response, but managed to get out only a small nervous laugh.

She looked genuinely worried. Not guilty. Or even remotely aware of what he had seen or might be thinking.

He lifted a hand, made an exasperated wave. "Wow, sorry. I just zoned out there for a second. It's work, I guess. Big board meeting tomorrow. Change in the air. That sort of thing. I'm fine. Sorry."

She looked at him funny and blew a wisp of hair away from her brow, then shrugged it off.

"So where's your cutter thing. For the pizza."

"That drawer." He pointed, and she turned around.

His finger froze in place when he noticed the jeans, with their familiar rips where his own knees had over time worn through the denim. They were his. She was wearing his pants, too. His heart did another flip-flop.

She returned to the counter with the pizza cutter in one hand. She looked at his pointing finger.

"Um, I got it." She waggled the circular knife at him.

He wondered if she'd gone though his closet and helped herself to anything else. He watched her cut the pizzas into quarters. Her feet were bare. She wore no jewelry, no wristwatch. He came up with a possible explanation: After the demo of her software that she'd given him earlier, she'd showered and had no doubt discovered she'd run out of clean clothes. She'd probably asked Alice if she could borrow some of his old things until she had a chance to launder her own clothes. She had, he reminded himself, arrived with very few personal effects, only enough to fit into a large duffel bag. Simple as that.

"Here." She slid a plate across the butcher block counter. "Eat."

It was probably nothing, he decided. He'd overreacted. Hell,

if he still found himself wondering about it later, he would just ask her. It was no big deal. Still, it had given him a small scare ... a normal response when he considered his history with women guests, he supposed. They just never worked out. The temptation to become more than acquaintances always seemed to get in the way. And while he and Kate had no hard rules in their relationship, they had made a deal of sorts: that if either had an affair, they would tell the other. So far, neither had had anything to say on the subject. He was pretty sure he wanted to keep it that way. Right now, he was starving.

He picked up his pizza and took a bite. "Delicious. I can't believe you don't do this all the time."

She stopped chewing. "I could," she said brightly, and a moment later she blushed, as though she'd said something to embarrass herself. "I mean, eat like this every night. But who has the time, right?"

Peter nodded and picked up another slice. He was thirsty.

"Wine. That's what we need."

"Red will go great with the stew," she suggested.

"Red it is." He got up and opened a nearby cabinet, revealing a floor-to-ceiling wine rack. His fingertips lingered on a particular reserve. He deliberated for a moment, considered tomorrow's board meeting. Then he selected a younger, less consequential vintage.

He opened the bottle and filled two glasses. He handed one to her, and for an awkward moment they stood there, unsure what to say next.

Ivy lifted her glass. "To new friends."

"New friends." He put a small emphasis on the last. They clinked their glasses, and Peter looked into his wine to avoid her eyes.

She savored the wine's good flavor for a moment, then set her glass down. "Let's eat." She filled two bowls with stew, he sliced a

crusty loaf of bread, and they went into the dining room with the meal. He started to go back for the wine.

She waved a hand at him. "Sit. I'll get it."

When she returned he noticed she'd topped off her glass.

They ate in silence for a while, both pleased with the delicious stew. Eventually, they picked up their earlier conversation.

"So what made you choose Stanford?" he said.

"This course they have. VTSS, for Values, Technology, Science, and Society."

"I've never heard of it."

"It's been around for a while." She set down her fork. "It's an interesting mix."

"Sounds like it. What do you like best about it?"

"The overlap, definitely. How one affects and impacts the other, and so on. The kinds of interactions you must think about all the time."

"Me?"

She snorted. "Sure, you. I mean, come on. Your work, your computers. They're founded in science and technology, right? And haven't they affected our society? Changed our values?" Her eyes glimmered with emotion. "You've democratized computing for the masses. Put it into the hands of the people. Given them a choice, an alternative to business as usual. I mean, consider the alternative. The only choice would be Future Processing–equipped clones running PCSoft's ugly operating system. And imagine if those rumors always floating around ever came true. If the two merged? Talk about world domination. It's scary to think what it would be like if you didn't exist. People wouldn't be able to choose for themselves. But thanks to you, they can. No more Big Brother, brother." She gave an appreciative nod of her head, then went back to her meal. "Anyway, that's what the course was about. I dropped it."

Peter sat with his fork hovering over his plate, ignoring this

last, still absorbing everything she had said. He was speechless, yet she didn't seem to notice. He set down his fork and refilled their glasses. He sipped his wine and studied her over the rim of his glass, as though he were seeing her for the first time. He felt the beginnings of an agreeable emotion crystallize. Which, in turn, raised a warning flag. Thin ice ahead if he didn't watch himself. Friends, he thought, silently repeating their toast. Just friends.

"Did you hear me?"

He'd lost track of what they had been talking about. "Where were we?"

"I said, that's what the course *was* about. I dropped it."

"But you sound like an expert on the subject. Why the change of heart?"

She gave a nonchalant shake of her head. "Music. Voice. This speech stuff. That's what I told you when I first met you. Remember?"

In fact, he did not remember. Moreover, it suddenly occurred to him that he didn't even know her last name. She'd been staying in his home for the last few weeks, yet he only knew her as Ivy. He worried sometimes about how he could completely miss certain points, obvious things others would probably pick up on at once. Had it affected his business sense? In the back of his mind, he wondered.

"I'm sorry. I don't remember, actually. Your last name, either. Did you even say?"

"My God, you're right." She finished off her wine. "I see what you're getting at."

"You do?"

"Sure. You're thinking, how could I ask if you remember that I dropped that course to get into this linguistics programming stuff when you don't even know my last name. I mean, it's not like we're old friends. Like you are all up on my life or whatever."

He went to take another sip of wine ... but then decided to hold off a bit.

"Anyway, it's Green. Ivy Green. Can you stand it?"

"It's certainly, ah, earthy."

"Very funny. But you're not completely off. I mean, the only green I think Rick and Jeannette had in mind when they named me was reefer."

He burst out laughing. "Why's that? And how come you don't call them Mom and Dad?"

"Oh, please. To hear them tell it? I'm like this post-sixties-rehash baby. The latter part of the 'Give-Peace-a-Chance-If-It-Feels-Good-Just-Do-It' set. They met at Woodstock, both of them really young. No kidding. A few years later, they just did it, made me, at some rock reunion or something. How it felt, good or not, I never asked." She paused for a moment when she saw Peter's amused reaction.

"Quit laughing," she said, laughing herself at the absurdity of her story. He apologized and made a valiant attempt to wipe the smile from his face. "Anyway, they moved to California. Lived at the corner of Haight and Ashbury for a few years. Later, my dad 'accidentally'—his term, I swear—started his own herbal tea company. Yes, it's the brand you've got in your kitchen cabinet. They moved to Mill Valley. That's where I grew up, with parents who told me to call them by their first names, so that our household would always be on equal footing. Or some shit like that."

"Sorry. I'm not laughing at any of it. Honest. It's just the way you tell it. It sounds very funny."

"Yeah, well. No problem. I'm still amused by them, to tell you the truth." Yet she didn't look amused, Peter thought, noticing the way her lips pursed, almost a pout. "Anyway," she said, blowing out a long stream of wind. "I think I'm a little smashed. Pardon me for a second." She excused herself from the table.

He hoped he hadn't offended her. Anyway, he wasn't going to worry about it. Nor was he worried anymore about the fact that she'd borrowed his clothes. Rising from the table, he realized that

Ivy Green presented no real threat. If anything, the opposite was true, as her mention of the late sixties aroused his longing for Kate.

He strolled to the adjoining living room and put on one of her CDs, then returned to the dining-room table and poured himself a little more wine. He leaned back in his chair and closed his eyes and let Kate's soft and folksy voice carry him away.

Peter had met the vocalist at a Sierra Club luncheon thrown in his honor, after Via had donated a batch of computers to the environmental organization. Kate McGreggor, the "softly outspoken" folk rock star, was the keynote speaker. He'd found it difficult to follow her speech, but not because she didn't have anything interesting to say. He caught himself trying to catch her hazel eyes when she would glance in his direction, and he was mesmerized by the way she occasionally pushed back her brown hair with its premature streaks of silver.

By the end of her impassioned twenty-minute oration, Kate McGreggor had captured Peter's heart like no woman ever had. Words to describe her flooded his mind. Intelligent ... pure ... true. And uncommonly attractive. What you see is what you get, he surmised. After lunch had finished up, she sang. Her voice was enchanting and perfect, and he knew he had to meet her. He introduced himself. At first she seemed reticent to stray beyond courteous chitchat. He guessed that her opinion of him was perhaps influenced by his participation in an industry notorious for its less than admirable track record with the environment. And maybe the eight-year difference in their age had something to do with it too. He didn't care. And when he invited her to visit Via the next time she was in the San Francisco area, she hesitated. He persisted, and eventually she relented. Arriving the following month, she surprised him with a special gift. A bottle of wine from her parents' obscure Oregon vineyard, where she'd grown up. He was touched by her thoughtfulness, and he made her promise to be the one to

share it with him when the company turned ten. After a long day of satisfying conversation, their attraction for each other was evident. And remained so, to this day. They were two people comfortable with themselves and each other, despite the huge contrast in their celebrity status. Kate maintained her home in Los Angeles, where she was constantly at work on her music or involved in various causes that benefited from her renown. She stayed with Peter between recordings and projects, sometimes for weeks at a time. Her independence meshed perfectly with his own, creating a foundation for what had become a lasting relationship that was coming up on seven years. The distance imposed by their careers generated a constant longing that kept their affection fresh. At times it was difficult to be so far apart, and he wished they could be together more often. Especially tonight, as his thoughts returned to tomorrow's board meeting.

His afternoon altercation with Matthew Locke flared in his mind's eye. It was ridiculous. And after tomorrow, it would all be taken care of. He was sure of it. Or as sure as he could be, in light of his conflicting feelings of betrayal and impending loss. And stupidity, he grudgingly admitted to himself. For not having realized sooner that things were not really as they appeared. With a sudden start, he wondered: Was he losing his touch? His acute perception and attention to detail, for reading complicated situations, reading others? He opened his eyes.

Ivy sat across from him sipping a cup of coffee, staring at him coolly. Had she made a pot? He hadn't heard her in the kitchen. He'd obviously nodded off after she'd excused herself. How long had he been snoozing here, with her watching? It was time to sober up.

"I could use some of that." He went into the kitchen and came back with a steaming cup. Unable to think of anything else to talk about, he realized how tired he was. He thanked her again for the wonderful meal. She assured him it was no problem, and

they sat there quietly sipping their coffee, Kate McGreggor's music drifting in from the adjacent room. Eventually Ivy spoke.

"So, I've been wondering. Is it true?"

"What's that?"

She waved her spoon vaguely in the direction of the other room.

"That you two are, like, totally lovers."

"True, very."

She nodded and started playing with an open packet of Equal. "In everything I read, *Vanity Fair, People,* they say you'll probably get married. To her, I mean."

He knew the right thing to do would be to agree with the speculation. Yet at the same time he hated to bend the truth. People in business had called him many things, but none could ever say Peter Jones was a liar. It simply wasn't his way. So he answered honestly.

"I don't know. It's a tough question to answer. We're both super-busy people. She's always recording or involved in things. And I've got Via."

On saying his company's name, his voice suddenly sounded funny. Not a crack, nor a tremble. Just a faint rise that lifted his curiosity. What he said about himself and Kate was true, absolutely true. But that wasn't what had gotten the small rise out of him. No, it was Via, he realized with concern. But that was true, too. He did have Via. It was his. At heart, anyway. And after tomorrow, it would be all his once more. Yet for some reason that he didn't understand he felt an uncomfortable tightness in his chest, a small bloom of dread.

And what Ivy was doing with the little blue Equal packet didn't help him feel any better, either. She'd dumped the sweetener onto the dark mahogany table and was now dragging the straight edge of the packet through the small white pile of grains, cutting out line after line of the substance, as though sharpening her technique for the real stuff.

The act had an unsettling effect on his changed mood. He'd had enough conversation for one night. He needed some sleep. Tomorrow was a big day. Wrap it up, he told himself.

"So, yeah. Marriage is a real possibility." There, he'd told a small white lie. In light of the way Ivy's own mood had shifted, it was the right thing to do. "Well, it's late."

This got through to her. A sudden look of embarrassment crossed her face when she realized what she'd done with the packet of artificial sweetener. She leaned forward and blew away the lines, then casually brushed up any remaining traces of the substance with her fingertips and briefly touched them to her lips. Her saw her tongue dart out, and he looked away. This small, unselfconscious act somehow challenged his estimate of her, that she posed no threat. Or did she?

She apologized with a laugh and he said it was nothing, unable to look at her. He picked up his coffee cup and moved into the kitchen.

She came in behind him, carrying their empty wineglasses. They steadily clinked together in her hand, a fragile ringing sound as though she were trembling, yet she didn't seem to notice. "How about some more wine?"

He rested his hand over the glasses, silencing them. "I've had enough. And I've got to get some sleep now. Thank you again."

As he moved to go, she moved too, gamely narrowing the already small space between them.

"Listen." He shoved his hands in his back pockets. "We can't. Please."

For a moment she didn't move as she weighed his sincerity; then all at once her shoulders slumped and she pressed herself against the doorjamb, giving him room to pass.

Careful not to brush into her he slipped by and moved to the living room to turn off the stereo. He hesitated, and decided to leave it on, allowing Kate's sonorous voice to prevail a while longer.

He loaded the multidisc tray with four more of her CDs and pressed the random button. On his way upstairs he said nothing when he passed the kitchen, where Ivy was busy loading the dishwasher.

Inside his bedroom, he closed the door, tossed his clothes on the floor, and dropped down onto his futon. He rolled to one side and lit the single candle he kept there for moments when he felt like this. He wouldn't go so far as to say he practiced yoga, or that he meditated, but both had some influence on the relaxation technique Kate had shown him not long after they'd met.

He set the candle at the foot of the futon and bunched up a pile of pillows behind him. He settled back and slowed his breathing in an effort to get his busy mind to do the same. Before long his eyelids fluttered, and the first falling sensation of sleep engulfed him.

But not for long. He started at the sound of her footfalls.

Ivy stood at the edge of the futon, between him and the candle, illuminated from behind. The outline of her willowy body showed through her sheer kimono, her blond hair encircled by a glowing halo of golden candlelight. Her voice was a whisper.

"Peter, I want to be with you."

He remained as he was, lying back, naked, unable to move or speak. He considered explaining to her the few close calls he had had with other guests. How they had ended in tears for the young women. How in all their years together, he had never been unfaithful to Kate. How in all their years together, Via had never been unfaithful to him, and how it was the same thing. He thought this only because he wanted her, right now. He had never felt this way before, with any of the other women. This close to the brink. Something had changed. And if he could cross over like this, could Via? Would its decision makers decide tomorrow to break their faithfulness to him? He was suddenly so mixed up.

But he voiced none of these things to Ivy. Instead, he heard

his own voice in his head, already forming an excuse: *I had a lot to drink ... it was the wine.* He was not drunk, yet he was already entertaining a defense for something that had not happened. Not yet. Nor did it have to happen.

She knelt before him, and in the dim light he noticed two powdery white rings encircling her nostrils. When she spoke again her voice was deeper, more forceful.

"Peter, it's like you've empowered me. Given me this whole new outlook and purpose. Like it's my future. Let me share this good feeling. Just that. That's all."

Her words had a breaking effect on him. He was both distressed and enlivened by her sentiment. He looked away. And in that instant he acknowledged his greatest fear, of losing everything so close to him. Now. Tomorrow. Beyond.

He reached out his hand and touched her neck, traced his fingertips across her smooth brow. He touched her lips and her breath hitched.

She moved over him.

They kissed.

Afterward, he felt a delirious sense of relief. As if it had all been a bizarre dream. One he was just waking from. He raised his head from the mat, and for a brief, wanting moment he saw Kate resting lightly on top of him.

Ivy stirred and lifted her head from his chest to look at him with a contented smile.

His mind collapsed. He couldn't catch his breath or move. He was momentarily frozen in place, racked by an unpleasant tightening in his stomach, remorse languidly bleeding into his heart. He wanted to turn back the clock, take back what they had done. Wanted tonight to be over. Tomorrow over. Both erased, another chance.

She sensed his unease but made no attempt to console him, and for that he was grateful. And she was grateful too, but not in the same way.

"Thank you," she whispered, then unsteadily rose to her feet and collected her kimono. She lifted a nearby comforter off the floor and dragged it over his naked torso. Then she blew out the candle and disappeared.

Unable to close his eyes, Peter lay there for hours, staring at nothing.

># CHAPTER 3

It was going to be a hot one. Not yet seven o'clock, it was already humid as hell, and summer was still weeks away. William Harrell braced himself for the cool comfort of the limousine's air-conditioned interior. He nodded to his driver, and the car briskly pulled away from the stately brownstone.

The commanding executive settled in for the half-hour crosstown commute, his course and destination the same today as they had been each business day for what felt like the last hundred years. His regal face had the precisely aged features of a character actor cast in the role of president of the United States. He wore glasses for reading fine print. At sixty-four, William Harrell's looks suited his position perfectly.

He stretched his legs until they touched the facing seatback. His calves responded wearily. Last evening's workout, the first in more than a week, had taken its toll. Busy working up his company's portable computer strategy, he had had no choice but to take a break from his ordinary workout routine. The sacrifice had

been worth it, despite the small aches and pains it had caused. He hadn't felt this charged up in years.

He picked up his copy of the *Wall Street Journal* and turned to the "What's News" column. There they were, as expected, the analysts' speculations on today's Via board meeting and quarterly earnings report. Harrell read with keen interest.

Sources revealed that the company's top two men were not getting along as famously as previously reported. A Via engineer who had asked to remain anonymous had this to say: "Jones has created a rivalry between his division [At Hand PC] and ours [Mate]. It's really distressing. Jones invented the Mate, yet he refers to anyone who isn't working on the At Hand as a 'bozo.'"

Analysts aired theories on how the company could turn around its dwindling market share. They cited Matthew Locke's prior career at International Foods, where his fondness for drastic reorganizations had more than once had a positive effect on the bottom line. A sidebar on the At Hand detailed the product's rocky first few months in the marketplace.

William Harrell folded the newspaper and tossed it to the floor. He smiled. Everything was going according to plan. His company's conservative strategy for its portable computer line was about to take a dramatic turn. But no one inside the company knew this. Not yet. It was all in his head. Where it would remain. For now.

The car turned onto the commanding block that boasted one of Manhattan's most extraordinary buildings. The driver parked before the enormous glass-and-granite tower, then climbed out to open his occupant's door. But Harrell was already out. Straightening the sleeves of his charcoal pinstripe suit, he squinted up at the world-renowned structure of corporate prestige and power, solely occupied by the company whose name was cast in stone above the building's entrance: ICP.

He entered the building and rode the elevator to its highest

level, greeted his secretary, then took his seat in his exquisitely appointed office, where he began his day as chairman and chief executive officer of the world's largest computer company.

It was the very title and position that Matthew Locke envisioned for himself.

Gathering his notes for the board meeting, he looked though his wall-size office window at the conference room halfway down the floor. The area just outside the boardroom was vacant. Apparently none of the members of the board or executive staff felt like engaging in the idle conversation that usually took place outside the room prior to the meeting.

His secretary, Eileen, was stationed at her desk just outside his office. She caught his attention with a small wave and pointed at the clock on the wall beside her. It was time. He nodded, picked up his notes and yellow tablet, and stood up. Eileen wished him luck. Unsure whether or not he would need it, he thanked her.

As he neared the boardroom he observed the huge table that had been set up outside, piled high with food: fruit salad, bagels, muffins, and juice. By the looks of things, no one inside the room had much of an appetite this morning, either.

He strolled in. The room fell silent, and he immediately noticed that Peter hadn't arrived yet. He nodded his greetings all around as he seated himself in one of two vacant leather chairs positioned at either end of the long glass-and-steel table. The room's amenities were simple and high-tech. Bleached wood paneling stood in stark contrast to a dark rug patterned with an abstract interpretation of the Via logo. The room's far windows offered a panoramic view across housetops and low buildings to the Santa Cruz Mountains, which rolled north toward San Francisco.

The six Via board members and most senior executives faced

this view, while the remaining vice presidents sat with their backs to the window. All were busy flipping through agendas on their At Hands or scribbling notes on the yellow tablets placed around the table. He sensed their unease. Even Hank Towers, Via's cofounder and vice chairman, appeared unusually distracted, glancing up only briefly from his leather portfolio to acknowledge the CEO's arrival.

Matthew's confidence began to waver when it occurred to him that each person seated around the table had been hand-picked by Peter Jones for his or her role in the company. Though Matthew was second in command, the others had all been with Via longer than he had. Did he honestly believe he could unseat Peter Jones from his place in this room, from these lives?

He abruptly shook off the thought and, glancing at Hank Towers, quietly comforted himself by recounting the prepara-tions leading up to this day. It all came down to Towers, who for the most part had agreed with Matthew's ideas on how to run the company. Towers had pored over the reports that he'd put together—particularly the Harvard Business School study, which found that by the time a business is ten years old, its original founders are almost invariably gone. There were exceptions, most notably Hewlett-Packard, whose founders had held directorial roles. And, closer to matters at hand, there was ICP, whose founder, Jonathan Holmes, had directed the company for a half century before turning it over to his son, Byron. The study went on to say that most departures were amicable, that the founders left to begin a new venture. However, in the remaining cases the founders were forced out because of their inability to grow with the business.

The door opened and the room went still.

Peter Jones strolled in wearing a faultlessly tailored Armani suit, crisp white shirt, and floral-pattern tie. He looked well rested and cheery as he scanned the table warmly and greeted the mem-

bers of his team. Except Matthew. It wasn't until Peter took his seat at the opposite end of the table that the two men made eye contact.

Neither looked away, and all eyes were on them as Martin Cohen, general counsel and liaison to the board of directors, called the meeting to order. Peter and Matthew maintained their locked stare as they waited for Cohen to proceed, neither willing to relent in this silent test of wills.

Cohen cleared his throat. "I won't be going over the usual agenda today," Cohen said, announcing a break from the meeting's customary pattern. "Matthew?" He nodded to Matthew, then diverted his attention out the window, escaping Peter's bewildered expression.

Greta Locke awoke with a genuine sense of purpose. She hadn't felt this focused in a long time. She looked at the clock and chided herself for not getting up sooner, when she'd heard Matthew getting ready for work. Poor thing. He'd tossed and turned all night. By now his meeting had begun. She said a little prayer for him, that everything would turn out the way he'd planned. For both of them.

She tossed off the blankets and hopped out of bed, stretched. Glancing outside the bedroom's rear window, she took in the rolling estate's sloping hillside lawns and gardens. The last flowers of spring were blooming nicely, and she briefly considered spending the morning out there among them. But she recognized this small change of heart for what it was—procrastination. No, today was the day. No matter how challenging it would prove, today was definitely the day to learn new things.

Strolling down the broad stairway, she took a moment to appreciate the lovely atmosphere she had created for them. Matthew had left almost every aspect to her, trusting her judgment

in furnishings, fabrics, artwork, all of the things she was passionate about. And she left him to his few but all-consuming passions. His small but well-selected library. His cars. And of course his computer. Which today she intended to get to know more intimately.

She thought about what she'd told Matthew last night, why she hadn't taken an interest in Via's products sooner. She hadn't told him the whole truth. About her undeniable fear of the keyboard more than anything else, all those orderly keys waiting to be struck in a certain, orderly way, the way anyone else would strike them. But she was different; her hands made it so. Since her accident her life had changed, and she had adapted accordingly, making little adjustments as necessary, accommodations that, with considerable care, went unnoticed by others. However, the At Hand's touch-type keyboard was not something she could convert to fit her special needs. She was at its mercy. And that cold reality more than anything else was what had kept her at arm's length from ever getting to know the computer better.

The Lockes' housekeeper, Dolores, came through the foyer carrying a bucket of ammonia water. They wished each other a good morning and then Dolores went back to her work. Greta strolled down the parquet hallway to the expansive, airy kitchen tiled in black-and-white marble. She opened the refrigerator and grabbed a cup of yogurt. An open bottle of Mumm caught her eye. They'd had most of it with last night's meal, a good luck toast to Matthew and today's meeting. She hated to see the little bit that was left go to waste. Why not, she decided, setting the yogurt and bottle on the counter. She went back for a can of Orange Fresh, and used a butter knife to pop open the metal tab. She poured the champagne into her glass and topped it off with the Orange Fresh. Her own version of a mimosa.

As she went to set the can back on the counter she paused to stare at the container in her imperfect grip. She rarely drank the

beverage, but when she did it never failed to remind her of its pe-
culiar consequence in her life. She experienced a moment of both
pleasure and pain. Her therapist had advised her to always reflect
only on the former at moments like this ... to the first time she had
met Matthew ... their first toast.

It was at an advertising agency. She'd been on assignment as a
hand model, her occupation before she'd become Mrs. Locke.
There she was, holding a can of Orange Fresh, then an all-new,
all-natural carbonated orange beverage. Over in the corner stood
the up-and-coming Matthew Locke, who'd dropped in on the
agency to discuss the soda's advertising launch. One of the camera
assistants told her who he was. His eyes had locked on her lovely
hand, bearing his newest marketing vehicle, then followed up her
arm to the face. They exchanged a look, and he hung around until
the shoot was over. It was early evening by then, and he offered her
a cocktail: International Foods' Winter Vodka over ice. She ac-
cepted the drink, then nonchalantly poured in some Orange Fresh.
In that instant, in that spontaneous mixing of the two fluids, Greta
had single-handedly invented a multimillion-dollar market seg-
ment for International Foods, one which would later garner con-
siderable praise for Matthew.

She blinked away the moisture in her eyes and took a sip of
the champagne-and-orange drink. It tasted funny this early in the
morning, but she finished it anyway, rationalizing that it would
help ease the apprehension she felt over what she was about to
do. She took her breakfast into the adjacent sunroom and seated
herself in one of the chaise longues. She used the remote to turn
on the TV, and between spoonfuls of yogurt she flipped channels,
pausing for a few beats on the different talk shows. She was stalling,
and she knew it. There was nothing left to do but begin. Yet she
couldn't quite bring herself to leave the comfort of the soft chaise
just yet. She surfed a little longer until a commercial stopped her
in her tracks.

It was a fast and colorful montage, quick cuts between a computer screen and what looked like everything in the world. Exotic locales. The solar system. Culinary spectacles. Artwork. Attractive men and women, darling children, spry grandparents. The rapidly flipping pages of an encyclopedia. A universe of possibilities. The ad ended with a spinning globe, around which the World Online logo revolved. She recognized World Online as the service Via had a special arrangement with, and she knew it was what Matthew used to access the Web. According to him, it was the most popular online service in the world. He'd encouraged her to try it, but she never felt any real desire to do so. Until now.

She clicked the TV off and tossed aside the remote, plucked her special pair of gloves from her jeans pocket, and marched straight for Matthew's home office, where his At Hand PC waited, ready to usher her into the well-connected Web set.

She felt energized and a little terrified, unusually optimistic about the notion that she was about to change her life. What she had no way of knowing was that her actions would change her husband's life, too. Neither for the better.

"Thank you, Martin," Matthew said as he rose from his seat at the head of the table.

Peter abruptly turned to Hank Towers for an explanation. This was a break in custom. Normally, Martin Cohen would read the agenda, then turn the meeting over to Peter. But Towers's attention, along with everyone else's, had shifted to Matthew. He began speaking.

"As you are all aware, Peter and I have been at odds over how to manage Via. In particular, how to see us through this phase of unprofitability."

Peter rigidly pushed himself away from the table. "What the hell is going on here?"

Matthew ignored the outburst and went on, his eyes roaming from person to person with measured fairness.

"Simply put, Peter and I have different styles, different strategies. Unfortunately, these differences are putting the rest of you in the middle. And this is bad for Via, making it impossible to move forward."

His throat was dry and he needed to wet it. A pause now would add just the right dramatic effect, and he poured himself a glass of water. However, seeing that Peter was about to interrupt, he hurriedly set the glass down and proceeded with his discourse.

"I see only one way to settle our differences. So I have decided to ask you, the board of directors and executive staff, to accept my resignation."

Just as he was about to protest, Peter's jaw dropped. He couldn't believe his ears. Here he'd thought Matthew was going to attempt to reorganize the company and take control of the At Hand PC Plus project. Instead, he was quitting. The unanticipated revelation was like an answer to Peter's prayers, and it saved him from the unpleasant business of having to fire Matthew. He felt a sudden pang of pity, his own anger and hurt turning to a strange mix of compassion and guilt for Matthew, and he wasn't sure how to respond. He searched for the right words.

"Jesus, Matthew. I don't know quite what—"

Before he could say more, Matthew Locke held up his hand. Apparently he hadn't finished. He shifted his focus from Peter to the people seated around the table.

"Unless, however, you approve my recommendation. To have Peter relinquish his duty as group vice president of At Hand. And as chairman of the board."

The room spun and suddenly all eyes shifted to Peter. He blinked and tried to focus on a single pair, but none held. He leaned back heavily in his chair. It made a strained sound. He looked up at the ceiling, and suddenly it all became clear to him. Matthew's little

game. He recalled yesterday's confrontation, and how Matthew had phrased it: *drastic changes.*

He tried to comprehend the full meaning of what Matthew had just announced. It was preposterous. He was this company's founder, its crown jewel, and he wasn't going anywhere. Except where he damn well pleased. The audacity. It was laughable. And that was exactly what Peter did. He laughed. So hard that his shoulders shook.

No one joined in on the fun. They simply sat there and stared, waited for him to pinch his eyes and straighten up in his chair and settle his clasped hands on the table, no more giggles. He spoke around an irrepressible grin.

"Phew. Sorry. I didn't mean to laugh. I mean, I know none of this is funny. It's just that you had me going there for a second. I really believed you were going to make my job easy." His smile vanished as he bored his famous blue eyes into Matthew's.

"But I guess you're not going to make it easy. So I'll spell it out for you, Matthew. You're fired." There. It was done. And now, out of courtesy, he would explain why this was the only option.

Matthew held his ground at the opposite end of the table, his fingertips resting calmly atop the yellow legal pad.

"It hasn't all been a wash, Matthew. You did a fair job of helping get the organization in place. Tightening the budget. Beefing up the sales force. And the other things you did. We don't need to recount them all here, but you did them. You did. But if I let you stay in your position any longer, this company will fail. I'm afraid I just can't do my job with us arguing the way we've been, Matthew. I'm sorry. I really am."

Unsure what to do next, Peter reached into one of the folds of his leather portfolio and extracted a sheaf of copies of his new organization, which, in addition to his current duties, showed him in the role of acting president and CEO. He was distressed to see that Matthew was still standing at the head of the table.

Peter sighed. "I'm sorry, I forgot." He glanced quickly around the table. "I'm sure among us we'll come up with a substantial severance package, Matthew. Full relocation, of course. Amicable references. The whole nine yards."

Finally, Matthew spoke up.

"Peter, stop."

Oh, wonderful, Peter thought. Now he's going to beg. He had no experience with this sort of thing, and he wasn't sure what to say to make it clear to Matthew that his mind was already made up. He apologized again, hoping that would do it.

Matthew took a slow sip of his water, casually returned his fingertips to the tabletop, and then went on.

"You're a brilliant young man, Peter. You've made this market what it is. We all know that were it not for you, this company would never have happened. Everyone here recognizes that, and is grateful to you." He was surprised by how easily his words were flowing.

It was turning worse than Peter had imagined. He considered using the power of his title to stop Matthew. But since he'd already said his piece, perhaps it was just best to let Matthew say whatever he wanted to get off his chest. After all, he'd hired the man, and if anyone was to blame, it was him, for not realizing sooner that a guy who knew potato chips couldn't be expected to understand silicon chips.

At this last observation he nearly started laughing again, and he bowed his head so no one would see. What he didn't notice were the sympathetic glances in his direction.

As crucial as today's meeting was, he found it difficult to concentrate on Matthew's drone. He wondered briefly again if he was losing some of his finer abilities to stay sharp, not miss a thing. He fought to pay attention, but his mind kept jumping to important matters that needed his attention. The battery problem, which this morning appeared to be fixed. Brighter screens. Easier-to-service

keyboards. And, as always, faster performance ... With an imperceptible shake he forced himself to focus on the session.

He sat up a little straighter in his chair when he sensed Matthew was winding down, and in his head prepared a thank-you to the departing executive for his candor, his service, et cetera.

"... and finally, because of your inability to effectively manage your organization, the At Hand PC Plus project has fallen behind schedule," Matthew said. His voice rose a notch. "All that must change."

Peter couldn't agree more with Matthew's last comment, and nodded to say so.

"So I have decided to ask each person here to vote," Matthew said calmly.

Peter Jones looked at the executive with genuine curiosity. "And what are we going to vote on, Matthew?"

"On us, Peter. On which of us is going to run Via."

For a few minutes she just sat there before it, warily considering its parts. She'd watched Matthew working on it enough to understand how it functioned. The basics, anyway.

Drawing on her tight gloves, she concentrated on the core device. The At Hand, with its light gray On/Off button on the front lip. The unit was closed, and seated neatly in its dock. This, Matthew had told her, was what turned the At Hand PC into a full desktop system. The other peripherals were all in place. The keyboard, which she merely glanced at. The mouse. Printer. CD-ROM drive. Scanner. And the monitor, which, she observed, was turned on but asleep.

The stylus pen, for drawing and writing directly on its screen, was stowed in the little tunnel in the side of the unit. Thank God, she thought. Because she was a lefty, the stylus terrified her. The

mouse, she supposed, was more forgiving, since it only had two buttons. She picked it up and moved it to the left side of the keyboard, then touched the power button to wake everything up. The screen blinked on, revealing the orderly At Hand workspace.

She made a few adjustments to her left hand, working the unique glove's special fitting into place. She settled her hand over the mouse and, taking a deep breath, moved the pointer to the Via logo. She pressed the button, moved the pointer to the writing program, and clicked. Moments later a blank page appeared. She lifted her hand from the mouse and poised it and her other hand over the keys. Since the accident, she had never touched a keyboard.

She toiled for an hour, relearning. Her impediment made it all the more challenging. The w, s, and x keys were particularly trying. She sweated, cursed. Willed her fingers to think differently. And eventually, she accomplished what she'd set out to do. Two letters. One to her widowed mother in Brooklyn, the other to Matthew's parents in Connecticut. In both she offered a brief greeting, and casually mentioned that she'd typed the letter all by herself, that she was finally catching up with the rest of the world on the Net.

The Internet in turn provided a welcome relief to the arduous letter writing. A few clicks of the mouse and she was connected to World Online. The colorful menu of icons appeared, each pointing out a different category. With so many to choose from she didn't know where to begin. So she began with the familiar, a subject she felt very at home with: shopping.

She spent half an hour roaming through virtual boutiques, browsing catalogs full of photographed merchandise. Before long her initial anxiety melted away and she considered running upstairs for her credit card. But then she remembered what Matthew had once said about online scams. Something about security. How

only some services were reasonably safe. She'd have to ask him later. Just looking was enough fun for now. And when she spotted the clock, she realized that she had been online longer than she would have imagined. She couldn't believe it. Her throat was dry, and she had to urinate.

She moved the pointer to the Goodbye button and clicked it. The program asked if she was sure she wanted to disconnect. But before she was able to click the Yes button, the At Hand beeped and a small paned window appeared in the middle of her screen, blocking the Goodbye box. She gave a startled gasp when she read the words in the new box.

"You bastard!"

She was momentarily frozen. And frightened. What had she done? She searched the small window for some explanation. Its title identified it as "Chat" message, from a person named "SFScooper." She could only assume this Mr. or Mrs. Cooper had mistaken her for someone else.

Seeing the reply box, she ventured to explain, wording her response carefully.

"I think you have the wrong number," she typed, then pressed the Send button.

"Fuck you, bastard!"

Her mouth dropped open. Brand-new to this strange form of communication, she resorted to straightforward language. The sort used to address a child.

"I am no such thing you nasty person. Who are you? And why are you calling me bad names?"

"You know who I am, fuckface!"

It had to be a joke. A stupid joke. And she'd had enough already. Now, where was the Goodbye box? But before she could figure it out, the Chat box flashed again.

"You'll be sorry, Locke."

Oh dear. Suddenly she understood, or close to understood

anyway. She was using Matthew's computer and online account. And somehow this rude person thought he or she was talking to Matthew.

"I am not Matthew Locke. I am Mrs. Locke. And I resent your behavior."

She quickly clicked the Goodbye button again, hoping it would disconnect her. She gave a grateful sigh of relief when the confirmation box reappeared.

But before she could click the Yes button, SFScooper's chat window appeared on top again. This time, however, it contained no profanity. Just one word:

"Oh."

She went to click Goodbye again, then reconsidered. This person had frightened and offended her, had called her husband terrible things. No, she was not going to let the creep get away with a simple "Oh."

"You should apologize," she typed.

She waited for a reply, staring at the little window. And waited. Had the person on the other end signed off? Was he or she sorry now for behaving so rudely? Or thinking of another foul response? She waited another minute or two. Still nothing. It was just as well. The last thing she wanted was to spoil her first day as an online citizen with this immature person.

Who then responded.

"I'm sorry. I made a mistake. I meant it affectionately. You know, 'You bastard.' Like, playful."

"You were wrong. My husband is not a bastard."

There was another pause, as though the person on the other end was weighing her response very carefully.

"You should create a personal ID for yourself. Your own online name. So people don't mistake you. Do you want me to show you how?"

She didn't know what to say. This person who had just offended

her was now trying to help her. It didn't add up. Yet she certainly didn't want what had happened to happen again. She had no idea how to do what this person suggested, how to create her own identity. What would it hurt to accept his or her offer to help, a sort of truce.

"Can I pick any name I want?"

"Sure. Anything. As long as it isn't taken. Think of something fun."

"OK," Greta typed, no longer aware of her thirst or full bladder. She was hooked.

"Show me," she typed.

"Now you're pissing me off, Matthew," Peter said as he rose from his seat. He picked up his pen and began pressing the button up and down. It sounded very loud in the nearly silent boardroom.

"I'm sorry, Peter," Matthew said. "But I'm perfectly serious. As president and CEO, it's in my power to conduct a vote. And that's what I intend to do. Unless you agree to what I've suggested."

Peter scoffed. "Matthew, you've lost it. A vote. I don't believe this. You want to vote. Hey, if that's what you want, go ahead. Make a bigger fool of yourself. Go on, Matthew." He waved his pen through the air, taking in the entire room. "Vote, then."

Peter shoved his hands in his pockets and began pacing. Then he halted and spoke excitedly. "No, wait. I've got a better idea, Matthew. I'll ask. Okay? I'll conduct your little popularity contest. This'll be fun."

Matthew gave an indifferent shrug. He had nothing more to say just yet.

Peter addressed the nearest executive, Alan Parker, general manager of the Mate division and Via's first executive hire. Short and rotund, Parker looked visibly upset as Peter set a hand on his shoulder.

"Hey, Al. What do you think of all this? Pretty awkward, I agree. But nothing we can't take care of nice and quick, get back to work. I don't need to repeat the question, do I, Al? Or am I just stupid? Am I crazy thinking you and everyone else here want me out of my company?"

Alan Parker swiveled in his chair to face Jones. "It's gone too far, Peter. You and your At Hand team have created a rivalry with my Mate group. Mate was this company's bread and butter up until At Hand PC was introduced. You've made us feel like second-class citizens. And now your product is practically driving us into the red."

Peter could barely hide his surprise at the restrained anger in Parker's voice. "Well, you've always been a little sensitive, Alan. Admit it. At Hand is where this company is going. Listen, you want in on it, fine. We'll shift you over into my group, soon as we can." He brightened, warming to the authoritative sound of his own voice. "And I'll tell you what: We'll throw a big party for the Mate team, okay? A big thank-you sort of thing. I'll even drop by to personally announce it. What do you say?"

Parker's face reddened. "That's not the point. Don't you see? You're doing it right now, Peter, just like you always do. Twisting things to suit you. Only you. And I'm sick of it."

Peter drew his hand away, incredulous. "You're kidding, right? I mean, okay, we've got our differences. Look, I know I leave something to be desired in the social graces department. It's something I have to work on. Yes, I admit it, I treat my engineers like gods. To me, they are. But you can't mean you're on Matthew's side. Tell me you're not, Al."

Parker turned back around in his seat and quietly cast his vote. "I'm sorry, Peter." He gathered his hands together and settled them on the table with a small thud.

Peter let out a disbelieving chuckle. "You're serious."

Parker nodded, then abruptly spun around to face Peter again.

"But Peter, wait. I don't think you should leave the company. We need you too much. To work on our future products. Just let Matthew handle what he's proposing—"

Peter lifted a hand to cut him off. "Save it, Al." He gave Parker a gentle pat on the shoulder and then stepped over to the opposite end of the window from Matthew. He crossed his arms and looked outside, the lord of his empire. No one said a word. They waited a full minute for him to turn around and face them once more, now wearing a bemused smile.

"So everyone thinks I'm a jerk, is that it? And our big-shot businessman here is a savior?" He flung a hand in Matthew's direction.

Matthew took a step toward him. "Peter, please. Alan is right. I—*we*—all want you here at Via. But you need to let me have the power to do what's right for our business."

Peter made a disgusted noise. "And I suppose you have that all figured out? Forget it, Matthew. And let's cut all this bullshit too, okay? Okay. Fine. If this is how you want to play the game, let's do it then. Around the room. No small talk. No sentimental crap. Just yes or no."

He pressed himself firmly against the warm window and looked over the table. "All right, who's next. Let's just move on down the line, why don't we. Denise. You. Me or Matthew, who's it gonna be?"

Denise Campbell had enjoyed a stellar career with Via. She'd started as a financial analyst. Brilliant with numbers, she'd eventually been promoted to chief financial officer. With anguished eyes, she turned around to face Peter.

"Peter, I know I don't have to tell you that as a publicly held company our first obligation is to our shareholders. And—"

He shook his head rapidly, eyes blazing. "No verbosity, please. Me or Matthew?"

"Matthew."

Peter gave a single nod and quickly moved to the next person. "Paul."

Regarded for his no-nonsense manner, sales and marketing VP Paul Crane uttered a single word. "Matthew."

And so on, the same name repeated again and again.

Through it all Matthew held his position at the opposite end of the window, his heart racing, rivulets of sweat running down his sideburns and into his collar while his face betrayed nothing. Until Peter, exhausted, exasperated, had come to the last person at the table.

Peter knelt before Hank Towers, the man who'd originally taken a chance and bankrolled Peter's dream.

"Hank," Peter said, his voice barely audible. "Jesus, Hank. Can you believe this is happening? I mean, can you honestly believe this? I can't." Peter drummed his chest. "You and I, Hank. You and I made this company. Made Via what it is today."

Towers sat perfectly still, but Matthew could see that Peter's words were having an effect on him. And on some of the others, as sounds of sniffing and little coughs, throats clearing, filled the room. He forced himself to not let his feelings get in the way of his own manner. It was important that he appear strong, stable.

What was going on inside was another story. His pulse doubled. Despite the so-far unanimous votes in his favor, Hank's influence was not to be underestimated. A vote for Peter would cause everyone in the room to reconsider his or her own vote, and possibly prompt a second vote.

"Hank, you have to trust me on this one." Peter gripped the armrest of Towers's chair. "Matthew isn't right for Via. If you let him have this, he'll turn Via into a second-rate company. All I want is what any of us wants, Hank. To be the best."

Matthew struggled to read Towers's stoic expression. It was impossible. Another cold stream of sweat trickled down his back. He felt his stomach rumble when it occurred to him that he might

have been wrong in his assessment of Hank's support. Had he been kidding himself in thinking he could turn Towers's loyalty against his cofounder?

Peter's voice was a rasp. "Damn it, Hank. Look at me. Don't you see what he really wants? His long-term plan? For Christ's sake, he tried to convince me that we should become compatible with PC-fucking-Soft's operating system. He even suggested once we should license our own OS to ICP. If that's not selling out then what the hell is? Come on, Hank. I'm your main man, and you know it. It's just you and me."

Matthew felt close to throwing up. While not entirely accurate, Peter's spontaneous assessment laid bare Matthew's ultimate motivation for all in the room to consider. They'd come down to brass tacks. It was now or never, and he held his breath.

Hank Towers looked the younger man in the eye, and slowly shook his head.

Peter made a terrible wrenching noise and dropped his head onto the arm of Hank Towers's chair. He stayed like that for a minute, trying to catch his breath. He could barely speak.

"Hank, no. You can't. We got through the tough spots before. We can run Via. Until we find someone who can cut it. Oh God, Hank."

Towers set a fatherly hand on Peter's bowed head. "No, Peter."

Peter looked up, fat tears rolling down his cheeks. "But this is my life here. I'll die if you don't save me, Hank. You're my only hope. Please."

"Calm down, Petey. Deep breath. Come on, now. Listen to me." He gave Peter's shoulder a bracing squeeze. "We're a big company now. At our most critical point in all our history. It's a big game out there now. One you're not equipped to compete in in an executive capacity. But you've got to stay on to do our big thinking. You've got to. All we're asking is that you let Matthew do

his job. You'll think it's all bad for a while, but then you'll under-
stand. And you'll wind up a lot happier for it. Mark my words.
You'll see, Peter." Towers let out an exasperated sigh. "Damn it,
Peter, we love you."

There wasn't a dry eye in the room. Except Matthew Locke's.
Pale with anxiety, lips pressed firmly closed, heart racing, he
struggled to remain unaffected by the raw emotion in the room.

Peter took a deep breath and stood, struggling to get himself
under control. The lapels of his suit were shining with wetness.
His tie was askew. He rubbed his sleeve across his forehead and
cleared his throat. He looked down at Hank, and with what little
defiance he could muster, he spoke.

"And if I refuse to agree to all of this?"

"Petey, I'm afraid it's the only option you've got."

Peter let Hank's words sink in for a moment, then turned to
look around the table. Everyone sat as they had through the whole
meeting, avoiding his eyes. Staring at their fucking yellow pads.
Maybe itching to lift their pens and start calculating what their
stock options might be worth after today's news got out.

And wasn't that what it all came down to? he asked himself
as he stood there unable to move or say anything. Wasn't that what
he'd used to lure each of them here? The bottom line. The riches.
But none of them understood that for him, it wasn't the money.
It was more than that. It was Via, and everything it meant. It was
his life.

And it was over.

He looked at Matthew, who mistakenly interpreted the glance
as a gesture of reconciliation. "Peter. It doesn't have to end like this."
He took a step toward the younger man.

"Don't come near me," Peter shouted, causing everyone to
jump in their seats.

He locked eyes with Matthew. "I can't believe you're doing
this. You're destroying my life." He shook his head in disgust and

quickly returned to his place at the table. He picked up his portfolio and hurried to the door, ignoring Hank Towers's plea to wait.

He paused at the doorway and turned to face the room one last time. He opened his mouth to say something, but no words came out. Instead he merely shook his head in disbelief, then departed.

The door slowly swung closed, sealing the executives inside the boardroom for the first time without Peter Jones at the helm.

All eyes were on Matthew Locke now.

William Harrell plodded through his morning in the usual fashion. Three meetings. Fourteen phone calls. Then on to his daily correspondence.

He kept a constant eye on his E-mail, awaiting confirmation from his secret partner. He knew it wasn't likely to come until early evening, but he kept checking anyway, in case the plan had gone awry.

At eleven-forty-five he left ICP headquarters for a ten-block ride to an exclusive men's athletic club. The membership list read like the Fortune 100. One of the club's perks was its "random matches," which pitted high-level executives from dissimilar industries against one another in squash and racquetball. The president of an insurance company, for instance, might be paired with the CEO from one of the major networks. Or, in William Harrell's case, the chairman of the world's largest computer company might compete with the chairman of the world's biggest food and beverage conglomerate.

Back from his workout, he glanced at the clock. In five minutes

his technical and business advisers would arrive to discuss the company's portable computer strategy. He took the free time to stretch his sore arms over his head. He was back in the game again, and it felt good. In fact, better than ever.

He thought back to a particularly memorable match, a little more than two years ago, against Rolland Worthy, head of International Foods. The game had changed his life. He gave an appreciative shake of his head as he recalled the match, when Worthy had asked him:

"What do you know about Via?"

The hard rubber ball struck the wall and blasted at him. Thrown off by Worthy's unexpected question, his judgment slipped and he overextended. The ball hurtled by, costing him a point.

Worthy gave a hearty laugh. "What, I hit a nerve?"

Harrell crouched. "They're a small Silicon Valley company that makes a proprietary portable computer." He bounced on the balls of his feet, ready for Worthy's serve.

The executive tossed the ball into the air and nailed it with his racket, then dropped quickly to a defensive stance, his actions fluid and youthful. They smashed the ball back and forth, and Harrell's fourth return forced Worthy into a corner, where he crashed, unable to save the ball.

"Gonna make it?" William Harrell joked.

Worthy rolled his shoulder and took position. "Serve the bastard."

As the match played out, Harrell's curiosity gnawed at his game. Why was Worthy interested in Via? The older executive's timing couldn't have been more apt. Or William's worse, as his curiosity started to cost him the match and he missed one point after another.

The small competitor had in fact been the topic of Harrell's meeting prior to the match. His business adviser had assured him

that ICP's new Business Partner portable computer had quickly gained nearly twice the market share of Via's older Mate system. But William Harrell knew too well how a tiny company could suddenly turn into a tremendous opponent. He'd learned that lesson with PCSoft, which had the giant ICP—and every other hardware maker—in the palm of its hand, earning a healthy licensing fee for every system that shipped with its prominent PortaPC OS. William would never live down his error of not buying PCSoft when it was still a fledgling start-up company. Now PCSoft ruled the industry, from portable to desktop to the Web, and its all-encompassing eye on the future searched even further, to computers in cars, in kitchens, in classrooms, and beyond, into the heavens, to the satellites that beamed consumer broadcasts around the world. They wanted it all. And partnered with Future Processing—makers of the CPU at the heart of ICP's and everyone but Via's computers—they were well on their way to having it all. Although ICP was many times larger than either PCSoft or Future Processing in billions of sales, the public nonetheless perceived ICP as a has-been player in the desktop and portable market.

Bottom line, William Harrell admired Via. Small as it was, Via was the only competitor playing to its own tune. And succeeding at it, however marginally. Despite the fact that Via's market share was dwarfed by the installed base of PCSoft/Future Processing systems, the public revered the legendary company. And it adored Via's eccentric founder, Peter Jones.

And that was what had William Harrell so troubled. Jones had been too quiet lately. Once the most outspoken voice against PCSoft's dominant and often suspect business practices, Jones had all but disappeared. He hadn't granted a public interview in more than a year. Harrell could only guess that Jones had something up his sleeve. Possibly big. Yet at the same time, Harrell had his

doubts. It was no secret that Jones was a poor chief, and that without proper guidance Via would eventually run itself into the ground.

So Harrell was caught off guard when, as they headed for the showers after the match, Rolland Worthy explained his interest in Via.

"This is completely off the record, my friend." William Harrell assured the older executive that it would stay that way, and Worthy continued. "They called one of my best guys. Matthew Locke. Flying him to California to interview for the president and CEO slot."

"Interesting," Harrell said casually.

Worthy grunted. "As you know, I've been grooming Locke to take my seat when I retire in a few years. Anyway, he came to me saying he'd gotten a call from a headhunter to go out and meet this kid named Peter Jones."

"Will he accept?"

Worthy shrugged. "Too soon to say. I think he wanted me to guarantee him my job now, retire sooner. When I told him I wasn't ready for that, he said maybe he wasn't either. He flew out to California this morning. What I don't get is what would some hippie computer nerds want with a guy who sells soda pop and chips?"

Harrell knew exactly what Via would want him for: the consumer market. Yes, Peter Jones had something up his sleeve all right. No doubt something huge. And to make it fly, he was trying to lure an executive who knew the consumer market inside and out.

Despite his hot shower, William Harrell felt a chilling apprehension creep in when he considered the possibilities. Not since his wife had begun her slide into the final stages of cancer had he felt that same uncertainty about the immediate future.

But that day was history. And, Harrell mused, history was being made today, at this very moment, on the opposite coast. Indeed, Rolland Worthy's surprise disclosure had disturbed William Harrell enough to cost him the match. But not the game. Indeed, his secret contender waited in the wings: a player who would

combine forces with Harrell and ICP to challenge the dominant PCSoft/Future Computing. The stage was set.

William Harrell checked his E-mail again. Finding no word yet, he waited. He was the leader of one of the most powerful companies in the world, a position he'd gained by operating at top speed, always anticipating the next move. But for once, he could afford to be patient.

He'd bet his career on it.

Peter charged out of the company parking lot and raced for the highway, tears streaming down his face. He was disgusted by his reaction. Instead of outrage, he felt anguish. Instead of opposition, defeat. The damage was done and he knew it was irreparable. Matthew had stolen the company out from under his nose. They had all turned against him.

Waiting for the on-ramp stoplight to change, Peter looked in his mirror at the Via logo, just as he had yesterday. The irony made his throat tighten, and he bit down on his lip to keep himself from turning hysterical. He looked away, then tore onto the highway, his foot heavy on the gas pedal.

How could he have let it happen? Missed the warning signs? Not seen that Matthew wouldn't be content with a second-place role? The tables had turned, and now Matthew was the star. He had played Peter as a pawn in a secret game of chance. And Peter had lost. Everything.

He hit seventy-five miles an hour and fantasized about cutting the wheel and ending it all in a terrific blaze. His knuckles were white. Even the car was a fucking prop. He thought of Matthew zipping around in the same model, and shouted to himself. Did Locke think it was all just a game of pretend? Take the top spot and suddenly you're an inventor? A visionary?

It was impossible to believe he was no longer in charge. He

tried to picture Matthew taking over the At Hand PC Plus project, marching into the engineering group with intricate schedules and an army of bozo project managers. And suppose Locke actually pulled it off, what then? Why, he would take all the credit for it, of course.

His stomach gave a painful heave as reality began to creep in. All he wanted was his company. His products. His life. Back to the way it was before all of this had happened. And then he remembered last night. What he had done. His heart raced faster. He'd blown it on that front, too.

Then it hit him. How any of this could happen in the first place. It was so obvious. He'd been used. They'd used him. All of them. Matthew. The executive staff. The board. They'd been using him for their own selfish gains. And when they were done with him they'd thrown him away.

His car phone jingled and he punched it, knocking it to the floor, then rubbed his eyes with the back of his bleeding knuckles.

No more talking. It was too late for that. They'd done enough damage. And he'd let it happen. Well, never again. No more being used. It was time for a change. Time to cut away from those who had stolen from him. It was the only way, he decided, and pressed harder on the accelerator. And after what he'd just been through, it would be easy.

He would start with Ivy.

"I think he answered but then he hung up," Matthew's secretary said as she put down her handset.

"Forget it," Matthew said. He closed his office door, took off his jacket, and dropped heavily into his chair. Leave it alone, he told himself. Leave him alone. It had to be this way. There was no other way. Though he had once sincerely cared for Peter, this was business, and nobody ever said business was easy.

He had hoped that things would turn out differently. That Peter would see the value in his suggestion to widen the business through alliances and the like. It had been a lot to hope for. Too much, really. Peter Jones was a renegade, and his unwillingness to change had cost him his company.

Matthew turned around in his chair to face his docked At Hand PC computer. His. He closed his eyes and let the thought fully sink in. He was dizzy with a strange mix of elation and remorse. The first phase of his plan had worked. They had chosen him to run Via, and Peter could no longer stand in his way. He was free to move on to the next step, and while this was what he'd wanted, he felt terrible when he pictured Peter's expression as he stood at the boardroom door looking back in disbelief, unable to speak.

He opened his eyes and stared at his At Hand PC's monitor, animated by a screensaver of spinning Via logos. He tried to envision a new logo. One that merged Via's far-reaching vision with the rock-solid might of the world's largest computer company.

The perfect design eluded him for the moment. He was getting ahead of himself. In time, though, all in time. He looked at the clock and calculated that it was going on 6:00 P.M. in the East. He scooted forward and moved the At Hand's mouse to wake it up. He loaded his E-mail program. He had worded the message a thousand times in his head over the last two years, never entirely sure how it would turn out. Until now.

He typed:

TO: wharrell@icp.com
SUBJECT: status

I have been granted full support by the board and executive staff to take over all senior management responsibilities at via, including the development of the At Hand PC Plus, which will be ready for release in three months.

peter jones has been chartered with overseeing the
development of future via products. it is unclear at this
time whether he will accept his new role.

we will proceed, and succeed, regardless.

—matthew

He clicked the Send button and let out an exhausted sigh
when the message vanished from his screen. At the same time
there was a soft knock on his door, and he turned around to greet
Laurence Merrill.

"You okay?" The young corporate communications officer
looked at him with genuine concern in her eyes.

"I guess it's the suddenness of it all." He wiped his shirtsleeve
across his brow. "It's still sort of a shock."

She nodded sympathetically. "Your statement's out to the
press." She handed him a printed list. "Here are the journalists
you're scheduled with."

He scanned the list. "Half of them were in the running for
the bio coauthor job." He stopped on one name. "How come Ellis
is crossed out?"

"I called each of them this morning to say you'd chosen Jan-
ice Lane of *Fortune* to coauthor your autobiography. They all took
it like pros, and wished you and Janice Lane the best of luck.
Except Joshua. He was pissed. He was sure the job was his, so he
quit the *Examiner* yesterday. Not very smart. Anyway, shall we get
started?"

Matthew briefly considered calling the dejected journalist to
offer a word of consolation, but then decided against it. He had
more important calls to make. He went back to the first name on
the list, a reporter at the *Wall Street Journal*. He picked up the

phone and dialed. And in the moment it took the journalist to an-
swer, the reality finally set in: This was his first call in his new role,
as Via's most powerful leader.

He was greeted warmly, and given the benefit of the doubt.

For now.

Unlike yesterday's sunny piano welcome, Peter this time arrived home to a cacophony of shouts of laughter, and what sounded like a robot reciting the alphabet. The combination had a dreadful effect on his already foul mood.

Charging to the back of the house he found Ivy sitting cross-legged on the floor. Eyelids drooping, long hair askew, she inhaled deeply from a fat joint. It took her a few moments to notice him. The room was a mess, littered with beer cans and junk-food packages, an empty wine bottle.

Two other young people, both men, appeared equally oblivious of Peter's arrival. The partying trio sat around a low table. On it rested an At Hand PC, connected to a monitor, cables, crude boxes, and a single microphone, into which one of the boys was speaking.

"Say cheese," the boy said.

On the monitor, a bright yellow smiley face blinked its black-dot eyes. And then spoke.

"Say cheese," the smiley face replied in a flat, robotic voice. At the same time, the words "Say Cheese" appeared in a little

balloon alongside the smiley face's mouth. Ivy had nicknamed the program "Myna Bird." It was a rudimentary experiment in speech recognition and synthesis that made it possible for the At Hand to "converse" in plain English. Its powers of interpretation were limited to a dictionary of several thousand common words.

The young man said more. "Goo goo."

The smiley face blinked but did not respond.

"I said, goo goo."

"I said ...," the smiley face said, unable to complete the sentence.

"I said goo fucking goo," the boy shouted.

"I said ... fucking ...," the smiley face replied, in deadpan monotone.

The boy laughed uproariously, but the others didn't join him. He looked at them with a buzzed and puzzled expression. Then he saw Peter standing in the doorway. He stopped laughing.

"What the fuck is going on?" Peter shouted.

"What the fuck is going on?" the smiley face repeated, minus the anger.

The guys bowed their heads in guilt while Ivy, breaking into a fit of laughter at the mimicry, got to her feet and stumbled over to Peter.

He was not amused. "What's so fucking funny?"

The boy with the microphone had the sense to switch it off before the smiley face could say more.

"You are," Ivy said, laughing so hard she could barely speak. "You are, love."

Peter looked at the scene and with a white hot fury managed the words "Get out of my house. Now."

The other young man stood, not sure whether he should run or stand between Peter and Ivy, who stood staring at Peter in stunned silence.

"I said get out. All of you. Get the fuck out of my house."

The visitors quickly disconnected the gear from the At Hand and packed up their knapsacks. Ivy lowered herself to the floor, still stunned by Peter's fierce outburst.

The young men made a wide berth around Peter and Ivy. "You can keep the beer, man," one of the guys said as they hastily retreated. They nearly collided with Alice, who came in to see what all the shouting was about. She began picking up the empty packages and bottles.

"Leave it, Alice," Peter said angrily. "Ivy will clean it up before she leaves."

The housekeeper hesitated for a moment, then departed with the few things she'd already collected.

Peter moved to the other side of the room, putting space between himself and Ivy.

"Peter," Ivy said quietly as she drew her knees to her chest. "I'm sorry, Peter. I'm sorry, I'm so sorry." She began rocking in place.

"You have to go."

"We were working on my program—"

"You're not welcome here."

"And I wanted to surprise you—"

"I should have never let you come here in the first place."

"And I wanted to surprise you with this dialect module I finished this morning—"

"I won't say it again."

She began crying softly, but he didn't care. He looked away. Stared at the smiley face gazing dumbly back at him. His mind was made up. No more free rides.

"But, Peter. I love you."

He fought the urge to run to her. To take her in his arms and say he was sorry for screaming at her. To let his own tears pour out as he explained what had happened. How his company was no longer his. How his life was over now.

But Ivy wasn't the one to cry to. For the first time since he'd bolted from Via, he thought of Kate, the only person he wanted to be with right now. A wave of guilt washed over him and he pressed his hands to his temples. His head was pounding. His heart was racing. He felt like he was going to throw up. In less than twenty-four hours his whole life had come undone.

"I'm sorry, Peter, but it's true. I'm so in love with you."

"No, you're not."

"Yes, I am. I love you." She spoke quickly, fidgeting nervously with the laces of her sneakers. "I almost died when I heard you were giving our commencement speech. I wasn't even part of the graduating class. What do you think I was doing there? I'd snuck in. Just so I could see you in person. Meet you. Because I knew. I knew, Peter." She rose to her feet and made her way slowly across the room, speaking with conviction. "That if you met me you'd be into what I was working on. And then you went and invited me here. Because you could feel it too. The way we connected. It's true. Just admit it."

"You're crazy. You used me. You even stole my clothes."

"No, Peter. God, it's not like that. What's wrong with you?" She reached out to him.

"Please. I'm sorry. But don't touch me," he said, shaking her off. He nearly stumbled to put more space between them. He crossed his arms over his chest. "Look, you can think up what-ever fantasies you want. You may even believe them. I can't give you what you want. But if you don't leave I can't be held re-sponsible. I'm at the end of my rope here." He heard himself say these things and knew he was speaking like a crazy man, yet he couldn't help it. He had to do this, protect himself, it was all he could do.

She clasped her hands together tightly. "But last night, Peter. What about last night. What do you call that?"

"Stupid. A mistake. A truly spectacular mistake. Please, please just leave."

She turned her gaze to the computer and shook her head sadly. "Don't you see? Peter, I did this for you. Because I care about At Hand. And Via. And you. Why do you think I changed my studies? For this." She waved a shaky hand at the smiley face. "Because I knew it was important. You know you care about it. You said so yesterday, when I showed you how far I'd gotten with it."

He said nothing.

She smiled bitterly. "So that's it? Wham, bam, fuck you ma'am?"

No response.

She nodded and wiped her nose. "All right, then. Well fuck you too, Peter Jones." She turned and ran upstairs. He heard the sounds of drawers opening, the closet door sliding on its tracks. A few minutes later she returned but did not look at him. He turned and pretended to stare out the window as he furtively watched her in the reflection.

She crossed the room and ejected a Zip disk from the At Hand PC and tossed it into her backpack, then she collected her small duffel bag at the doorway. She paused.

"You're gonna regret this, Peter. I promise."

He said nothing.

And then she was gone.

He turned around and frowned at the smiley face. It stared back. Passive. Obedient. Waiting for input. Just like everyone else, he thought morosely, it wanted something from him.

Dropping down heavily onto the sofa he felt something poke his side. A wine bottle, shoved between the cushions. He lifted it. Red wine. And then it hit him. It was the bottle Kate had given him on their first date. The bottle they'd vowed to drink together when Via turned ten years old. Like him, it was nearly depleted.

He looked from the bottle to the insipid smiley face and shook his head sadly.

He hurled the bottle at the happy face, nailing the fucker right between the eyes.

Matthew called out his wife's name as he charged up the stairs, taking them two at a time. He found her in the master bedroom, soaking in the tub.

"I did it," he said, showing her the headline in the afternoon paper he'd picked up. In just the few short hours since the showdown his attitude had already started to change, not so subtly, as though whatever remorse he felt was purging its way out of his memory. He was only vaguely aware of the change, and when he did recognize it he told himself it was a form of self-protection, a way of coping.

"Darling, hooray for you! I saw it on the five o'clock news!"

Whipping off his tie, he glanced at the reading tray Greta had set across the tub. She set down what she had been reading, the slim At Hand PC manual borrowed from his office shelf. "Come over here this instant." She stretched over the side of the tub and puckered her lips.

He kissed her cheek and seated himself on the closed toilet seat.

"Goodness, Matthew. You must feel like you're on top of the world."

"I mostly can't believe it. I'm relieved, that's for sure. I knew it would happen, it had to. But you just never know until it's all said and done." He studied his own photo in the paper, a stock corporate portrait, positioned beneath the huge headline: "Via Heads Change Hands."

"Oh, Matthew. I would love to have seen that little pest's face when the ax fell. Tell me. Did he cry? The little boy who broke his favorite toy? Did he, Matthew?"

"Greta, you're brutal. And yes, there were tears. It was very upsetting. He couldn't believe it at first. Then when he realized it was for real I was afraid he was going to have a heart attack." He left out the part about feeling like his own insides were being torn up. She wouldn't want to hear it, and besides, he had to guard against turning sentimental.

She closed her eyes and smiled as she tried to picture the confrontation in her head.

He studied her with secret fascination. Her right hand lay across the side of the tub, bare, exposed, lovely, while the left lay hidden in the sudsy water.

She opened her eyes and let out a satisfied sigh. "Darling, be a dear and pass me that oil," she said, pointing to the nearby shelf.

He handed her the bottle and she held it between her knees, so that she could unscrew the cap with her right hand. She dropped the cap on the floor and squeezed a long stream of the rose-scented red oil into the tub.

Matthew momentarily lost track of his thoughts, mesmerized by how the color bled into the water. She handed the bottle back to him and closed her eyes. She settled deeper into the water and gently oscillated her shoulders and hips, mixing up the oil and water. His memory flew back in time, the scene flashing vividly in his mind. The International Foods yacht party thrown for him to celebrate the success of Orange Fresh. One minute laughter, cheers. The next, horror, shouts. Her scream. The water, frothy with blood. The splashing in his face—

He gave a start when he realized that she was flicking bathwater at him, bringing him back to the present.

"Greta, my shirt. You're staining it."

"Oh, shush. The water's perfect, darling. Come on, dive in."

He absently wiped at the pink dots on his shirt as he rose to his feet and formulated an excuse. "Honey, I can't. I have to go check and see if William Harrell got my E-mail message."

Wait, that's the header. Let me format properly.

"Oh, come on. I'm sure he's following the news. Take a breather, for crying out loud. Please, Matthew. Just this once."

He briefly considered how she must see things. When he had doubted the viability of his plan, she was there for him. Encouraging him. Saying all the right things. Her unflagging confidence in him had helped him through the moments of doubt. Until finally he too fully believed it would work. And that, he understood now, was when it must have happened. When his love for her had slipped completely from his grasp.

It had started to recede after the accident. They'd struggled to act normally. But over time they quit pretending. Stopped making excuses, and making love. And settled into a companionable life together. He focused on his work, she on her things. The house. The garden. Parties. And on him, supporting him in his career. He couldn't remember the last time they'd made love, not in the real sense.

And now? He knew what she was thinking. Hoping. That things would suddenly be different between them. Better. Closer. Stronger. But in his heart he knew nothing would change.

He remembered the object, which he kept hidden in his briefcase. That was precisely how he thought of it, as the object of his lost affection. He could not bring himself to destroy it. Or to reveal it to her, even though it rightly belonged to her. It was his secret, all that remained to remind him that he had once loved this woman completely.

Thumbing his wedding band on his ring finger, he turned the conversation back to her. "So did you do it, darling? Sit down with the computer?" He alternated his attention between his wife and the newspaper story.

Rising above her disappointment, she smiled with evident pride. "Matthew, I couldn't believe it. It was so easy. I did not one but two, two letters. I went online. Browsed some boutiques. And had my first brush with a hacker or online fiend or whatever you call them."

"Really, a hacker?" He was only half listening.

"Well, a rude person. A Mr. or Mrs. Cooper. They never said either way, now that I think about it. Anyway, this he or she called me all sorts of dirty names. And then it occurred to me. That they thought they were talking to you!"

"Hmm. An angry Via purist, I bet. I get those sometimes, E-mails mostly. Know-it-all kids or engineers who want to tell me everything I'm doing wrong with the company, and how I can save it if I'd just listen to them. It's nothing."

"Maybe not to you, but I was shocked, Matthew. So I created my own identity. 'The Gret One.' After some great hockey player. At least that's what this Cooper person said. Do you like it?"

"That's my Gret. The one and only. Have fun with it, darling. But be careful. There're definitely crazies out there, scammers and that sort of thing." He folded the paper under his arm. His attention had moved on to other, more pressing things. He smiled at her. "All right, then. Back to work for me. I'll be down in my office."

Her merriment turned to disappointment once more, and he didn't want to leave her like this.

"Hey, how about this. You keep practicing with my computer, and when the new At Hand PC Plus is ready in three months, I'll get you one of your very own. Sound good?"

"Sure, Matthew. That would be lovely." She scooped up a mound of suds and blew them at him. "You sure you don't want to come in?"

"Gret."

"All right, all right. Go do what you have to do. I've got my own computer work now too." She picked up the At Hand manual and pretended not to notice her husband's grateful wink.

He hurried downstairs to his home office. Greta had moved the mouse to the left side. Yes, a computer of her own was exactly what she needed. He hoped she would become fully engrossed in her new hobby. It would make things so much easier. He knew bet-

ter than most how time flies when one is seated before a computer. He picked up the mouse and put it back where it belonged, on the right side. Then he restarted his At Hand.

An erotic thought occurred to him as he waited for the machine to start up. Glancing at the mouse again, he thought not of his wife's hand resting on it, but of Laurence Merrill's. He recalled yesterday's galvanizing phone conversation with her. He on his car phone, she on his office phone, patched in by his secretary. Had she touched his system, his mouse?

The computer was ready now, but he wasn't. He went to his library's toilet and closed the door. He dropped his trousers and got ahold of himself. He closed his eyes and concentrated, hardened.

He considered the act the secret of his success. He'd discovered it at the early age of ten, and it had forever altered the course of his life. His special study tool, through grade school, high school, college. Whenever girls distracted him from his studies he simply got himself off, and back on track. Of course there'd been some real contact with women, brief affairs, but none worth the time or energy for anything longer lasting. It was a small price to pay to come so far, so fast. And he'd never fully grasped its relevance until he met Greta, a woman worth marrying, with hands that were more expert than his own.

But hers were not the hands he thought of now, holding him, stroking him. These were the youthful hands of another, and moments later they worked their magic.

He'd been lying in bed for hours, staring at the ceiling. Time didn't matter anymore. Every now and then he took a gulp of Scotch from the bottle he had opened after Ivy left. He never drank hard liquor, but today seemed like a good time to start, the most natural thing in the world. He needed help, something to let him escape his own mind and force him to sleep. Or unconsciousness. Right now,

that was the most appealing option. It was too soon to try and think things through.

Through? How, he wondered, does one think through being through? With each swallow of the burning spirit the questions grew more complicated, more impossible to answer.

What he wondered most was what they would do for the future. What would Via do? His instinctive reaction to anything that threatened Via—in this case, his own ejection from the company—never failed to force him into action. But this time he was unable to intervene.

Almost ten years, he mused. All spent on Via, where everything began. It seemed like a lifetime ago.

He drifted.

He'd always been an oddball student, unable to fit in with the jocks or pot heads or other groups. He was an orphan most of his life, given up as an infant by a poor unwed mother he never knew. He grew up in San Jose, raised in an orphanage governed by an elderly couple, Clayton and Clara Dodson.

He was used to spending time alone, reading or going for walks in the nearby wooded hills. He pretended he was Henry David Thoreau, observing nature, lost in his own thoughts, comfortable with his life of solitude.

When forced to spend a few trial days with potential foster parents he turned sullen and despondent. He always waited until the last day with the hopeful parents to throw a tantrum. It never failed to turn them away. He needed no one, nothing—except maybe his collection of science fiction novels.

Eventually the Dodsons stopped sending him off to potential families. He made no trouble, and helped out where he could around the orphanage. With Clayton's encouragement, Peter was

granted a scholarship to Cal Poly. He won the award not because of his grades, which were below average, but because of a heartfelt essay on the value of the home computer as a companion. He described a device that was easy to use and small enough to take with you wherever you went. Yet it was powerful enough to do everything a big computer could do. Its interface, he imagined, would be unlike anything anyone had ever seen. It would learn from its owner, pay attention to his likes and dislikes, anticipate his needs. The more it learned about its holder and the world around it, the more loyal and dependable a friend it would become.

How exactly this computer worked, what technologies it used, was not of interest to Peter. It was of interest, however, to the review board that had granted the scholarship. The school was in fact researching many of the concepts the then eighteen-year-old had described.

He failed miserably as a student. He skipped classes to pursue his own interests in the library or labs, ingratiating himself with seniors and faculty. By the third quarter he had made friends with two bright engineering students, John Dulin and Rick Caruso. He described his dream machine to them one night over beers and pizza. They discussed the feasibility of a computer like the one he imagined, and decided that only its most basic features could be brought together for a price that would be attractive to consumers. Then let's build it, Peter suggested. The boys laughed at him. He told them he was serious and wagered that if they would help him put together a prototype, he would find the funding necessary to turn the idea into a reality.

Luck was on his side. By the end of the school year the boys had created a working version, code-named Mate. It was smaller than any portable computer on the market, and featured an integrated contacts and schedule organizer, word processor, and communications program dubbed Easy Does It.

Of course none of it actually worked, but the concepts were there, just waiting for the capital. Peter packed his prototype into a cardboard box, grabbed the next bus to Sunnyvale, and paid an unannounced visit to a man named Hank Towers, whose company was the world's leading maker of electronic display panels used in a variety of devices, from submarine instrumentation to medical monitors to gauges on the space shuttle.

Politely informed that Mr. Towers was unavailable, Peter thanked the secretary, then took a seat on the comfortable sofa in the reception area and waited. By the end of the day Mr. Towers was still unavailable to see him. And so the next day he returned, asked to see Mr. Towers, and was told the same thing. He parked himself in the lobby and waited another full day, to no avail. He waited the next day, and the next, until finally Hank Towers had to see for himself this kid who would not go away.

The rest was history, the stuff Silicon Valley legends were made of.

Were, Peter thought hazily. Were made of. He drifted in and out of sleep, drunk, disoriented.

The phone's relentless high-pitched warble forced him awake. He squinted at the late-afternoon sun cutting into his bedroom. Reaching out blindly for the handset, he knocked over the bottle of Scotch, spilling it onto the hardwood floor.

He lifted the handset to his ear, but before he could say anything an anxious voice said his name. A woman's voice. It was her.

"Kate." It came out as a moan.

"Peter, I heard. My God, I don't know what to say. Are you all right?"

He was unable to speak. He pressed his fingers to his eyes, said her name again.

She spoke very fast. "I caught the tail end of it on CNN. A reorganization. I called your office. Ben said you took off. He was so upset. Peter, what the hell is going on?"

"It's over." His words slurred together.

"What do you mean 'over'? How?"

"Me. Via. Everything."

"Petey, talk to me. Are you drunk?"

"Mmm."

"Talk to me, Petey. What exactly happened?"

"I was fired. Sort of. From my own company."

"I can hardly hear you. What do you mean 'fired'? How can that be?"

"Fired!" he shouted, and immediately regretted it. The sting in his head diverged, spread. His heart did a strange jig. Somehow the word "mate" punched its way into his head. Mate. It was what they'd called their first computer. And it was what Kate had become, his soul mate. Wasn't she, he reflected, behind his inspiration for the At Hand PC? Wasn't their nomadic relationship what had inspired him to design the world's most truly portable computer companion?

And now it was being taken away from him. How long, he wondered, before Kate was gone too? The more aware he was of this feeling, of losing everything close to his heart, the more he wanted to tell her what had happened last night. He had to tell her. But not like this. Not over the phone. He would wait until he saw her in person.

Kate asked him to explain what had happened at Via.

"Matthew's in control. They want me to sit in an office. Be a thinker. Isn't that funny? A thinker."

"Then you're not fired, Peter, right? You're not really fired?"

"Good as. Nothing left for me to do there. They've taken all my power." For some reason this sounded funny to him, and he laughed.

"Baby, listen to me. I'm in LA at the studio. I'm leaving right now. I'll be on the next plane up there, as fast as I can. Hang in there, okay? I'll be there before you know it."

"Okay."

"I love you, Petey."

"You too," he said, sounding horrible to himself. He hung up the phone and picked up the Scotch. "It was the Scotch," he said to the empty room, then uttered a broken chuckle that bordered on hysteria. He had to get a grip.

He searched for the bottle's cap, but then saw that he wouldn't need it. It was all gone.

And so was his life, he thought, rolling the bottle away. Via. And maybe Kate, too. These things come only once in a lifetime. And had become his lifetime. Once you've lost them, he reckoned as he began to drift off to sleep, you never again get, or deserve, anything as good.

Teetering on the edge of consciousness, he struggled to re-call the lyrics of an old song he used to love. Something about you can't always get what you want, but if you cry sometimes, you get what you need.

He knew he was off, but it was close enough.

And so he cried.

Returning by limousine to his palatial home, William Harrell proceeded directly to his impressive home office. He powered on his Via At Hand PC and reflected on his day as he waited for the system to start up.

Word of the coup at Via had spread like wildfire over the company's E-mail system. It was the top story on all the afternoon business wires and news programs. Wall Street reacted negatively to the news, sending Via's stock on an eight-point plunge by the close of the day.

Because of the Via shake-up, William Harrell's afternoon meeting with his two most senior advisers had been extremely trying. His advisers saw Via's suddenly vulnerable position as a huge opportunity for ICP. They suggested to Harrell that he immediately accelerate the development of the BPX ultraportable computer, which was currently in the proof-of-concept stage. His marketing expert produced hastily composed figures and charts projecting the potential market share Via might achieve if it proved successful in getting its rumored At Hand PC Plus to market in the next

three months. He asserted that ICP's window of opportunity to announce its own competitive product was small, and they had to act fast.

Ordinarily, Harrell would have agreed wholeheartedly with his advisers, and approved the additional budget and manpower required to speed the BPX to market. To his advisers' astonishment, however, he objected, saying that the company would continue with its plan to upgrade its current, more conventional BP portable model.

What his advisers had revealed was exactly what he and his secret partner, Matthew Locke, already knew, and were betting on. His advisers had no way of knowing that their fears of Via's cutting into ICP's potential market share would hardly be a worry in the not-too-distant future. On the contrary, it would be cause for celebration. The deal was under way, but ICP's part in it was a secret, and would remain so for the time being, until the next phase was complete.

Sitting at his antique desk, Harrell smiled when he imagined how his advisers would react if they found out he was using an At Hand PC at home, instead of ICP's more traditional clone PC. He started the At Hand's E-mail program. More shocking, he thought, would be the dinner conversation he and Matthew Locke had had here in his home, a little over two years ago. They would have thought him mad.

And at the heart of the matter, he was, but not the sort of mad associated with insanity. Rather, his was the get-even kind of mad. The type of anger that can force a man in William Harrell's position to think very hard about his competition and how to crush it. And he wasn't thinking of the tiny Via, either. His sights were set on a more formidable nemesis: PCSoft. And to a lesser, but no less meaningful, extent, the software giant's partner in global PC domination, Future Processing, which manufactured the CPUs

that ran PCSoft's PortaPC operating system. Together, they ruled the computing world.

It was William Harrell's greatest ambition to challenge that reign, and eventually topple it. But despite ICP's size, he knew he could not do it on his own. He would need a partner.

And in Matthew Locke, he had found it.

He owed it all to that squash match with Rolland Worthy, when the International Foods chairman had mentioned that Locke was being pursued by Via. Instead of returning directly to his office after the game, he asked his driver take a slow spin around Central Park. Flipping through news channels on the limo's portable TV, Harrell paused on a commercial that never ceased to amuse him in its audacity. It was for the Remington brand of electric shaver. The commercial in which Victor Kiam says he liked the product so much, he bought the company.

And then it hit William, the germ of the deal. He picked up his car phone and dialed Matthew Locke's office at International Foods. Locke was away on business in California, his secretary said. Thanks to Worthy's disclosure, William knew why Locke was out west—he was being interviewed by Peter Jones for Via's number two spot. William asked the secretary to please have Locke call him as soon as he returned, and he did. Harrell invited him to dinner later in the week, and spent the next few days formulating his pitch. He knew it was a long shot, but he was enthused just the same. He was grateful too, for the idea was the first diversion powerful enough to distract him from grieving over the loss of his wife, Martha, who the year before had finally succumbed to a dreadful battle with cancer.

The two businessmen sat with cocktails in Harrell's library. Locke said frankly he was puzzled by Harrell's invitation, and

wondered if it had anything to do with Rolland Worthy. William admitted that Worthy had told him about Locke's trip to California to interview for the CEO job at Via. As the two men carried their drinks to the dinner table, Locke joked that he wasn't interested in interviewing for the same spot at ICP.

Harrell's response surprised Matthew. "That's not exactly what I had in mind. Yet." They sat down to the meal, served by Harrell's butler.

"I'm not sure I follow," Matthew said. "Via builds portable, proprietary computers that aren't compatible with the best-selling clones running the PortaPC operating system—your own computers included. Those aside, ICP's real business is in mainframes. Communications. The heavy stuff. Why the dinner? To size up a potential rival? I can't see how Via or I would concern you that much."

Harrell cut into his steak. "First, let me ask you something. Is there any real chance of you going to Via?"

"I'm seriously considering it."

"Clever of Jones to think of you. He's got something up his sleeve, doesn't he? Something he thinks might be a big hit with consumers. Which is obviously why he's calling on you, a champion in the market."

"Thank you. And yes, he is up to something. Maybe big."

Harrell set down his knife and took a sip of wine as he pushed his plate aside. "I'm going to be frank, Matthew. And if what I have to say does not interest you, I'll understand. All I ask is that you entertain the idea."

Matthew Locke nodded noncommittally. He felt no obligation to stop eating while the other man talked.

"A few years ago I made the biggest blunder of my career when I didn't buy PCSoft. As you know, we built the first PC. And then the first laggable PC. Both outfitted with a Future Processing CPU. We'd contracted PCSoft to write the original operating

system, and we sold a shitload of PCs. We were number one in the business. But it never occurred to us, to me, that the OS would end up being what really counted. We're a hardware company. We think in units. PCSoft wanted us to buy them. We didn't. Two years later, when the cheap clones started eating our business, I realized what a terrible mistake I'd made. Now look at us. We're number five in PC sales. You're right, big hardware is our mainstay. But that may not always be the case. The smaller PCs are beginning to take over on the server side of the Web. And while we and a few others own that market right now, PCSoft's next-generation OS is being taken very seriously. So they not only have the PC market, they're also making a huge push into the server and big-business MIS side too."

Mathew had forgotten his meal. He was intrigued by this elder executive's grasp of the industry. However, being brand-new to it himself, he did not see how Via fit into any of it, and said so.

"That's the kicker," Harrell said. "Which is where you come in. And my secret plan, for lack of a better term. To make ICP the PC giant we once were."

"But I still don't see how—"

"Exactly. And neither will the competition. Surprise is the element. And here's how: you, Matthew Locke. While Via may not be the market leader in portable computers, they are by far the most innovative. I've toyed with the idea of spinning out a Via-like group of rebels here at ICP, but the board wouldn't buy it. They figure we count our losses, toe the PCSoft line, and keep licensing the OS for our systems just like everyone else. But I want to change that. I want to have our own OS. I want Via."

Matthew stared in disbelief. If he understood Harrell correctly, he was proposing that the two enter into a high-stakes business game, a big-league version of Monopoly, but with real billions of dollars instead of play money. It was insane. Bombastic. And utterly compelling.

"Why me?"

Harrell stood up and wandered over to the liquor cabinet. He poured two glasses of Scotch, and suggested they continue the conversation in the library. They sat in stately leather armchairs. Harrell sipped his Scotch and sized up Locke over the rim of his glass.

"I've done my homework. Matthew Locke: youngest vice president in International Foods history. And one of the youngest ever VPs in the Fortune 100. Accountable for ten times as many millions as your closest peer. The feather in your cap? Orange Fresh. The fastest-moving soft drink brand in history. Brilliant."

Matthew acknowledged the astute assessment with a small tilt of his tumbler. "But computers are a whole different game. Who's to say I'll have the same success?"

Harrell brightened. "Ah, but there's Peter Jones. Smart, innovative. But a dreadful exec. Which is why he needs you. To run the business, while he invents the products. It's a marriage made in heaven."

"I'm not so sure. He's got very strong ideas, possibly the strongest I've ever encountered. Why don't you just offer to buy his company?"

Harrell chuckled. "You know what he calls us? IC-Pee-Pee. He's gone on record saying that we're so big we piss all over ourselves like a puppy when it comes to thinking small. And he's right. Which is why I want him, and his company." Harrell waved his glass expansively. "Say you accept the job. You go in there, learn the business, learn from Jones. And at the same time, you work on him. Subtly at first. Small suggestions. Ideas on how Via might consider partnering with ICP. Start with compatibility. Move on to licensing. Small steps. Until eventually, we merge."

Matthew's mind was racing. He had a million questions. But before he could speak, Harrell leaned forward in his chair and gave the final push.

"Look, Matthew. I'm just a few years from retiring. To this day, everyone in the company, the industry, still thinks me a fool for not having bought PCSoft when I had the chance. And they're right. I was a fool. I made a terrible mistake. And because of that mistake we, once the leader in the PC business, are at their mercy. For now, it's small-scale numbers on our bottom line. But the public perception has us down as a loser. And the future? The PCSoft server software is moving in at an unprecedented rate, so God only knows.

"But I know one thing. By the time I retire, I want ICP to be well on its way to commanding the fastest-growing market, the micro-notebooks, handhelds and palm-size devices. I believe Via can get us there. And with your track record, I believe you can get us there.

"I can see what you're thinking: What's in it for you? Let's just say when I retire, you could very well find yourself sitting in a very powerful position. So, what do you say?"

"Yes," William now whispered to himself, years later, as his E-mail program revealed the message he'd been waiting for from Matthew Locke. He read it quickly, and was mildly concerned by how it ended. The news reports had been vague about where Peter Jones ultimately fit into today's upheaval at Via. According to Locke, the chances looked slim that Jones would agree to stay on in a development role. While losing Jones had always been a possibility in the deal, it was one that William Harrell sincerely hoped to avoid.

As he moved to turn off the computer, he paused to consider his fingertip resting on the At Hand PC's trackpad. It amazed him that a device could evoke such a feeling of continuity, repose. That a computer could look so gorgeous, unlike anything ICP or any other PC company had ever created.

It caused William Harrell to wonder: Without Peter Jones, could Via hold on to its prized disposition?

It was a disquieting question.

Peter groggily awoke to a familiar, comforting scent. He threw an arm over his eyes to block out the overhead light and lay there listening to her moving around in his room, opening and closing his closet and drawers.

His head was pounding and he moaned.

"Hey, you," Kate said tenderly.

He uncovered his face to find Kate crouched before him. He propped himself up on one elbow, then plopped back down on the pillow, too dizzy to rise just yet.

"How you doing?"

He shrugged and met her eyes. He had to tell her. He knew it was best to just come out with it. Get it over with. Let the last twenty-four hours go down as a complete failure. He propped himself up again, shook his head, unable to speak.

"It's okay. I'm here now."

He nodded, looked past her, and saw the luggage.

"What's all that for?"

"We're going away for a bit."

He yawned. "We are?"

"Yep. To the Maine house for a little while."

"Okay," he said, offering no argument.

She rested her cool hand on the back of his neck and kissed his forehead. "But first we're going to give you a good hot shower. Come on." She gently helped him up and out of the room.

In the bathroom she went about undressing him while he held on to the towel bar to keep from tipping over. She turned on the shower and dipped her hand in the stream and adjusted the temperature.

He thought of Maine. The sun. The sea. The distance. It was a brilliant idea. And once they arrived, maybe then it would be easier to tell her. He looked at her. Yes, he would definitely wait to tell her.

"Kate?"

"Hmm."

"You're an artist."

"Mmm-hmm."

"Well, I was wondering. About when you've created something. When it's something really good."

"Like a CD? Or, let's see, a handheld computer?"

"Yeah. Like those."

She helped him over to the shower, and he paused before stepping in.

"So when it's all done, you have it to hold in your hands, and you're really finished with it. You can keep going back to it, but no matter how great it is, it's history. So I want to know: Do you ever feel when it's like that, done, you'll never be able to do it again? Anything ever again?"

"All the time, love. All the time." She took his chin in her hand and kissed him lightly on the lips. "But no matter how impossible it may seem, it comes back. If you did it once, you can do it again."

"Promise?"

"You know it."

"Good. Will you come in here with me?"

"Yes."

# PART II

Eating breakfast in the nearby café had become part of Peter's morning routine. The waitress greeted him as he sat down with his usual pile of newspapers. She brought him a cup of coffee, a scone, and a glass of orange juice.

For years Peter had retreated across the country to the quaint town of Camden, Maine, popular in the summer with executives and their families from the eastern cities. He was grateful for the privacy that his vacation home provided. He'd let his hair grow longer, and maintained a close-cropped bright blond beard. With his deep tan he looked more like a surfer than a high-tech legend, and over the past three months he'd been recognized by only a few executives around town. Today, however, anyone reading the *New York Times* would see a small picture of him on the front page of the business section. It was one of the older stock photos, maintained by Via's public relations department and distributed to news agencies upon request. Beside it was a more recent photo of Matthew. Any local readers who suspected it was Peter they'd spotted skulking around town would have no doubt now. And after

finishing the story, it was entirely possible they might feel a pang of sympathy for him.

### VIA UNVEILS IMPROVED
### HANDHELD COMPUTER

San Jose, CA – Via, Inc. today announced a more powerful version of its handheld computer, the At Hand PC Plus. The device offers a faster processor, more built-in memory, an external CD-ROM drive, a modem, and a brighter display. Analysts say the computer's most significant improvement is its handwriting-recognition software, which advance testers report is "99 percent better than the original; it's incredibly accurate." Most blame the original At Hand PC's clouded handwriting-recognition software for the product's stymied sales.

No pricing information was announced; however, sources at CompuStore, the nation's largest computer dealer, report the new At Hand PC Plus will retail for the same price as its predecessor. The company plans to upgrade existing At Hand users "at a very low price."

Industry watchers are calling the introduction of the new model a feather in the cap for Via chairman and CEO Matthew Locke, who three months ago wrested power from the company's cofounder, Peter Jones, in a boardroom showdown.

"The At Hand PC Plus demonstrates Locke's ability to manage a high-tech company," said Elizabeth Leahy of Quest Market Research.

"We're very excited about the At Hand PC Plus," Locke said in a telephone interview. "We were caught in a perception problem. While the handwriting input method is only one way to work with the At Hand PC, early reports led potential buyers to believe that the

unit didn't work. That wasn't entirely true then, but it is especially untrue now. The handwriting recognition is solid, fast, and accommodating of everyone."

In his new role as Via head, Locke reorganized the company's formerly separate engineering groups, consolidating resources on the completion of the At Hand PC Plus, "speeding the new and improved model to market three months ahead of schedule," according to company spokesperson Laurence Merrill. To enlist the support of software developers, Locke took to the road with early prototypes of the At Hand PC Plus. The company said three times as many applications will be available for the At Hand PC Plus by the end of the quarter.

PowerBase Software president Andrew Davidson believes today's Via introduction will make the At Hand PC Plus more appealing to buyers. "Via really delivered with the new [At Hand PC] Plus. We're ecstatic. It's got more room for bigger applications, which means our corporate clients can now consider it over the less-remarkable clones." PowerBase is the leading developer of large-scale database software. "We were frankly worried when Peter Jones departed," Davidson continued. "But Locke came to our offices in person with his engineering managers and showed us what they had. We jumped on it and we're now about 90 percent complete with our ProBase client software, which we ported over from the PCSoft version. I think Locke will do all right in his new role."

According to Merrill, Jones is "on sabbatical" in New England. A source close to the company said that Jones was offered a "visionary-at-large role" after being ousted by Locke and the company's board of directors. However, Via officials declined to comment on whether

Jones intends to return to the company in a nonmanagement role which renders him essentially powerless. "Matthew Locke and the rest of the executive staff are eager for Peter Jones to return after his vacation," Merrill said.

Jones could not be reached for comment.

Peter folded the newspaper and sipped his orange juice. The news of Silicon Valley felt very far away. Everything felt very far away. He closed his eyes and turned his face up into the warm sun.

A moment later a shadow moved in front of him, blocking the sunlight.

"Think you'll go back?"

Peter Jones opened his eyes to find an elderly man before him, a copy of the *Times* tucked neatly beneath his arm.

Peter eyed the stranger. "I don't know."

The man placed his large tanned and weathered hand on the back of the vacant chair opposite Peter. "Okay if I join you?"

"Sure." Peter leaned back in his chair and watched the man settle down with an appreciative sigh. He removed his cap and signaled the waitress with a wave and an easy smile. Then he fixed his attention on Peter.

"Congratulations on the new product," he said. He unfolded his newspaper and laid it over Peter's copy. "Your whiskers threw me for a second or two, but I used to slack off on my shave now and then. Though not because I was trying for a low profile, nothing like that."

"It wasn't my product," Peter said, stroking his light beard unconsciously.

The man drew a pen from his pocket, lifted his thumb and winked one eye shut to look Peter over like an artist gauging his subject. "Hold still. I want to get this right." He then proceeded to draw a mustache and beard on Peter's newspaper photo.

Peter was amused.

"Well," the man went on, taking up their conversation without looking up from his sketch, "you weren't there for the big show. But it is your product, just the same. Congratulations, son."

Peter shrugged and did his best to smile appreciatively.

The waitress arrived and greeted the man with familiar warmth. The man shoved the newspaper across the table for the waitress to see. "What do you think? Resemble our man here?"

She viewed the photo and smiled politely, unaware that she was looking at the same person. She seemed to take it all in stride, as though the stranger joked like this all the time. "Let's see. A mineral water and a bagel, very lightly toasted, with just a smudge of low-fat cream cheese, right?"

The man smiled graciously. "Precisely, my dear. Thank you. And anything for you, Mr. Jones?"

"I'm fine, thanks." Peter sipped his coffee, while his companion closed his eyes and turned his smiling face into the sun. Looking at him, Peter felt a dim recognition. Had he met the man before? There was something about the cynicism in his eye. The way he had addressed Peter so frankly. Like he knew the business. Resting as he was, it was plain to see that he was well into his retirement years. Maybe seventy-five years old, Peter estimated.

The waitress returned with the man's breakfast. "Here you are, Mr. Holmes."

Peter heard the name but didn't make the connection. Not right away, anyway. Instead, he was distracted by the man's eyes. Open as they were, he suddenly looked ten years younger. The stranger's gaze fixed on Peter.

"Isn't easy walking away from something you've given birth to." He squeezed some juice from the lime slice floating in the glass.

The statement was phrased like a question and Peter felt oddly compelled to respond. "No. It sure isn't." It was the first he'd spoken of his departure to anyone but Kate.

Except for her weekend visits from Los Angeles, he'd been alone the past three months. He'd spoken with hardly anyone, and then only when necessary. Ordering meals in restaurants. Paying for goods at the general store. Picking up his bundles of forwarded mail at the post office. He'd forgotten how good it could feel to talk to someone, even a stranger. Especially a stranger. But at the same time, Peter sensed that this man wasn't just any stranger.

"I hear you," the man said. "Same thing happened to me, sort of. Gave them fifty years of my life. Started when I was twenty. Not all that different from you. Yes sir, I remember how it felt."

"How's that?"

The man's voice turned solemn. "Like somebody chopped a chunk of my heart off." He gave Peter a searching look, his lively blue eyes full of understanding. "Sound about right?"

Peter looked into his empty coffee cup and nodded. They sat in silence while the man munched on his breakfast and sipped his water. He finished half the bagel, then pushed the plate aside and rubbed his hands together.

"Son, you're a bright boy. I know all about you. How old can you be, thirty?"

"Thirty-three."

"Hell," the man chuckled. "When I was your age, I was just warming up."

Peter crossed his arms and considered the man. What had the waitress called him. Mr. . . . ?

"Yes sir. Same age, in fact, when I invented a new system design. Sucker became the standard for the next many, many years." He sipped more water, jutted out his lower lip. "Still is."

"And what design was that?" Peter said. And then suddenly he knew. Before the man even answered, Peter deduced that there could be only one computer that had been around that long.

"The 990."

Peter tossed his head back and, for the first time in months, he laughed. Of course. Byron Holmes, inventor of ICP's 990 series. The mainframe design around which ICP had built its business. Byron Holmes, son of Jonathan Holmes, founder of ICP.

"What's so damn funny?"

Peter touched the man's arm. "No, no, not funny. Crazy. That the two of us would meet like this. Please, go on. What did you do after the 990?"

"Revise, revise, revise."

"I bet. Things sure moved slower back then, huh?"

"Back then? You make it sound like ancient history." Peter could see that Byron Holmes was enjoying this as much as he was. "You kids from the Valley think your teensy computers are going to replace our big machines very soon, don't you?"

Peter picked at his half-eaten scone. "I wouldn't know. I've pretty much dropped out of the game."

Byron Holmes rapped his fist on the table, causing Peter to jump in his seat. "Now that's a load of crap and it doesn't fly with me. The sour-face routine."

"Well, it's true," Peter said, meeting Holmes's intense stare. "I made that company what it is. And then it was taken away from me."

"That's craziness," the older man said with a dismissive wave of his hand. He scooted his chair closer. "Boy, I'll tell you something. After I made the 990 what *it* is, they moved me into top management. Sure, it was my dad's company. But I had the right education for it. Double master's, the hardware, and the business side. So I could have done it if my heart had been in it. But it wasn't. All I wanted to do was make those big, beautiful machines. And management knew it. They suggested a 'change.' So eventually I stepped down, and they moved in another fellow. I felt like I'd maybe made a mistake. But in the long run, it was the right thing to do. Now he's the head honcho. And we're old friends to this day."

Peter's expression registered disbelief. "And you just sat back and let him make all the important decisions? Decide the fate of your products?"

"Damn straight. And I stuck around for a long time. Oh, I had a nice title, vice chairman, but I really only worried about the machines. I spent years evolving the 990 into the design it is today, which will probably see them through the year 2010, maybe a little longer."

"And then you just left? Retired? The way you talk about it, it sounds like it's still in your blood. Like you're still at it today."

"Had no choice. Heart attack. Makes a man reconsider things." Holmes paused and scratched his lightly sunburned nose. "Anyway, me and my wife have been enjoying ourselves like youngsters ever since. Not bad for seventy-four years young, you think?"

"I'm impressed," Peter said. "But it's not the same. I could run the company. With all due respect, you inherited yours. But I started mine from scratch. I know it better than anyone. They just didn't give me a chance."

The older man discounted the younger with another grandly dismissive wave. "Nah. You'll come around eventually. Can't have both, you know."

"I could."

Holmes's tone turned serious. "Listen, that's just pure, one hundred percent poppyshit." He poked a finger at Peter's shoulder. "You need to squeegee all that anger out of your system. Get over your hurt feelings. Then pick yourself up and get back out there. Do something bigger, better."

Peter was about to object when a handsome woman carrying a bag of groceries arrived at their table. She wore a light summery outfit and a wide brim hat. Byron brightened at her arrival.

She graced Peter with a warm smile. "Is this old man filling your ears with World War II stories?"

"I haven't even gotten to those yet." Byron stood up, took the bag from his wife, and introduced Peter. "He's the boy who invented those pesky little computers everyone's running around with these days. He's also the best conversation I've had in a while. Mr. Jones, it's been a pleasure."

"Likewise."

The two men shook hands.

"We're not done with our discussion, Mr. Jones," Byron Holmes said with a pleasant smile. "How about you drop by our house for dinner, Sunday night?" He patted his shirt pocket for a pen.

"Thank you," Peter said, "that's very kind. But I've been pretty much sticking to myself. I'm not exactly the best company right now."

"Nonsense." The older man scribbled the Holmeses' address on a paper napkin. "Eight P.M."

Peter relented. "I'll be there," he said. "But I have a friend coming. Would it be all right if I brought her?"

"Can she dance?" Byron said.

"No, but she can sing."

Grace Holmes shushed her husband and smiled apologetically at Peter. "Of course," she said. "Please, bring her too."

The couple said good-bye and strolled off holding hands, leaving Peter to reflect on the encounter.

It wasn't completely unusual, since Camden was where many men like Byron Holmes spent their summers. Even so, it had been quite a kick to shake hands with the man whose surname was synonymous with the world's first tabulating machine. Small world, Peter mused. But then he modified his assessment, reasoning that he was from the small world, while Byron Holmes was from the big world. Yet as Holmes had pointed out, in the long run it didn't matter how big or small your brainchild. When it's yours, it's yours, and no one can ever take that away from you.

He looked at Holmes's fleeting sketch of him and smiled. For the first time since being forced from his company, Peter Jones felt the smallest flicker of optimism.

Greta read the *Times* coverage of Via with interest and frustration. Sipping her morning tea, she scrolled to the bottom of the Web version of the story and smirked at the mention of Peter Jones. While she was absolutely thrilled the pest was no longer on either her or Matthew's mind, things hadn't exactly advanced as she'd hoped they would.

Her progress with the At Hand PC was nothing short of prodigious. And Matthew was impressed. However, her expectation of recapturing his full attention now that Peter Jones was out of the way went unsatisfied. It seemed like Matthew spent more time in the office than before the boardroom coup. He'd become obsessed with the development of the At Hand PC Plus. He'd promised to get her one of the new models for herself, and at least that was something pleasant to look forward to. No one was more surprised than she by her interest in the computer. It had begun to change her view of not only Matthew's business, but the world at large, as crazy as that sounded.

She'd fallen into a satisfying routine of sorts, settling down before the computer each morning with her tea. First, her horoscope and the top news stories. Next, the arts and entertainment sites. Depending on what she read, her interests then sometimes shifted to the online shopping districts, to browse a favorably reviewed book, or perhaps to select an especially well received wine highlighted in one of the fine cuisine sites.

But she never spent more than an hour or so on this part of her routine. No matter how compelling a particular news story or topic, her anticipation to get to the really interesting stuff always

won out. She still felt a little naughty about it, as though she were somehow deceiving Matthew or being unfaithful. It was ridiculous, and she knew it. But at the same time, it was all so new, so *liberating,* that she couldn't help but feel she was doing something not quite right.

She closed the Web browser and switched over to the World Online chat groups. Checking her list, she saw that several "friends" were logged on at the same time. She still thought it strange to think of these people as friends. She had never met any of them in person. Yet in some ways she felt closer to some of them than the "real" women friends she'd made here in California. Most of them she saw only at functions or dinner parties, the occasional baby shower. She never felt like she fit in. Most of the Silicon Valley wives bored her. Most had impressive educations, impressive estates and belongings, and flawless plastic surgery. They behaved like an elite sorority, to which Greta wasn't welcome. Her lack of a college degree probably had something to do with it. But in the company of so many seemingly perfect women, Greta became all the more aware of her shrouded imperfection. The gloves helped to cover it, but she believed they all knew what she was hiding. It was so embarrassing.

She glanced at her gloved left hand resting on the At Hand PC's keyboard. After the initial struggle she'd regained almost all of her impressive typing skills, making small adjustments to the keystrokes as necessary. Her friends on the other side of the screen knew nothing of her imperfection, and that was fine with her.

Also fine was the good friend she'd made, who greeted her now.

"Morning, the Gret One!" her friend typed.

"Hi, Gregor," she responded.

"We have to stop meeting like this. ☺."

He'd taught her how to use the At Hand's special function keys to create expressions of happiness, sadness, indecision. It was

a whole new way of communicating, and she'd begun to express herself like never before.

"Down, boy. I've already told you I'm a married woman!"

"☹."

"Now, now. No pouting, Gregor."

"Ah, but look. You didn't say happily. Happily married."

"Nice try. Well, maybe not *perfectly* happy today."

"Oh?"

"It's nothing. My husband is a very busy man, as I've mentioned. That's all."

"Mentioned, yes. But you've never said what it is that keeps him so busy. Are you sure he's not … Well, it's really not my place to suggest such a thing."

"Having an affair? Heavens no. No, the love of his life is his work. And today is an important day for him. Big news."

"Such as?"

Greta hesitated before going any further. She'd had only that one horrible encounter online, the first time she'd used the At Hand PC, with that Mr. or Mrs. Cooper person, whom she'd never again run into. She'd met Gregor during her second day online, when she'd nonchalantly dropped in on the Northern California Adults forum. He sent her a welcoming message, to which she politely responded. They chatted briefly, and when she realized he was trying to figure out if she was single, she immediately told him she wasn't. Even so, he remained the gentleman. And over the last three months she had grown quite fond of him. And she supposed she trusted him. It wouldn't hurt to tell him a little more. She typed:

"You said you use an At Hand PC too, right?"

"I love it. It's great. And I positively can't wait to get the new one they announced today. It's so cool!"

"Yes, well, that's what my husband does. He works for Via in an important position."

"I'm impressed!!!"

"So is the press, by what I've read. So that's good. But Gregor, I have to admit, the company really does work its employees hard."

"But from everything I've read, the employees love putting in long hours."

"Hmm. I suppose. I don't love it, though. I think it's unhealthy."

"☹. Poor Gret One. How about a hug."

"You're sweet. Thanks. I'm just feeling sorry for myself. Maybe after today, with the new computer done, my husband will finally take a breather. Plus, our anniversary is coming up in a few days, so maybe that will help things along. Anyway, enough about me and my life. How about you? How is your book coming along?" He'd revealed that he was working on a novel; however, he was very secretive about the details.

"Up and down. I hate the freelance crap I have to write to pay the rent. I wish I could afford to just write the novel. And then there are my medical bills, from throwing out my back at the gym that time. The doctor says I could fix it with this new microsurgery they do, but who can afford it? I told you I don't have health care, and with this preexisting condition I can't get coverage to take care of it. I know, I know, drag out the violins...."

"Poor Gregor. Well, you won't tell me a bit about your book, but from the way you write here I have a good feeling about it. You have a way with words."

"Thank you, Gret One. And now will you finally tell me your real name?"

"Not a chance. I've probably said too much already."

"Nah. You're safe with me, Gret. Or is it Gretchen? That's the most obvious guess."

"No."

"Hmm. Greta?"

She paused.

"Aha! Greta. Well, Gret One, your real name is lovely."

"Wise guy! Okay, is yours really Gregor?"

He paused.

"Aha yourself. Gregor. That's a lovely name."

"Gregor and Greta. ☺."

"Right. The two Net addicts who should be busy doing other things than talking online."

"You're right. But Greta, if I may say something: I'm very happy I know you."

"You too, Gregor."

"I mean, really, really happy. ☺ ☺ ☺."

"Me too." She felt herself blush. She was flattered and touched, and even a little excited. She couldn't remember the last time a man had spoken to her this way, least of all Matthew. "See. There you go. So smooth with words."

"Well, I mean it. I'm sorry. You probably think I'm coming on to you again. Don't worry. I promised you I wouldn't try to pick you up."

She didn't know what to say.

"Uh-oh. Now I've blown it. I've offended you."

"No. Just … I don't know how to say it so I will just say it. Thank you, Gregor. You're kind. And if things were different …"

She pressed the Send button, but then instantly regretted it. It wasn't right to lead him on. She was a married woman. He was a single man. She had no idea what he even looked like. He had no idea what she looked like. It was crazy. And thrilling. She looked at a photo of herself and Matthew, on the bookshelf beside his desk. They were both smiling. It was at least ten years old. She turned back to the screen.

"Greta, I'll just say this once. I'm here if you ever need me. For anything. To talk to. Or meet F2F sometime for coffee or a drink, or whatever."

"F2F?"

"Face-to-face."

She looked sadly at her gloved left hand. And she wondered: Would she have been unfaithful to Matthew by now if she didn't have her handicap? Then an even more disturbing thought entered her mind: Would she even be considering it if her hand hadn't been destroyed? It was one of those unanswerable questions, impossible to consider the one without the other—which was exactly how she felt about her once-perfect pair of hands.

"Greta, are you there?"

"Yes. I'm sorry. And I have to go now, Gregor."

"I've upset you. ☹."

"No. You've just caused me to take stock, that's all."

"I hope you like what you see."

"Not exactly."

"Oh, Greta. I'm so sorry. I've messed up. Listen, I bet you are beautiful. I can tell by the way you talk."

"Thank you, you're very sweet, Gregor. But you can't tell such a thing by how someone types."

"But I can! I can tell. What do you think of me?"

She felt suddenly nervous. "I don't know."

"Come on. Try. I'll help you. I'm thirty yrs old. Dark brown hair. Nice smile. Gray eyes. And, let's see ... I work out at a gym."

"So you're Tom Cruise. And I'm Nicole Kidman."

"Perfect match!"

"You're crazy."

"About you, Greta. ☺."

His unbridled sentiment startled her and she touched her hand to her chest. She'd gotten into a conversation she couldn't get herself out of now. The troubling thing was that she felt unusually attracted to him. With the few specifics he'd given her she formed an abstract picture of him in her mind. A young man. With a lovely smile. And a nice manner. And his lips? Enough, she told herself, feeling silly all of the sudden. This was getting out of hand.

"I really must go, Gregor. I'm sorry."

"Same time tomorrow?"

She paused. "Yes."

"All right, great. But wait. One more thing. Close your eyes for a second."

"My eyes?"

"Yes."

"But how will I see the screen?"

"Just do it."

She closed her eyes, waited a moment, then opened them.

"Kiss."

"Oh," she whispered in surprise, unconsciously touching her gloved fingertips to her lips.

Without another word she disconnected from the service and sat there for a long while, considering his final word and the oddly stimulating effect it had on her.

>CHAPTER 8

Matthew Locke sat in his office and shuffled through a pile of transparencies, arranging them in the correct order. Today was an important day, and he wanted everything to be just right. He'd gotten his hair cut yesterday, the occasionally unruly black waves clipped a bit closer than usual. He wore neatly pressed khaki pants, a striped oxford shirt, burgundy loafers, and an irrepressible grin. Everything had come together perfectly over the last three months, and he was ready to move on to the next phase of his plan.

He looked through his office window to the opened boardroom door. Outside, the executives milled about the table piled with breakfast foods and beverages. He thought back to the last time they had all been called together like this, when they'd voted Peter out of the company. The contrast was obvious. But he warned himself against overconfidence. What he was about to propose would come as a surprise to the attendees.

His intercom beeped softly and he looked at his secretary, Eileen. She tapped her wristwatch. It was time.

He collected his presentation materials, thanked her, and nearly collided with Hank Towers, who was just coming out for seconds. They exchanged a pleasant greeting as Hank refilled his cup of coffee. Matthew waited for the vice chairman and then followed him back inside, relishing the quiet impression it would give the others: the company's two senior executives coming in together.

Matthew picked up at once on the good-natured feeling in the room, as the members of the board and executive staff finished their muffins and casual conversations. He set his transparencies beside the overhead projector and took his seat.

Hank raised a hand for quiet. "Before we get started, I just want to offer a word of congratulations, Matthew. Yesterday's unveiling of the At Hand PC Plus was a huge success. Dealers are falling all over themselves to get their hands on as many units as possible. Congratulations." The others around the table followed with congratulations, and someone clapped. Another pair of hands joined in, and then another, until the entire room was applauding his success.

He swept the table with a warm smile and thanked them, adding that the real congratulations should go to Alan Parker and his team of engineers for pulling off the job sooner than expected. No one mentioned Peter's name or contribution to the project. And that suited Matthew just fine.

Martin Cohen stood and announced the agenda, a copy of which rested before each person. The last item on the list was Matthew's presentation, titled "The Whole World in Your Hand: Opportunity Knocks."

The group spent ninety minutes covering the usual business, and then Matthew was up. "Should we take a break before I start?" He knew the title of his presentation had them all intrigued. This would be the first time anyone but Peter Jones had presented a major company strategy for Via. No one stood or motioned for a break.

"Good." He strolled over to the light switch and dimmed the room's overhead lamps, then returned to the table and turned on the projector. He showed the first slide, the Via logo.

"At Via," he began, "we've focused on the individual. One person, one computer. Truly personal computing. True to our company's corporate culture, which prizes the individual."

He changed slides, revealing a pie chart highlighting Via's share of the handheld market. Via's take was a mere sliver when compared with the rest of the pie, colored largely by the PortaPC standard owned by the combined efforts of PCSoft and Future Processing. He paused for a moment to let the image sink in.

"This is what we're up against. While the At Hand PC Plus is a far superior product to the clones, they nevertheless dominate the market. This is due in large part to their compatibility with PCSoft-based desktop computers. Exchanging documents and E-mails between the desktop and PortaPC systems is easy, because they share exact or custom file types. One look at this chart is all it takes to see that we're merely a bit player in the larger scheme of things."

None of this was new to anyone around the table; however, it was important to reiterate before making his next point. He settled his next slide on top of the one already in place. The huge PC-Soft/Future Processing section of the pie was now cut up into several smaller slices.

"But when you look at it this way, we're not so tiny after all. Many of the various PCSoft-compatible hardware makers are smaller than we are. The company owning the largest slice of the PortaPC handheld market is, of course, ICP." He took a sip of water, then continued. "International Computer Products is every-where. There is hardly a big business, organization, or government in the world that doesn't use an ICP mainframe or minicomputer for its processing. Which is why we need them."

Matthew's true meaning of this last went unnoticed at first—until he projected his next slide, which showed ICP and Via together sharing the single largest slice of the handheld market pie. Chairs squeaked as several of the executives leaned forward to settle elbows on the table. A questioning murmur rippled through the room.

He felt momentarily overcome by a profound feeling of power. Here he stood in the position that for the last decade had been occupied by Peter Jones, famous for his resentment of ICP and every other player in the PCSoft/Future Processing game. Yet with that one slide, it was plain for everyone to see that Matthew felt differently. As did everyone in the room. The murmur was building to a disconcerted chatter. He knew they would be surprised. And he also knew that it was up to him to turn that surprise into understanding. He spoke quickly.

"Please, before you jump to any conclusions, let me explain." Several executives voiced questions and concerns. Matthew lifted an open palm. "Please," he repeated, his voice rising slightly.

Hank Towers suddenly rapped his knuckles on the table. "Come on, people. Let's have quiet. Go on, Matthew."

"Thank you, Hank," Matthew said. He placed the next slide. The illustration showed the At Hand PC Plus alongside a row of popular PCSoft applications.

This time it was Hank who abruptly interrupted, his voice bordering on outrage. "Wait a minute, Matthew. Are you suggesting we build a clone, like everyone else?" The room erupted again with urgent questions.

"No, Hank. Not at all. Please, if you'll let me just explain."

Hank lifted a hand in apology. "I'm sorry. All right, no more interruptions, I promise. Go on."

Matthew tried to lighten the moment with a small chuckle. A

cold sweat broke on his back. He silently sucked in a deep breath, then pressed on with his plan.

"Am I proposing we build a clone? I wouldn't think of it. Rather, I'd like you to imagine something. Imagine if the At Hand PC Plus were compatible not with PCSoft programs, but with the data they create. The word-processing documents. The spreadsheets. The E-mail messages. Contacts and schedules. All of the information created by the most popular PCSoft programs."

He flipped the next slide into place, depicting a PCSoft word processing document on a clone screen, and the same document on the At Hand PC Plus screen. He spoke calmly and clearly as he voiced the first tangible piece of the secret deal.

"My suggestion is this: that we align ourselves with ICP to create the translation software to enable people to use the At Hand PC Plus as companion to their PCSoft-based desktop computer. I've had preliminary discussions with ICP's chief, and he is willing to proceed. A strategic alliance between our companies would mean we bundle the ICP-created translation software with every At Hand PC Plus, giving us instant credibility with the large corporations that have so far resisted our product. And while ICP would continue to sell its own PCSoft-compatible handheld device, we also discussed the possibility of ICP co-selling the At Hand PC Plus as well, earning a royalty for each unit they ship. If the numbers are good enough, our strategic alliance could eventually mean that ICP would label their own version of the At Hand."

The room was dead quiet as the full weight of Matthew Locke's extraordinary proposition settled in. He quickly returned the combined ICP/Via slide to the screen, illustrating the huge chunk of the action that his idea projected. He noticed the sharpening looks around the table. He perceived in their calculating expressions their underlying interest: sales. Which would mean higher stock

prices. Which in turn would translate to greater riches for every one of them. As Matthew had anticipated, it always came down to the bottom line.

And so it came as no surprise that the first person to speak up was Hank Towers, the company's largest shareholder.

"It's brilliant," Hank said.

"Thanks for the vote of confidence, Hank," Matthew said, shaking hands with Towers, the last person to leave the boardroom. The door silently swung closed behind the cofounder, and Matthew dropped heavily into one of the chairs. He crossed his hands behind his head and let out a huge, satisfied sigh. He closed his eyes and spent a few moments basking in the good feeling of his accomplishment.

He'd done it. The hardest part, veering Peter Jones's once-loyal followers toward ICP's wide-reaching arms, was over. With the support of the board and executive staff in the bag, the launch phase of the deal had finally moved into the open. He felt enormous relief, more confidence than ever. William Harrell would be equally delighted with his success. Their success. Things could not look brighter. The rewards would be astronomical.

At the sound of the door he opened his eyes. He smiled at the sight of Laurence Merrill.

She looked so refreshing in her light linen suit. Her straight honey-colored hair framed an intelligent face. She was carrying a bundle of press materials against her chest, and his eyes shifted briefly to her hands.

"How did it go?" Laurence asked.

"Great. Really great."

"That's wonderful, Matthew." Her enthusiasm was genuine. It

was one of the things he liked most about her. "Ready for our meeting?"

"Absolutely." He rolled out the chair beside him. She seated herself and moved in closer to the table, and he edged a little nearer, very interested in what she had brought.

"First, let me give you a quick update on the autobiography project. Janice Lane would like to speak with you by phone this weekend about her next step, starting the actual first draft. She's read everything available on Via, and the articles about you and your career. She's also finished interviewing most of the friends and peers you suggested. And gone though all of the brainstorming notes you sent her. She sounds very enthused."

Matthew nodded his approval. He made a mental calculation, counting out the next nine months. The autobiography's publication date would coincide almost exactly with the final stage of the deal. It would be perfect. He would become the most talked-about businessman, sought after for all the important magazine covers. All the interest and publicity would serve as free advertising for the book. And this realization so pleased him that he almost blurted it out to Laurence. But he caught himself. Only he, his wife, and William Harrell knew the full extent of the deal.

Laurence spread out the materials she'd collected. "I got everything you asked for. ICP's employee handbook. Current and past annual reports. Day care center guide. Conduct manual. Ads. Banners. Brochures. And even these temporary tattoos they put in with the computers they sell to the education market for grade-schoolers. They sure are a big company. And I had to be pretty sneaky getting some of it. How does it all fit in with your strategy?"

He began sifting through the various articles. "Perception. I want to understand ICP's corporate culture inside and out. You know how Via employees feel about 'Big Business' and companies like ICP. I've got to convince several thousand rebels that aligning

ourselves with ICP will only make us more successful." He paused for a moment to glance at his wristwatch. "We've sure got a lot of ground to cover. How about we order in some lunch?"

She looked relieved. "I was afraid you were going to skip it. Yes, please. I'm famished."

"Me too," Matthew said, stealing another look at her loveliness.

"Hey, you ready yet?" Kate said, appearing in the bathroom doorway.

Peter stood leaning over the sink, carefully dragging a razor across his chin. The scruffy beard he had maintained since departing from Via was on its way out.

"Hallelujah!" Kate said.

Peter paused for a moment to wink at her in the mirror, his face foamy with shaving cream.

She leaned a shoulder against the doorframe and stood watching him. "I'll like your face smooth, Petey. It feels better on me."

"Ouch." He jerked the razor from his face. A dot of blood instantly formed on his chin.

Kate slipped off her robe and hung it on the door hook. "So, Lancelot, what do I wear?"

"Anything you want. It's just a neighborly sort of thing." He rinsed his face and pulled the skin on his neck taut to inspect his work, noticing her full naked reflection. He turned and smiled at her.

"I think it's more than that," she said.

"What's more?"

"The dinner. I think this Byron Holmes guy is probably excited he's met you, and wants to get to know you better."

"Yeah, maybe. Me too. I could use a friend here. I only see you for two or three days at a time." He crossed his arms and rested his rear against the sink, looked her up and down with a playful grin. "You know, for a forty-year-old lady, you're quite a knockout."

"Oh yeah? Well for a thirty-something boy, you're not so bad yourself." She moved over to him and slid her fingertips beneath the waistband of his Jockey shorts at the small of his back. She rubbed her cheek softly against his. "Mmm, definitely better." They stood holding each other for a while, quietly appreciating the closeness.

He pulled away to look into her eyes. "What is it about us? That makes us work? Worth only seeing each other so little?"

She thought for a moment. "Well, we're a lot alike." She kissed the tip of his nose. "And a lot unalike. Which makes for an interesting blend, I'd say."

He touched his forehead to hers and looked down at their pressed hips. "Do you think maybe we should be together more?"

"Maybe. Sure."

"More permanently?" He gave a small thrust of his hips.

"Maybe."

"Maybe?" He sought her eyes.

"Petey, we work great because we both have things in our lives that we believe in."

"Had."

"Have," she said, lifting his chin. "You're just a little dry right now, that's all. You have to give yourself some time to let things happen." She kissed his brow. "It doesn't all just suddenly change overnight, babe."

"I know. But I've been thinking." He hesitated, unsure how to

go on. He still had not told her about what had happened with Ivy. And now, standing here as they were, Via and Ivy and everything else that had gone wrong seemed so far away, so irrelevant to his life now. Their life together. Would telling her about Ivy accomplish anything other than to absolve his guilt? He knew Kate would be hurt. And he did not want to hurt her. No, he decided, there was no point in telling her.

"And?"

"About if, I don't know, maybe we should settle down. Split more time between here and California. Together."

She smiled at him knowingly. They'd had this conversation many times in the past, usually at times such as this, when he was feeling depressed. "Babe, you know neither of us would really be happy if we settled down. Not yet, anyway."

"No, I don't know that. We might. I mean, what if it was official. If we were to, you know—"

"No."

"But maybe—"

She pressed her fingers to his lips. "Peter, you know the minute you get going on something again you won't feel this way."

He shrugged. "Okay, okay. So maybe no wedding bells. But I've been thinking how I'm not getting any younger. I remember the first time I saw a kid using a Mate computer. Kate, it was so incredible." He tightened his grip around her waist and pulled her closer. "God, imagine if ... you know ..."

She lowered her head and he knew he'd gone too far. Her eyes were moist when she looked up again. "Peter, you know I can't have a baby," she said. "You know that." She moved his hand around to her taut belly. "Closed for business, sorry."

He hugged her tightly. "I'm sorry, Kate." He kissed her eyelids. "I didn't mean like that. I meant maybe adopting. But listen, I'll give it a rest for now. You're right. I know you are. I'm just feeling sort of lost and mixed-up. I'm sorry."

She nodded and he gently thumbed away her tears. She spoke softly in his ear. "It'll come again, Peter. I know it will."

"Promise?"

"Cross my heart," she said, and kissed his cheek. "Now put some clothes on. I'm getting cold and hungry and we don't want to be late for your new friend." She slapped his rear, then turned and went into the bedroom.

An instant later his underwear whizzed past her head, grazing her long hair. She set her hands on her hips and turned around to face his mischievous grin.

"Isn't it fashionable to be late?"

"Dinner in five minutes, Matthew," Greta said, standing in his office doorway. He spun around, startled. She leaned to one side to see what he had behind his back. "What are you hiding?"

"I wanted to surprise you," he said. He drew his hand around, revealing a brand-new At Hand PC Plus. "It's for you, Gret. Your very own. I was just moving all of your files and things over to it."

"Matthew, it's beautiful."

The company had changed the color of the newest model to midnight blue, with a lightly textured surface that felt soft and almost pliable to the touch. He held it out to her, and she accepted it in her gloved hand. She looked at him expectantly, waited for him to say what she'd been waiting all day to hear.

"Pretty slick, huh?"

That wasn't quite what she was hoping to hear. She smoothed the fabric of her dress, hoping to draw his attention to it, but he didn't seem to notice. Maybe he was just waiting until they sat down to dinner to say it. Surely he remembered. The present proved it. She kissed his cheek anyway. "Thank you, darling. It's perfect."

"All yours. And look in back. There's a pullout phone cable now, so you can plug it in anywhere."

"You mean anywhere but in your office, darling."

"Well, not really. You can keep working in here if you like. I just thought maybe you'd want to use the drawing room or one of the guest rooms for yourself. Your own home office. I can bring home a printer too, if you want. Whatever you want, Gret, I'll get it for you."

She thanked him and set the unit on his desk. "I'll take it upstairs later. Now, come on. I don't want dinner to get cold."

"Right behind you," he said, but he remained in his office a little longer, tinkering with Zip disks and connections and his own new unit, which he'd been updating with his existing documents and programs as well. He looked at his desk and groaned. It was piled with notes and charts, schedules, technical documents—all of which he still had to consolidate into a cohesive strategy. He'd put off working on the ICP alliance strategy in favor of configuring the pair of new At Hand PC Pluses. And now he was behind schedule. He could probably finish the report by morning, so long as he hurried through dinner.

He was momentarily disoriented when he left the light of the bright office. The house was uncharacteristically dark. He padded down the long hallway and passed the closed dining-room door, crossed the foyer, and rounded the corner to the family room and kitchen area. Except for the range light, the kitchen was dark too, and there were no plates or utensils set on the table where they usually ate, facing the family room and the big-screen TV.

He turned back to the kitchen, observed the pots and pans with their lids askew, knives and spices and assorted other preparations scattered about the countertop. "Greta?"

"In here," came his wife's voice softly.

A flickering glow caught his eye at the far end of the kitchen,

coming from the adjoining dining room. He'd passed its other entrance, from the foyer, on his way through.

His surprise was apparent when he found her sitting at the formal dining table. The room was bathed in soft candlelight, creating sparkles in the crystal glasses and silverware place settings. Between the settings was an arrangement of serving plates and a basket of warm bread. Poached vegetables and steaming potatoes sat beside a covered serving dish. To one side stood a grand bouquet of flowers from Greta's garden.

"My word," was all he managed to say as he seated himself at the head of the table, to her right.

"I gave Dolores the rest of the day off," Greta said. "I prepared the whole thing myself."

"It smells wonderful, Gret." He smiled, a bit puzzled by the formality and candles. They took meals in the dining room only when entertaining guests.

She withdrew a bottle of champagne from the standing silver ice bucket at her side and held it out to him. "Would you, Matthew?"

"Well, well," he said, "my favorite." He undid the wire cage and popped the cork, expertly filled the flutes and handed one to her, then held up his own. "Cheers, darling."

They clinked their glasses together and he winked at her, tasted the champagne. He made an approving sound, unaware that she had not taken one sip. He set his down and went straight for the covered serving dish.

"Oh, boy. Another favorite." He gestured for her plate, selected a delicate squab for her, two for himself. He ladled sauce over his birds and vegetables, took another sip from his glass, and then dug into his meal with unbridled gusto.

Watching him, she felt like crying. She took her first taste of the champagne. Some celebration. She knew her husband so well. Barely two minutes into his dinner and already his mind was elsewhere. She'd misinterpreted the At Hand PC Plus as a present.

Well, she'd been wrong. No, he hadn't remembered, and admitting this to herself caused a strange, aching feeling in her left hand. The doctors had warned her the sensation might manifest itself on rare occasions. An itching or throbbing or tingle, as though everything were in its right place, like normal.

The same was true, she thought wanly, of her marriage. How at times it tricked her into thinking it was still all there, like normal. But not now. He'd flat-out forgotten. As though in protest, her left hand suddenly shook with a small spasm, causing her untouched utensils to loudly collide. The silver tines of the fork made an enchanting sound that slowly faded into a silence so pronounced it finally attracted Matthew's attention.

He looked at her with a curious expression and wondered why her eyes were shimmering. Before he could ask what was bothering her, she spoke.

"Happy anniversary, Matthew." She raised her glass and downed the contents.

"Oh, Gret." He set down his utensils and for the first time really noticed the details. The glossy shine of her lips. The extra touches around the eyes. The exquisite silk dress. The light scent of perfume. She blinked and a teardrop fell and painted a dark trail down her cheek. Ashamed, he looked down at his plate. Their anniversary dinner. He lifted his hands in a helpless gesture.

"Greta, I am so, so sorry. With all the work … the new product … the alliance coming together. I just, well, I just honestly forgot. Can you forgive me, Gret?"

She dabbed at her cheek with a napkin and reached her good hand across the table. He took it in his own, touched his lips to the soft material.

"It's all right, Matthew. It's all right." She withdrew her hand and put on her best forgiving smile. Her husband, the busy executive. Why should tonight be any different?

Refilling her glass, he made an effort to cheer her up. "It's delicious, Gret. The best I've ever had. Really. We've eaten in all the best places and I'm telling you, I've never, ever had it this good."

She smiled her gratitude and picked up her fork, speared an asparagus. She chewed slowly, trying to think of something to talk about. She took a long sip of her champagne and observed her husband's eager appetite.

"Matthew, you could at least slow down and enjoy it."

He looked up, a dribble of sauce getting away from his lower lip. "I'm sorry, honey. It's just that I have to call up my coauthor tonight to go over the biography outline. It's, what, going on ten-thirty her time? Plus, I have more work to do tonight." He wiped his chin with his napkin. "For the trip."

"The trip," she repeated sarcastically as she set down her fork and hefted the bottle of champagne. She refilled her glass and ignored his. "What trip, Matthew? What are you talking about?"

"Tomorrow. New York. I told you I was meeting Harrell on Monday. Didn't I? I must have. I'm sure of it."

"No, Matthew. You didn't."

"God, I could swear I said something, honey. I'm sorry. But you see what I'm talking about? I'm so overwhelmed." He let out a dramatic burst of air, then gulped the rest of his champagne.

"Well if you're going to New York tomorrow, can't you meet this writer woman while you're there, rather than call tonight?"

"I am. And that's why I have to call tonight. So she can hear my comments on the preliminary outline, tighten it up so we can go over it when I arrive tomorrow night. Then it's all day Monday with Harrell."

She frowned. "It's amazing. The way you're changing. And if you'll forgive my candor, I don't mean pleasantly."

"Hey, what the hell's that suppose to mean? Come on, how about a little understanding? I said I was sorry already."

"Saying it and meaning it aren't the same, Matthew. I swear, since you got rid of Peter Jones you've become so involved in that company."

"Look, I said I was sorry. I meant it. You're just upset because I forgot our anniversary, and so you're attacking me."

"No, Matthew. That's exactly what I'm talking about. The way you're behaving. Right now. You're trying to convince me of what you think, without hearing a word I'm saying. And who was famous for that? Who was it you used to come home saying the same thing about? Does replacing Peter mean that you have to take on his awful behavior as well?"

"Jones has nothing to do with this."

"Jones? No one despised him more than I, but Jones? Even during your worst arguments you always called him Peter. And Harrell? You keep saying Harrell this, Harrell that. Whatever happened to William, your friend?"

"Friend? Did I ever say friend? He was never my friend, Greta. He's my business partner. To be blunt about it, more of an accomplice, really."

"Accomplice. How charming." She let out a disgusted sigh. "Like us, I suppose. Wouldn't you say, Matthew? Partners is too kind. Accomplices, yes. That sounds truer. His and her accomplices."

He gave her the look to indicate he'd had enough of this discussion. She poured the last of the champagne into her glass and sat back with one arm across her breast, cupping her elbow in her hand. She looked at her plate. She'd hardly touched it. She gave a sad shake of her head. Their anniversary dinner had turned into a disaster. And their marriage? What word would she choose to describe it?

"Matthew, I'm sorry. You're right. I'm upset. But doesn't that mean anything to you? Doesn't tonight, our anniversary, mean anything—despite however busy you are? What's happened to us?"

"Greta, it's too late for this conversation right now. We'd go in circles for the next hour. I'm sorry, I can't. I'm going to be up until six in the morning as it is. I've got an early flight. I'll just be able to get in a jog and a shower, if I'm lucky." He tore a slice of bread in half, wiped up the last smear of sauce from his plate. He spoke with his mouth full. "We'll talk when I get back if you'd like."

She grimaced. "God, you make me sick."

He shrugged, not caring enough to disagree.

"Fine then, Matthew. Take your trip. Don't even bother to ask if I'd like to go with you."

"It's one day, Greta."

"It's Manhattan, Matthew. You know how I miss it."

"Darling, you know you can go anytime you want. Have I ever stopped you from doing whatever you want, Greta? No. I didn't think so."

"I believe we were talking about you, Matthew. When will it stop with you?"

"What stop? Jesus, Gret. No more to drink. You're not making sense now."

"This. You. Us, like this. All of it. Damn it, Matthew, you're obsessed with Via. Obsessed with your big secret deal. You're worse than Peter ever was. It's horrible, seeing you turn into this."

"It's not an easy job replacing him."

She scoffed. "That's how you see it? That you've replaced him? Dear God, you're worse than I realized."

He wiped his lips and carefully set his napkin down beside his place. "I've got a job to do, Greta."

"Well don't let me stop you." She waved him away, and covered her eyes with her gloved left hand, waited for him to leave her alone. But what he did next completely surprised her. Had she finally gotten through to him?

He came around the table and settled a hand on her shoulder. Softly, he spoke. "Greta, whether you understand or not, every-

thing I do is for us. The things I'm making happen at work are very complicated. And very important. Things that will change our lives together forever." He rubbed her neck. Too briefly. Like everything else. Hollow promises. Shallow meanings.

She dropped her face into her hands and shook her head. "You've changed our lives forever already, Matthew. That's what's so sad. You just don't see it. How bad it is. How it's already happened."

He slipped his hands into his pockets and turned around to go, pausing for a moment. "I'm sorry, Gret, but I have to get back to work now. Please try to understand. And don't worry. Nothing bad will happen to us. Nothing. I won't let it."

And then he was gone, leaving her to sit in the flickering candlelight with her unfinished dinner, her empty glass. She turned and looked beyond her own reflection in the window, at Silicon Valley glittering in the distance.

"Then maybe I will," Greta Locke whispered.

"Poppyshit," Byron Holmes said with a dismissive wave at Peter, seated at the other end of the dining table.

"Dear," Grace said, patting her husband's arm affectionately. "Don't get too worked up. You don't want to scare off our new friends."

Kate and Peter chuckled good-naturedly. They were enjoying themselves immensely.

"I disagree, Byron. It's not, ah, poppyshit," Peter said. "Kids are only as strong as what you feed them. It's everything around them. How many good examples can you honestly name? Movies? Television? MTV?"

The foursome sat around an antique Shaker table, situated near the living-room hearth. The home was decorated in a simple and warm country style. The effect was homey, comfortable,

like Byron and Grace Holmes themselves. Peter and Kate felt instantly at ease the minute they walked in the door. Outside, dock lamps dotted the inlet and a few boats bobbed silently in the lulling bay.

"It's funny, the way kids take so quickly to computers," Peter said. "We'd invented the Mate with no one in mind but ourselves, computer guys. But almost at once parents bought them for their kids."

Grace said, "I wonder what the ratio is. Between the computer haves and have-nots. It must be enormous, when you consider how costly they are."

"True," Peter said, "And at Via we—" He paused for an instant to correct himself. "I mean, they ... they are always trying to figure out how to make them cheaper, so that the education market can afford them."

Peter's longing tone hadn't gone unnoticed by the others. Byron took a shot at lightening him up. He pointed his mustard-smeared knife at Peter's dinner plate. "That's all well and good, son, but if you don't eat my Gracie's cooking I'll have hell to pay."

Grace smiled at Peter. "They have one of your computers at the foster home where I volunteer a few hours a week. The children spend hours on it, doing their homework or playing games. They talk in a language all their own, and it's remarkable to see how it brings them together and gives them something in common to share. They interact with one another in wholly new ways."

The discussion carried on some more, and halfway through the meal, even with Byron's demands, Peter stopped eating. Grace excused herself and began clearing the table. Kate stood up with her. "Let me help you."

Byron briskly rubbed his hands across his chest with evident satisfaction.

"Everything was delicious," Peter told Grace. "I just haven't had a very good appetite lately."

"That's all right," Grace said, removing Peter's plate. "You can take leftovers home if you like."

"Too late," Byron said, snatching the uneaten sausage. "And wait till you see what's for dessert."

When Kate and Grace were out of earshot, Byron leaned into the table and lowered his voice. "You're a lucky fellow. She's lovely."

"She sure is," Peter said. He felt an uneasy stirring in his chest when he thought once more about not telling Kate about Ivy. He'd already decided that there was nothing to gain by telling her, yet it kept coming back unexpectedly, to gnaw at his consciousness. He wondered if he'd just forget about it someday.

"Come on," Byron said, pushing away from the table. "Let's get some air while the ladies fuss and giggle." Peter had a quiet laugh at that one when he tried to picture his feminist Kate "fussing" about in the kitchen.

Heading outside, Byron drew a small pouch and a briar pipe from his jacket. He filled it in silence as they strolled out onto the dock. He lit up when they reached the end, the glow of his match flickering in the black water below their feet. That's just what I need, Peter thought, a spark to go off inside my brain.

Byron shook out the match and worked his pipe, regarding Peter for a moment. "You know, boy. I like you."

"Thanks. You're a good guy, too."

"That's what my wife tells me," Byron said, exhaling a cloud of blue smoke. He pointed the mouthpiece of his pipe at the boat docked alongside the landing. "You and I ought to take her out for a float before the season's completely finished."

"The *Net Work*," Peter observed aloud. "Pretty fitting name."

"Aye," Byron joked with a pirate's voice. He sat on the edge of the dock and gestured for Peter to join him. Their feet dangled a few inches above the low tide.

Byron took another draw from his pipe and looked up at the

stars. He puffed out a few smoke rings, then turned and looked at Peter. "Listen, I'm gonna tell you something. And I want you to promise me you'll think about it, okay?"

"Sure."

"You're a bright fellow. But if you don't mind me saying, you're walking around with this long look on your face. Like a little boy who's lost his old dog and blames the world for it."

Peter didn't know what to say. He knew it was true, and felt embarrassed that it was so plain for everyone to see. He stared down into the dark water and shrugged.

"Son, everything dies. It's how life goes on. Your ol' pooch? He's gone. That's how you have to think of it. Things live, and they die. Now it's time to go pick yourself a new puppy. Train it, love it, make it great."

"It's easy for you to say," Peter said. "You've done it all, and it lasted a long time for you, so much of your life. A whole career's worth." He gestured toward the softly lit house behind them. "You have your success and your wife and you're happy."

Byron scoffed. "You think the 990 was the only thing I ever did with ICP? No way. I did all sorts of things, new products. The difference is I stayed on board. And times were different then. I was trained to do the things I did. You're different."

"Why's that?"

"Simple. Son, you're a rebel. With a cause, for sure. I was too, but in a different sort of way. You're a genuine risk taker, but not for the sake of taking risks. No, you do it because it's the only way you know how to be."

"Right now I feel like the only way I know how to be is lost."

"That's fine. But is it the end? Naw. You just have to understand and accept that it takes healing, over time. Sometimes longer than you think. There's nothing like time, and you have to respect it."

"I know that, I do. And pardon me for saying this, but I feel like time is running out for me. I can't explain it."

Byron gave a hearty laugh. "Less than half my age, and you're feeling old are you? Ha. Let me tell you about time and age, son. Hell, I've been there and back already. And I almost died along the way. True story."

Peter turned to him. "Died?"

Byron nodded thoughtfully. "Yes sir, after that heart attack I mentioned the other day. And why? From not letting go. Almost bought the farm. But worse, after I got out of the hospital, I almost lost my wife. I'll spare you the gruesome details, but let's just say you'll get through this one. And it may not be the last time it's going to happen, either. The more you invent, the more you run the risk of failing. I won't say you were just lucky your first time at bat, but that was quite a home run you hit. And you'll have more. And you'll strike out too. Maybe more of those than homers or even decent base hits. But either way you'll get going again. And take it from an old man, it's true what they say."

"What's that?" Peter asked with genuine interest.

"That everything gets better with age."

Peter gave an appreciative nod. Staring at the water, he forced out what he found so hard to say. "But it hurts."

Byron patted him on the back. "Yeah, I know it. But you'll pick up and dust off pretty soon."

"Well, like you said. Only time will tell." Peter turned and looked back at the house. Through the kitchen window he could see Grace laughing at some story Kate was telling, gesturing wildly with her hands.

Byron withdrew his pipe from his mouth and poked Peter's arm. "Boy's blind, too. I see a lady in there who looks at you with a real fancy in her eye. She standing strong by you, son. I can tell."

Peter nodded. "I'm lucky, I know. I feel like Kate's all I've got now."

"Yeah, well how about I try to broaden your horizons a little. I'll give you something to think about."

Peter looked at him attentively. "Such as?"

"Mmm, let's just say I've been bored lately. Yeah, I love it here, and our home in Connecticut, and we've been talking about maybe traveling again this winter. But I've got this sort of itch, like I have to find something new to play around with. The way I used to feel, a long time ago. You ask me, I think there was a reason for us running into each other the way we did."

"How so?"

"I don't know, exactly. Not yet, anyway. But I've got a sneaking suspicion it's got something to do with our difference in thinking. I mean that in a good way. We come from very different worlds, yet they're rushing toward each other. Yes sir, if you and I put our heads together, I bet we could really show the rest of them a thing or two."

Peter was intrigued by the prospect. "You really think so?"

"Son, I know so," Byron said, stuffing his pipe in his shirt pocket. He lifted himself to his feet with a laughing groan and rubbed his belly. "Come on, let's go get us a wedge of that apple pie."

She set the dirty dishes in the sink and wrapped the leftovers in foil. On the counter sat a cranberry-and-apple crumble she'd fixed. The bourbon sauce, meant to be warmed and drizzled over the piping-hot dessert, sat hardening in a saucepan. Seeing no point in heating it, she dumped it down the drain and left the dishes for the maid to deal with in the morning.

Matthew was back in his office working away, while here she stood in the dark, quiet kitchen. Happy anniversary, she thought wryly as she opened the refrigerator to withdraw a bottle of wine.

She looked at the label. Not her favorite, but it would do. If Matthew was going to work the night away, then she would celebrate by herself. She set the bottle on the counter and grabbed a clean glass from the cabinet. The glass fumbled in her shaky left grasp and fell to the floor, shattering into a hundred bits.

She swore out loud, and the sound of her own broken voice unleashed a flood of anger and sadness. She slumped against the counter, the numbing effect of all the champagne now setting in, and wondered if Matthew had even heard the glass break, her shout. She cried and waited, but he didn't come. Evidently the sound hadn't carried all the way back to his precious little office. Or if he had heard, he didn't care.

She thought about his "gift" to her, the new At Hand PC Plus waiting in his office. It gave her an idea. If he wouldn't celebrate with her, she was pretty sure she could find someone who would.

She opened the utensil drawer and withdrew a corkscrew. Kicking aside the largest broken shards on the floor, she took down another glass and carried it, the wine, and the opener through the dark foyer to the library and Matthew's adjacent office.

She found him on the phone, pacing back and forth in front of his desk. He turned and saw her standing with the bottle of wine and gave her a disbelieving look. "Excuse me," he said into the phone, then cupped his hand over the mouthpiece. "I'm speaking with my coauthor."

"Good for you." She waved the bottle at him. "It's not for you, anyway. Just open it." She held it out to him and he took it, then the corkscrew, and resumed his phone conversation as he proceeded to open the bottle.

"Yes, yes," he said, "I like that angle. Sort of, 'Go west, young man.'"

Greta snorted and glanced around the room. One of the yard lights shone into the library through the rear windows, illuminating her brilliant salmon bowl. Seeing it made her feel even sadder.

She turned around and picked up her new At Hand PC Plus and tucked it under her arm. Matthew handed her the open bottle of wine. She took one last look at him, but he was already pacing again, as though she weren't even there.

"Happy fucking anniversary," she said loud enough for his dear coauthor to hear, then turned and ran out without looking back, smiling a bitter smile all the way up the broad staircase to the second floor of the mansion.

She ambled down the long hallway to the guest room farthest from the master suite. Her own private office, she thought cheerily, paying no attention to the room's unlived-in air. She set everything down on the antique secretary desk facing a window that overlooked the rolling Stanford hills. She poured herself a glass of wine and took a sip, then set about plugging in the At Hand PC Plus's power cord and phone cable. Between her studies of the first unit's manual and the Plus's ingenious plug-and-play design, even Greta, bombed, could get it started.

Unlike Matthew's configuration, she had no monitor or external keyboard, no extra mouse. Instead, she would have to make do with the smaller built-in screen, compact keyboard, and stylus pointing device, which popped out of the side of the unit. She picked up the instrument and looked over her shoulder, down the long hallway. It was dark and empty, yet for some reason she felt uncomfortable, as though Matthew might come up behind her at any moment and unexpectedly catch her doing . . . what?

She knew what, but she wasn't quite ready to admit it to herself. She pressed the Power button and waited for the unit to start up. True to his word, Matthew had moved all of her files over, including her preferences and World Online settings. She started the program and a moment later she was connected.

Before she could even check to see if any of her "friends" were online, her screen flashed. It was Gregor.

"Greta! Where've you been? I've missed you ☹."

She glanced nervously over her shoulder again, then got up and closed the door. She locked it and, turning around, hesitated for a moment as she considered the little room and her place in it. She looked at the bed, the armoire, the fresh flowers she'd placed in here earlier that day. The setting struck her as curiously exciting— more like some exquisitely appointed hotel room than a home office. So anonymous, she thought. She swayed a little and reached out to the dresser to get her balance, then seated herself at the secretary desk and began typing.

"Gregor, I'm sorry. I've been ... busy."

"Happy anniversary, Greta. It's tonight, isn't it?"

A sudden tear dropped down onto her keyboard. She hadn't realized she'd been crying. "Yes," she typed. "☹."

"Aw, Greta. What's wrong? Why are you sad?"

She plucked a tissue from the nearby dispenser and wiped her nose. "Let's just say things didn't go as planned. I made a big dinner. But he forgot."

"I'm sorry, Greta. Maybe you'd rather be alone ...?"

"No! I was hoping you would be here."

"You were? I was afraid I'd frightened you away the other day. I'm sorry if I upset you."

"It's okay." She was dizzy with so much to say. Her touch was fast and loose, as though she were speaking freely, drunkenly, but of course with her hands instead of her mouth. She typed away— it was so easy to just say whatever she wanted to say, anything at all.

"No, Gregor, I was touched. I was surprised. I blushed I think. And here you are again. I wasn't sure if you'd be here." An unexpected pang of jealousy stopped her for a moment. She wondered: "Gregor, you seem to be here a lot. Do you have a lot of 'friends' on here?"

"Lots, yes. But you mean women friends, don't you?"

"Sort of." She held her breath, thinking for a moment how crazy this was, how she could feel jealousy about someone she'd never met in person. It was an oxymoron. But she was curious and concerned, just the same.

"No. Just you, Gret."

"Really, Gregor? Honest?"

"Cross my virtual heart. The reason I'm here so often is because I have a second phone line that I'm always connected to. I have my World Online configured so that when you come online, a special little bell ring-a-lings. So if I'm working or close by, I can come running to see you."

She was touched. "That's so sweet."

"Yeah, yeah . . . and now comes the part where you remind me you're a married woman."

She didn't respond. She wasn't sure what to say. She waited for him to make the next move.

"Greta? Come on, say it. That's what you always say."

She waited.

"Greta? Are you still there? If you don't respond, I may say something crazy."

She waited, watching the little clock in the corner of the display tick off a full minute and ten seconds before he said more.

"Greta, come on. I'm warning you. This silence is getting a 'rise' out of me."

She didn't make the connection as she watched another minute roll by, unbearably, thrillingly, before he finally prompted her into action with his next line.

"I wish you were here with me, Greta. I wish I could see you."

"Gregor."

"Greta, tell me what you are wearing. Did you dress special for the dinner?"

"Yes. I put on a black silk Gucci dress. My emerald earrings.

My best gloves." She pressed Enter, then suddenly gasped, realizing too late what she had typed.

"Gloves?"

She thought quickly. "In case we were going to go out for a stroll."

"Oh. You mean fancy gloves. Not the keep-warm kind. Okay. Go on."

Her heart was still racing from her slipup. Gloves. She'd actually typed gloves. She closed her eyes and considered again what she was doing. It seemed so crazy to be describing herself to him like this.

"Anyway," she typed, "it doesn't matter. Matthew didn't even notice. He had his head up his ass over work. As usual." She refilled her glass, noticing that she'd polished off nearly half the bottle already.

"What could be more important to him than dinner with his beautiful wife?"

"Oh, his big deal with ICP. It's all he thinks about now."

For the first time in all of her online conversations with Gregor, he didn't immediately respond.

"Gregor, are you there?"

"Yes. I'm here."

"You got so quiet of a sudden."

"I'm sorry. I was just ... I'm sorry. Shocked, is the word. That a man would be that, well, obsessed with his work, to ignore his wife."

"Now you know how I feel."

"Do I? How do you feel, Greta? Right now? I mean really feel. Sexy?"

"Oh, Gregor. You always make me laugh."

"I'm serious, Greta."

"Sexy, no. Drunk, yes."

"I'll bet I can make you feel sexy."

"No, no. I don't think so."

"Oh, I bet I can. If I were there with you, I bet you would feel sexy."

"Yes, well. That's neither here nor there, is it?" Her heart was speeding up in a strangely familiar way, as though she were reading a novel in which a seduction was unfolding. It was so detached and unreal, yet somehow his words were getting to her, touching her.

"I can make myself a little there, you know."

"Beam yourself here like in *Star Trek*," she typed, laughing aloud without even thinking about it.

"In a way, yes. But just a part of me."

"Gregor, you're getting awfully weird on me. Dare I guess what part?" She giggled, surprised by her own candor. She would play along with his game. What would it hurt?

"The middle."

"Just the middle. I'm disappointed. Why not all of you?"

"That can be arranged. But just the middle for now. But you have to make a deal with me."

She laughed again, amused by her own frivolity. She sipped more wine, making it last.

"What's the deal."

"That I get to see you, too."

"Why, of course, Gregor. I'll just beam my middle to you, too."

"I'm serious."

"You can't be. It's not possible."

"But it is, Greta. That's what I'm trying to tell you. Hasn't anyone sent you a photo of themselves over the Net?"

And suddenly what he was talking about made sense. He meant a picture. That he would send her a picture. And by the sound of it, a very personal picture.

"Greta? Oh no, I did it again. Scared you off."

"I'm here."

"Well? Do we have a deal?"

"Gregor, this is all so new to me. I don't know what to say."

"Say yes."

"I can't. It would be ... unfaithful."

"No, it wouldn't. It's just a picture. Tit for tat, so to speak."

"Gregor, I'm trying to be serious."

"I'm sorry. But listen, you don't have to send anything too re-vealing if you don't want. Not right away, anyway. But at least agree to the possibility."

"But how? I don't even know the first thing about sending a picture of me this way. I'm not that advanced."

"I'll help you. In fact, I'll send you everything you need. And explain to you how to set it all up."

"I don't know, Gregor."

"There's nothing to be afraid of, Greta. It's just like exchang-ing photos with a pen pal."

"But you said your middle."

"Okay, so not exactly like pen pals. You know I'm drawn to you, Greta. So I'll take the first chance. I want you to see the effect you have on me. I'll capture a photo of myself right now with my little digital camera here and send it to you. You look at it, see if it does anything for you. But at least promise you'll consider it, okay?"

She didn't see any harm in what he suggested. What the hell. "All right, Gregor. It's a deal. Go on, send away. Show me what you're made of!" She laughed with gusto.

He told her to wait for a few minutes while he prepared the image. She stood up and strolled over to the corner window and looked outside, sipping her wine.

Matthew's office lamp cast a glow onto the lawn. She could see his shadowed profile leaning forward at his desk, before his own At Hand. Dear God, she thought, when it occurred to her that she and her husband were living in the same huge mansion, yet both were up to their own private business, a million miles apart. She

shook her head in astonished disbelief. Had her obsession turned as intense as his? It made her wonder, as she glanced longingly at her At Hand computer and realized how much its connection to the outside world had come to mean to her.

Just then, the computer announced she'd received new mail. A shiver of excitement raised the hairs on the back of her neck. She seated herself a little unsteadily, picked up the stylus, and tapped her E-mail box, revealing a single new message from Gregor. Unlike the plain text messages he had sent in the past, this one was earmarked with a tiny slide icon, indicating it contained a graphic. She hesitated. It felt so wicked, yet at the same time she was delirious with curiosity.

Taking a deep breath, she poised the stylus over the slide icon. With her free hand she picked up her glass of wine and finished it off in a single swallow, while at the same time tapping on the new mail message. With wide eyes she watched as her until-now-unreal seducer's naked torso unfolded in all of its tan, lean, muscular, and forcefully rigid glory.

She reacted with a start, and for a second time that night the wineglass slipped from her gloved hand and fell to the hardwood floor, a final shattering exclamation point to the Lockes' anniversary gone astray.

"Mr. Harrell, Matthew Locke has arrived."

"Send him in, please," came William Harrell's voice over the intercom on his secretary's desk.

Matthew was surrounded by the opulence afforded only by companies at the highest reaches of the Fortune 500. Plush carpets, rich wooden desks, fine art originals, and staff that address one another as Mr., Ms., Mrs., and sir. The overall effect provided a sobering contrast to Via's compact, Herman-Miller partitioned offices, open-air buildings, and first-name protocol. Matthew could hardly believe that less than three years ago he had occupied a Manhattan office not unlike this one, so expansive it seemed more like a penthouse apartment than a place of business. His office at Via was barely larger than any other manager's, just enough space to move around in.

He'd felt queerly out of place entering the massive ICP building, surrounded by such abundance and magnitude. He'd even forgotten how long it took for elevators to climb tall buildings; Via's

biggest structure was only three stories high, and most everyone used the central atrium staircase to travel between floors.

William Harrell's secretary rose and escorted Matthew into the chairman's office. Matthew pulled his sleeves and straightened his suit, mindful of yet another difference between West Coast Wizardry and starchy East Coast Business. Indeed, California had affected him more deeply than he'd realized.

He carried his briefcase and a large binder containing all of Via's product plans, financial summaries, and forecasts, as well as the strategy he had worked on two nights ago—his and Greta's anniversary night, he dryly reminded himself. Anyway, he'd brought along his new At Hand to polish the strategy on yesterday's flight out, then printed the final document on a portable printer in his hotel suite.

The binder felt heavy in his hand. He had come to think of it as his clay, molded into the shape of the new Via, a onetime grassroots company turned serious. Since last week's introduction of the new Plus model, Via's stock had climbed six points, and the reviews were positively glowing.

It was all very exciting. So much so that it had seeped into last night's sleep, a shadowy dream in which he was cast as a double agent, transporting a covert document to some untold organization. Showered and neatly turned out with his briefcase and the binder, he'd strolled out of the hotel with the feeling that he was holding his fate in his hands. His life, and the lives of so many others, would now change irrevocably. And then a macabre thought entered his mind, a dim leftover from his exotic dream: the cyanide pill. At least that was what he recalled from the spy novels he'd read, that the agents hid a cyanide pill in a molar, to bite down on in case a situation turned hopeless. Striding down Park Avenue he laughed at himself for trying to remember if that was how the dream had ended. It was unclear—and preposterous, he told himself as he made his way downtown to ICP's headquarters.

As Matthew strolled into William Harrell's office with the binder firmly in hand, his mind flashed again with murky snatches of the dream. He shifted the binder under his other arm so that he could accept Harrell's outstretched hand as the two met in the middle of the office suite. They exchanged a hearty greeting, and Harrell asked if he would like coffee or some other drink. Matthew declined, and moments later the secretary returned with a tray of beverages anyway, coffee, tea, sodas, and pastries, then silently departed.

"Let's get started," William Harrell said. "I got your E-mail, and I'm pleased to hear everything went well with your executives and board. It hasn't been all smooth sailing on my end. My advisers went ballistic when I revealed our alliance plan. They'd been on me to build something to 'blow the hands off Via,' as my tech adviser put it. To his dismay, I've informed my executives that we'll pursue a strategic partnership with you." Harrell eyed the binder. "Is it all in there?"

Matthew was pleased with Harrell's disclosure. It meant that Via and he were even more valuable to ICP now than when they had first met to secretly discuss the deal. He briefly considered the irony of the arrangement; he now had ICP in the palm of his hand. He gave the binder one last heft, weighing its import, before turning it over to Harrell.

"It's all here," Matthew said. "The complete strategy."

Harrell opened the binder in his lap and began flipping through it, getting the gist, smiling at what he saw. He looked up.

"Oh, yes. This is a trade, after all." He picked up a folder from the table and handed it to Matthew. "Here are all the file compatibility specs for the PCSoft OS extensions, as well as all the popular applications."

Accepting the slim folder, Matthew's spirits dropped a notch. The folder carried none of the weight of the binder he had just turned over. No girth, no satisfying heaviness in his hand. In fact, it

was of little personal use to him. He would hand it over to Alan Parker and his engineering organization, and they, in conjunction with ICP's team of engineers, would turn it into a graceful suite of software tools that would make the At Hand PC Plus compatible with the millions of desktop computers running PCSoft's OS and applications. Still, the actual exchange felt oddly uneven, though he knew that was hardly the case.

William slipped on a pair of eyeglasses and read a section with interest. "Tell me more about how you plan to handle the actual announcement when the software is ready."

Matthew stood and slipped his hands into his pockets. "In approximately four months we'll announce both our strategic alliance and the compatibility software around which it's based. Our statement will detail Via's new direction into Big Business, while yours, I suggest, focuses on Via's advanced technology. How Via's comparatively lean organization and extraordinary design enables ICP to offer a broad alternative to the PCSoft and Future Processing way of doing business. It's going to knock their socks off."

Harrell grinned broadly. "It'll give me no small satisfaction to stick it to those two. And this is only the small stab. The big jab comes next. Where are you on that?"

Matthew seated himself again and leaned forward with his elbows on his knees. This was his favorite part. "Here is where timing will matter most. Assuming things go as we planned—that ICP's co-selling position substantially drives up At Hand PC Plus unit sales—we'll then begin the merger process. This would occur somewhere between six and twelve months after the strategic alliance announcement. ICP will reveal its move to standardize on the At Hand PC platform for its handheld line, and our companies become one."

William snapped the binder closed. "Excellent."

Matthew nodded his agreement.

"It's exactly how I envisioned it, in some ways better," Harrell said, and was pleased to notice that Matthew had caught the subtle ambiguity in his comment. "You've managed to smooth the transition with the alliance aspect, so that the merger unfolds a little at a time. In stages."

"That's the idea. But you said 'in some ways.' Meaning what?"

Harrell removed his eyeglasses and sipped his coffee. "Meaning exactly that. In some ways, our plan is progressing better than I ever imagined. For instance, your idea to slap a 'Via/ICP SoftLink' logo decal on every At Hand PC we sell creates the unconscious impression for the user that our two companies fit nicely together."

Matthew nodded in agreement; however, his concern was obvious. "But in other ways, you're not as pleased?" In the back of his mind he knew what this was leading to. For months he had absently wondered how long it would be before the subject came up. He locked eyes with Harrell.

"No, not exactly." Harrell set down his coffee cup. "I mean Jones, of course."

"Jones?" Matthew said, trying to sound surprised. "What does he have to do with any of this?"

"That's right. Precisely what I've been wondering. What *does* he have to do with any of this?"

"Your point?" Matthew said, unable to hide the defensiveness in his voice.

"Jones himself. Have you been in touch? Has any of your staff heard from him? A phone call? E-mail?"

"No. He's in self-exile."

"I see." Harrell stood up and strolled to the window to stare out over the neighboring buildings.

Matthew turned on the sofa and slung one arm over the side. "Why do you ask? Is there a concern?"

Harrell kept his back to Matthew. "More a curiosity, really.

How he's spending his time. What he's planning on doing. Whether or not he'll return to Via anytime soon."

"I can't say," Matthew said; then, in an effort to assure Harrell, he added, "but he still holds a large amount of Via stock. So technically, he's still with us."

"Mmm. But will he be with us when we reveal our alliance? When we proceed with our merger? I have to admit that he, more than the products themselves, motivated my initial idea for the deal. I'd always hoped to get Jones as well."

"And as we had discussed more than once, the chances of that were fifty-fifty, at best. His taking off as he has was no surprise, when you recall the way he responded after I tried to feel him out on the idea of compatibility and aligning ourselves with ICP."

"Yes," Harrell said calmly, turning around. "Yes, indeed we did. And you're right, Matthew. I'm merely pointing out that the ideal outcome would be for Jones to stay with Via. Paints a rosier picture, don't you agree?"

Matthew didn't respond.

"Think you can convince him to come back?"

The thought had never crossed Matthew's mind. He was perfectly content with the distance Peter had put between them, and had adjusted accordingly. "I can't say."

Harrell moved over to the sitting area and eased into one of the facing chairs. "I guess we'll just have to wait and see. Anyway, you needn't worry, Matthew. It's not going to change our arrangement."

"No, of course not," Matthew said with a forced smile. Inside, he was furious with jealousy and loathing for Peter. When would Harrell and the rest of them think of Via as *his*? And when they merged, would people still refer to the former Via as "the company founded by Peter Jones"? It made Matthew's blood boil,

but he forced himself to hide his feelings. It wouldn't look good to come undone over Peter in front of Harrell. After all, it was this very office Matthew intended to eventually occupy, and control was everything.

Harrell picked up the binder again and opened it. "Anyway, I'll need to read through this and then we'll talk again about some of the finer points." He glanced at his watch. "When do you fly back?"

"I'm scheduled on a flight out tomorrow morning. But since we're finished already, I think I'll change it to tonight." He stood and collected his jacket, and Harrell rose as well to see him out. The executives shook hands, and William wished Matthew a safe return trip.

Pressing the Down button at the elevator bank, Matthew noticed that his hand was a little unsteady. Harrell's piqued interest in Jones had gotten a hell of a rise out of him.

"Come on," Matthew whispered angrily, pressing the Down button again. After what felt like an eternity, the elevator arrived. He let out a grateful sigh, pleased to be going home sooner than expected.

He boarded the elevator and pressed the Ground-Floor button, impatient for the first time at the thought of how much longer it would take to complete the deal. He counted down the levels as he descended, wishing things would move faster.

"Hey, where are you off to so early?" Kate said, lifting her head from the pillow.

Peter nearly tripped himself up as he worked on his jeans. "Uh-oh. I woke you. Sorry, I was trying to be quiet." He zipped up the fly and knelt beside the bed. Her hair lay spread around the pillow, and he combed it with his fingers. He kissed her lightly. "Would you mind taking a rain check on our trip to Boston?"

She closed her eyes and shook her head, then settled deeper into the bedding, trying to hide her face.

He touched her chin and tilted her face to him. "Hey, what's the big grin for? I thought you wanted to go to Boston."

She lifted her hand from beneath the quilt and gently knocked her knuckles on his head. "Circus is in town."

He looked embarrassed by the fact that she could read him so easily. "Well, I've been thinking."

"Mmm-hmm."

"After talking to Byron the other night and all. You know, outside on his dock."

"Thinking, huh? Like when I kept trying to talk to you yesterday at the park, and you were off in outer space? That kind of thinking?" She laughed.

"Yeah, I guess then too," he said. "I don't know, it's weird. This concept that just sort of popped into my head. I want to talk with him about it, see if he can help me think it through. There's something missing, a link I guess."

"Sounds to me like you're going to be busy. Maybe I'll head down to Boston myself, then back to L.A. That okay with you?"

"Yeah, sure. If it's cool with you." He locked his hands behind his blond head and looked at her with those intense blue eyes. "I just have to talk to him about this."

She was overjoyed, and she told him so. "Petey, I'm ecstatic you don't want to go to Boston. Go talk to Byron. I'll be back next weekend. If, that is, you still want to see me." She pretended to pout.

He gave her a funny look. "You're such a goof sometimes." He kissed her again and went back to dressing.

She laughed at him. "Hey, who's calling who a goof?" She tossed a pillow at him. "You're all inside out, Einstein."

"Huh?" He looked down at his shirt and saw that he had put it on inside out and backward. He pulled it over his head and put

it back on. "What would I do without you?" He leaned over and kissed her good-bye.

"Don't mention it," she said. "Knock 'em dead, champ."

On his way out he stopped in the kitchen to leave her a yellow Post-it note. He drew a smiley face and wrote, "I'm a lucky guy," and stuck the note on the coffee machine, where she was sure to see it.

His mind was racing as he quickly covered the short distance to the Holmeses'. With tourist season over, the town was cool and somber. A few cars belonging to the last vacationers and winter holdovers remained. Fewer boats bobbed in the lagoon, the rest transferred to winter storage until next season.

As he set foot on the Holmes front lawn he ran into Grace as she was coming around the side of the house, carrying a sizable potted plant. "This one isn't going to make it, I'm afraid."

"Bummer," Peter said sincerely, and Grace agreed. "Is Byron here?"

"Out back." She smiled and lowered her voice, as if to reveal a secret. "I'm glad you came by. He's been mumbling about some idea he says he wants to tell you about. He'd planned on dropping by your place today, after he finished up with the boat. He'll be glad you're here."

Peter thanked her and trotted around the house to the dock. He spotted the top of Byron's white-haired head above the *Net Work*'s side. He greeted the older man as he climbed aboard the boat.

"I see you got your tennis shoes on," Byron said, looking up from his work. He made a few last wipes with an oil rag over the vessel's teakwood bulwarks. "Good. You're ready to sail."

"If you say so."

"I say so. You saved me a short walk, you know. I was going to come over to see you." He replaced the lid on the oil and placed it and the sodden rags into a plastic bag. "Here, stow this, son,"

he said, tossing the bag to Peter and directing him to the open bin inside the cabin. Peter took a moment to appreciate the boat's impressive interior, crafted from fine teakwood and brass fixtures. The effect was clean, elegant, sharp—much like its captain, Peter thought.

"Cast off," Byron ordered, indicating the boat's mooring lines.

Peter hopped to the deck and unwrapped the lines from the cleats. The engine churned to life.

"Now give us a good shove," Byron said.

Peter heaved his weight into the vessel, then jumped aboard. Byron applied power and the boat lurched. They motored for the inlet, the water ahead rolling in small swells.

"Is it going to be windy enough?" Peter asked, shading his eyes to observe the ocean that lay a half mile out.

"Here," Byron said. He handed over a pair of spare sunglasses.

Peter put them on and looked again. He spotted a few craft in the distance, whipping along at a respectable clip with their sails fully puffed out.

Byron eyed the younger man's shaky legs. "Sail much?"

Peter shook his head. He leaned against the side and gripped the rail with both hands, anchoring himself as he watched Byron handle the wheel.

"Your legs'll settle down in a minute." Byron pulled his pipe from his shirt pocket. With his elbows he steadied the wheel, while at the same time he expertly applied his windproof lighter to the pipe's bowl. He nodded his head at Peter's knees and chuckled. "Just go with the flow, son."

By the time they reached the quicker ocean Peter was able to stand up straight. And just in time, for Byron began shouting orders to bring up the sails. Peter followed with coltlike shakiness, slipping a few times, but equal to the task. Within minutes the mainsail and jib were fully swollen in the eastern breeze.

Byron cut the engine, and Peter was immediately enraptured

by the silence, by the power of the wind as it pushed the sleek vessel along quickly and quietly. It was a blissful sensation, but before he could just hang back and enjoy it, Byron had him back to work.

"Here," the older man said, stepping away from the wheel. "Hold it where my hands are."

Peter placed his hands beside Byron's and braced himself. His body gave a small jerk when Byron let go, and he returned his hands and helped Peter find his grip.

"That's it. Just keep her steady," Byron said, and released his grip with an approving nod. He headed back to the cabin and disappeared for a moment, then reemerged with two cans of Heineken. He popped the lids and handed one to Peter. "Top of the mornin' to ya." He tipped his head to Peter, then took a long swig from his can.

Peter made a queasy face. Definitely not his idea of morning juice, but what the hell. He took a small sip, and it tasted surprisingly good, despite the early hour.

The two men shared a few minutes of silence. Eventually, Peter spoke up.

"So, I've been thinking."

Byron squinted at him. "Mmm. Me too." He turned to the distant shoreline and sipped his beer. "You first."

Peter nodded. "It was about what you said the other night. About our differences. The good ones."

Byron took a thoughtful suck of his pipe and nodded agreeably.

"And I started to think about your experience with big-system stuff," Peter went on. "And what I know about small systems."

Byron let out a great plume of smoke, listening with keen interest.

"And it really hit me more than ever how the two are coming together, the way you mentioned. Via's handhelds are helpful, but they're not tightly integrated into the bigger systems the way they could be. I don't just mean dialing up and connecting. I mean more. As a genuine extension of the desktop and online systems.

But more actively than the way portable devices today behave. More … proactively."

"Mmm-hmm," Byron intoned, encouraging Peter to continue.

"Imagine, say, a handheld that goes the extra mile. But different from everything out there. No compromise. Reengineered from the ground up. Sure, all the obvious stuff—fast processor, memory, connectivity—but then some. Truly handheld. I mean, this small." Peter traced a rectangle in the palm of his hand. "About the size of a wallet. Maybe it even flips open, like a cellular phone. Net-ready, from E-mail to pocket-size Web and newsgroup browsing. From huge databases to desktop syncing of all your important stuff, contacts, schedule, messages, the works. But a whole new interface. A whole new design, unlike either Via's or PCSoft's PortaPC OS. I mean really revolutionary. A no-brainer. You plunk it down and it does what you want it to do, and then some, anticipating your next move by learning from your past actions. By knowing you better and better the more you work with it." He paused, winded, to gauge the older man's reaction.

Byron took out a key and worked off the pipe's metal wind cap. He checked the tobacco, then leaned over the side of the rail and carefully rapped the pipe against his weathered palm, spilling the black ashes into the ocean. He returned the pipe to his shirt pocket and pushed his sunglasses up on his nose, then took a swallow of his beer and looked at Peter.

"You're talking about intelligent agents. Little software helpers that run in the background and pay attention to what you're doing, what you're not doing, then act on their own, on your behalf."

"Yes, exactly. We only started scratching the surface of agent technology at Via. It was never at the front of our design. We worried about the hardware first, then the OS and the applications. It's that kind of thinking that probably cost us the market. PCSoft works the other way. They do the software, and leave the hardware

up to everyone else. But even PCSoft, as far as I know, hasn't really taken agent technology anywhere. Yet. You see what I'm saying?"

"Hell yes. And the bugger of it is, it fits in nicely with what I've been knocking around." Peter was impatient to say more, but he kept quiet and let Byron talk. "I'm tired of all this bellyaching over the Net. It's the world's greatest source of information, yet getting what you want out of it is a bitch. Some sites are trying to make sense of it for you, but none with any genuinely uniform method. Sure, they're all talking about it, and eventually they'll get there, but it's going to take time. And I started wondering, what better venue than those handy little computers you know how to build. Yet even those are too damn complicated. It needs to be simpler. Especially on an accessory handheld like you describe, keeping it in sync with your desktop system, so when you come back with it everything gets put back in order—Web sites you visited, E-mails you picked up or sent, new contacts. But in the blink of an eye, with no fuss."

"Yes, exactly," Peter exclaimed with a pointed finger, which inadvertently caused the boat to lean. He quickly returned both hands to the wheel and got her under control again. He carried on some more, and Byron jumped in intermittently, sharing his own ideas on the subjects and concepts they covered. Eventually they took a breather, and Byron went below for fresh beers. He handed one to Peter.

"I didn't realize you kept up on all this stuff," Peter said, popping open his second can of beer.

"Hell yes. What, you think a guy like me retires and then just unplugs? Not a chance. Fact is, I've got a report on various agent technologies, back in my office in New York."

Peter gave a reflective nod of his head. "You know, it looks like you were right. I mean, that we have more in common than I figured."

Byron shrugged and focused on the horizon for a minute. He

seemed suddenly serious when he turned to Peter again. "I guess it's time I fess up."

Peter looked at him with questioning eyes.

Byron sniffed, and adjusted his sunglasses. "See, I'd been watching you in that café ever since you first showed up. I knew who you were, saw the way you looked. And the way you didn't look, too. At anything around you. It was written all over your face that you wanted to be left alone. I'd read the news, knew everything that had gone on at your company. So I waited. Until the other day, when that new Plus model was introduced. Hell, I figured there was no better time to throw a drowning fellow a line. Since the first time I saw you I'd had this feeling we'd maybe enjoy a sort of meeting of the minds. Like we are now."

Peter smiled, moved by the older man's humility and frankness. "So what do you think? Want to check out some of this stuff we're talking about, the two of us?"

Byron scratched his ear and grinned. "Sounds like I've got me a new hobby." He raised his beer. "Partners?"

Peter touched his can to Byron's and smiled.

"Partners."

Greta's memory of what exactly happened the other night was vague.

She knew a few things for certain. Or as close to certain as possible. That her behavior with Gregor had been questionable. That she'd made some sort of promise to him, the specifics of which she couldn't entirely recall. That she'd emerged from the guest room hours later with her black silk dress draped over her shoulder, and that Matthew hadn't even noticed because he was still downstairs working. And that she'd received a package from Gregor, just as he had promised she would. She hadn't mustered up the courage to open it yet. Or do much of anything since.

The next morning she'd awakened briefly to Matthew's activity, in from his jog and then his shower. She supposed now that she was still drunk at the time, pretending to be asleep as he dressed and packed for his trip to New York. She dimly recalled waiting for his clean aftershave smell to come close, a good-bye kiss on the cheek. Either he'd skipped it or she'd fallen back asleep,

because the next thing she knew it was late morning, and he was long gone.

At noon she'd put on a robe and ventured downstairs. She remembered eating a cold leftover squab at the kitchen window, then returning to the bedroom with a bottle of wine, which she polished off through the afternoon, alternately crying and drifting off to sleep. She couldn't bring herself to go into the guest room and contact Gregor. She could only cry and drink and doze. Later that evening she returned to the kitchen. She found frozen lasagna in the freezer. She washed down three Tylenols as she waited on the microwave, promising herself that tomorrow morning she would get it together, clean up, no more wine, start anew. Retreating once more to her bed, she pulled the shades and climbed under the covers.

Monday morning rolled around but she hadn't felt like getting up. Sometime in the early afternoon Dolores, the housekeeper, had knocked gently on the bedroom door to check on her and give her a FedEx package. She'd asked Dolores to leave the package at the foot of the bed, where it still sat. She said not to bother making anything for dinner, and gave the housekeeper permission to leave early if she felt like it.

Anguish, mental exhaustion, nausea, and headache kept her in bed until now, early Monday evening. Matthew was due back tomorrow afternoon, and she would have to pull herself together by then. And Gregor? What was she supposed to do about him? She knew now that she was genuinely attracted to him, yet at the same time she felt horrible, torn between her commitment to a husband who no longer needed her, and a man she knew only by his online persona. And don't forget the other, she guiltily reminded herself. The photo. The image was burned in her memory, where it stirred up an endless stream of vivid fantasies.

When was the last time she'd fantasized about Matthew? She couldn't remember. Yes, she loved him. And she couldn't help but

wonder if her unusual attraction to Gregor was simply a reaction to Matthew's rejection. Maybe. And that was what hurt the most, his rejection. That she'd really lost him.

And thinking this, it was impossible not to acknowledge her own, more personal loss. She moaned at the irony of it, of having lost the upper hand that had originally drawn Matthew to her in the first place. God, so many years of suffering. And not just after the accident. Even beforehand things had been less than perfect. Particularly where his unconventional sexual tastes were concerned, how he preferred mutual masturbation to intercourse, which he always complained was too tiring.

She lay there trying to count how many emotional ups and downs she'd pulled him through over the years. When his self-confidence would flag over this marketing campaign or that, or when he'd had such a hard time deciding whether he should make the move to Via. But no more. He came to her no more. Not for bolstering his ego, or even for his singular style of sex.

And that was the crux of it, wasn't it? In the last twenty-four hours she finally admitted it to herself, the reason. The accident. That was when their break had happened. She heard his voice in her head, so many promises, new beginnings, a change that would turn everything for the better. After the accident. After they moved here. After his plan was under way. After last week's introduction of the new computer. After, after, always after. How many times he'd promised it would all begin soon, Greta, soon.

Now what? she wondered. She would have to face Gregor eventually. If not in person—never that—then with an E-mail message. Yes, that was what she would do. She would write him. Apologize for the other night. She wasn't sure if she had anything to apologize for, but she would do it anyway. And she would thank him for his kindness and then get his address to return whatever it was he'd sent her.

To meet him in person wasn't an option. Not because she was

considering committing adultery, but because she couldn't bear the heartbreak of feeling more for him than the thrill she already felt. Of falling in love, and then losing him the way she'd lost Matthew. All because of her deformity.

The thought of losing touch with Gregor, even as an acquaintance, made her heart ache. Her experience with the At Hand PC had changed her life. She'd originally hoped learning how to use the computer would bring Matthew closer. But the opposite had happened. It was as though he'd found a surrogate companion for her, something to keep her entertained without bothering him. Her plan had backfired on her, and perhaps the best thing would be to stop using the computer after she sent Gregor her good-bye message.

She wiped her eyes and warily climbed out of bed. She might as well do it now. But first she would clean up. She'd gone all day without a drink and was feeling somewhat better, though her head still hurt a little. She eased into the shower and let the hot jets wash away her aches and pains. Yes, saying good-bye to Gregor was the right thing to do. And enough with the masquerading too, she decided while creaming her bare hands with lotion. For the first time since the accident she stood up from her vanity without the protection of a fresh pair of gloves.

She slipped on a clean robe, picked up Gregor's box, and set it at the top of the stairs for a moment while she went to the kitchen to select a bottle of wine and a glass. Just one glass, she vowed, to help ease her nerves. She struggled with the opener for a moment, then found it was much easier this way than with the gloves. Back upstairs she went to the guest room and set down her glass and the bottle, then returned for Gregor's box and stuck it in the clothes closet. Tomorrow morning she would call FedEx to pick it up.

She sat down to her At Hand PC Plus, connected to World

Online, ignored Gregor's six new E-mail messages in her in-box, and began composing her farewell letter.

She never finished it. He was there, online, waiting for her. He bombarded her with a stream of apologies and questions, and she listened, watching line after line scroll by, her heart beating fast, challenging her resolution to end her affair with him … if that's what it was.

Eventually he got to the box, and asked if she'd opened it.

"I can't, Gregor. I'm sending it back."

"Greta, no. Wait. Please, listen."

"No, Gregor. I can't. I may have gone too far already. I can't even remember." She eyed her wineglass and decided to leave it where it was. It had gotten her into too much trouble already.

"But Greta, we had a deal."

She apologized again, but he persisted.

"Greta, I want you to see me again, now."

She typed with trembling hands, recalling the photo of his naked torso. "No, Gregor. We can't. I can't."

"Just listen. See the little eye icon in the corner of your Chat window? That's the 'live view' feature. Click it."

"No."

"Yes, Greta. Just do it. I'm presentable. I swear."

Her resolve wavered. She took a sip of wine, just a small taste. Maybe seeing him would make it easier to stop seeing him, she rationalized.

She clicked the eye icon.

And there he was, framed in a small window in the corner of the screen. The resolution was a little blurry, and she leaned in for a closer look.

"Greta?"

She jumped in her chair. He had said her name. Not by typing, but with his voice.

She typed: "Your voice, I can hear you."

"Yes," he said, nodding on the screen. Her first impression surprised her. He was not quite as attractive as she'd pictured. His face was rather longish, with mussed dark hair hanging nearly to his eyebrows. Plus, he had one of those raffish goatees, which she wasn't fond of. He cocked his head to one side.

"Hello, Greta."

"So there you are," she typed. He smiled, and her impression changed a little. He looked so young and earnest, concerned for her.

"Now will you open the box?"

"It's one of whatever you've got there, isn't it? So that you can see me, too?" She glanced at her left hand on the keyboard.

"Yes. Will you?"

She hesitated. "You won't like what you see."

"I bet I will."

"I bet you won't. I'll prove it." She steeled herself against a sudden wave of sadness, tears building in her eyes. But she knew she had to do it, show him her terrible flaw. "Tell me what to do."

She retrieved the box from the closet and set it on the desk, then followed his every instruction. She connected the small egg-shaped camera to the At Hand PC Plus's rear port, set it beside the unit so that its lens was pointing directly at her. He told her to run the installer program on the included CD, and she did. He said she would have to restart her computer before the device would work.

"Come right back," he said, and she promised she would. Without giving it any thought she refilled her glass while she waited for the computer to restart. She launched World Online, and accepted Gregor's invitation to join him in a private chat. A moment later he appeared on her screen again. And so did she, in her own small window, right below his. She leaned close to the screen to see herself and realized that she couldn't look directly into her own eyes. That it was impossible, because the camera was off to one side, rather than in the center of the screen.

"Greta, you're lovely," Gregor said softly. "Look this way, into the camera." She turned her head, stared into the tiny lens. She smiled nervously and covered her face in embarrassment.

"Say something for me, Greta. Please."

"Gregor."

"Your voice is lovely." He flashed his beguiling smile and she shook her head.

"So you see, I'm an old woman." She laughed.

"Hardly, Gret. You're lovely. Really. Would you move back a little so I can see more of you?"

She glanced at her left hand. "Yes." She laced the fingers of her left hand around the bowl of her glass and scooted back in her chair a little, providing him a fuller view. She slowly raised the glass to her lips, sipped her wine, watching her own actions in the little screen, waiting for his reaction. Tears began to well in her eyes.

But he didn't seem to notice.

"Lovely," he said.

"Look closer," she said.

His face loomed closer in the window and he squinted his dark eyes.

"Lovely."

"Closer."

"I can't get any closer, Greta."

She let out an exasperated little cry and set down her glass, then flattened her left hand over the breast of her clean light blue robe, fanning out her fingers.

"This, Gregor. Now do you see?" Her hand was trembling.

"Oh, Greta," he said, tilting his head to one side.

She studied his face, watched for signs of revulsion.

"Is that it, Greta? That's what's supposed to be so ugly to me? Well it's not. See for yourself. Go on, Greta, look. Really look."

She blinked away tears, tried to see herself in a new light, as

he was seeing her. But she could see only what she always saw, her flawed left hand as stark and shockingly off-putting as always.

"Greta, don't cry. It's no big deal."

She scoffed. "No big deal?" She stuck her left hand out in front of her, waggled her fingers. "I can't say I agree with you on that one. The missing one I mean, of course."

He was nonplussed. "How did it happen, Greta? Tell me."

"It's too horrible to tell."

He reclined a little in his chair. "Tell me."

It suddenly occurred to her that he really wasn't shocked. She was the one who was upset, not he. He truly didn't seem to care. And if he didn't care, what would that do to her plan to stop "seeing" him? She rubbed her nose with the sleeve of her robe and sipped some more wine.

Then she took a deep breath, looked straight into the tiny orb's lens, and told him everything.

"It was horrible, Gregor. We were aboard a yacht on a windy lagoon. Celebrating a new soda of Matthew's that was a big success. I'd had a lot to drink. At one point I was standing off to one side by myself. Or swaying, is probably the more accurate way to put it. I was poking my ring finger in the little hole of an empty soda can, thinking about how successful Matthew had become. How lucky I was. How we were going to start a family. I was just sort of daydreaming, I guess. It was nighttime. Apparently we were getting ready to sail some more. I remember the flashes, they were taking Matthew's picture. The flashes popped and I closed my eyes for just a second. At the same time the boat rocked underfoot. I lost my balance and reached out for the rail. I couldn't see. The flashbulbs had blinded me for a second. The can was still dangling on my finger when I finally got hold of the rail to stop myself from falling. I felt rope and metal and the worst pain all at once. I'd grabbed between the support line and the rail. The can was caught in between. I think that was when I started to scream. I was leaning

over the rail, trying to free my hand. And then the boat lurched forward, and I went over. My finger didn't come with me. Matthew was standing at the rail screaming hysterically. Someone jumped in. It was dark but somehow I saw the blood anyway, everywhere. I remember reaching out for the white life preserver, the blood so dark against it. Then seeing what had happened. Really seeing. The bright white nub of bone, the rest gone. The next thing I remember I was in the hospital, my left hand bandaged so I couldn't see it. I thought it was just a bad dream. But it was really gone. It's really gone."

Her gaze was fixed on her left hand and where her ring finger used to be. A strange sense of contentment washed over her, and she was surprised by her dry eyes.

She looked up and faced him.

He pressed his fingertips together in a prayerlike position, touched them to his lips, and softly said her name. He moved his face up to his camera and looked her in the eye. His nose was slightly crooked, she thought, as he whispered that he wanted her now more than ever. That she was beautiful and none of it mattered. Not her hand, not her marriage to Matthew, not any of it.

He asked her to slip off her robe.

And she obeyed.

Afterward, they talked. About how long it had been since she'd felt this way, and about Matthew and his obsession with Via. This interested Gregor. He was very curious about Via. He told her he was a big fan of the company, that he had scraped together enough to upgrade his own At Hand to the Plus. He asked her more about the deal she'd mentioned the other night, and she said she couldn't recall what she'd told him. He pressed for details, saying that as an At Hand enthusiast he was worried about the fate of the company with Peter Jones out of commission. The mention of Peter's name

incited her to tell Gregor all about Matthew's secret deal and why it was justified.

And then, as though the mention of his name had summoned him, she heard Matthew calling her name. She looked over her shoulder, aghast.

"Gregor, he's home!" she hastily whispered to her lover. "He wasn't due back until tomorrow. But he's home already. My God, I have to go."

"Greta?" Matthew called again. Judging by his voice he was on his way up the stairs. "Are you up there?"

"In here," she called back, her voice unusually cheery. She turned back to Gregor. "Go now, go. I'll see you tomorrow. Go." Gregor seemed at once amused and shocked. She couldn't tell, and right now it made no difference—Matthew had reached the top of the stairway and was coming down the hall. There wasn't enough time to disconnect the small egg-shaped camera. She looked over her shoulder and smiled at her husband, trying to gauge whether he could see it.

"Just doing some online shopping," she said, quickly twisting around in the seat. She snatched the camera and drew it into her robe, to hide it between her legs. For a freaky instant she watched in horror as her own viewer window followed the camera's every move on its way to its hiding place, the folds of her robe, a flash of pink flesh, pubic hair, then darkness. For a split second she caught Gregor's astonished reaction before she fingered the Power button, making it all go away.

"All done," she said, turning to face Matthew just as he reached the doorway. His suit was rumpled and his tie was loose. He'd picked up his mail from the kitchen table and was casually flipping through it as he checked in with his wife.

"You're home early," Greta said.

"We finished sooner than expected, so I grabbed the next flight out." He frowned. "Are you feeling all right? You look flushed."

"I'm fine."

His eyes lingered on her for a moment before drifting to the open box on the floor. She held her breath.

He was about to ask her about it, but then he noticed the half-empty bottle of wine and his expression changed, as though it explained her reddened cast.

"Anyway," he said, glancing at the letters in his hand, "I've got a few things to do before bed. See you in a bit." He turned and headed back downstairs.

She extracted the camera from between her legs and un-plugged it. She tossed it into the box and hid it in the closet, then moved to the window and looked outside at the dark ground below.

A moment later Matthew's office light switched on. She watched his elongated shadow on the lawn as he moved to his desk.

She let out a gigantic sigh of relief, for once grateful that her husband had chosen his work over her.

William Harrell rose from his reading chair and stretched. He'd spent all evening with the binder Matthew had brought him.

The strategy was perfect. Locke had put together a plan that would let William eventually stick it to his dual nemeses, PCSoft and Future Processing. By the time he retired, Via would be a sub-sidiary of ICP, earning him new respect and putting him back at the forefront of the industry.

He reflected briefly on how Matthew's attitude had changed since they'd first devised the deal. His once-agreeable unfamiliar-ity with the business had turned to an edgy self-confidence that bordered on arrogance. Not inappropriate for a man of his posi-tion and stature, William thought, but worth keeping an eye on just the same.

Of more concern were Matthew's obviously adversarial feelings toward Peter Jones. While William had every intention of following

through with their deal as planned, he was nevertheless disappointed to hear that Jones was keeping such a low profile. It raised a dim concern in the back of his mind, not unlike his old curiosity about Jones, before the deal was even conceived, when he had kept a casual but envious eye on Via's and the young upstart's every move.

He wondered: Could Jones become a potential threat to the deal if he were to resign from Via and go off on his own? Harrell knew the young inventor had substantial financial reserves. Combine that with the venture capital he could secure by simply picking up the phone, and Jones would easily have the necessary resources to become a serious player again. But William had been in the business long enough to know that reputation went only so far. That even Silicon Valley's wunderkind would face major obstacles at this stage of the game. The biggest obstacle would be Jones himself. He was not an organization man, which was why he'd hired Locke in the first place. And this insight gave William Harrell a certain sense of security, however short-lived.

Shutting off his reading lamp, he was momentarily startled when the phone rang. He glanced at the wall clock. It was nearly midnight, and he answered curtly.

"Billy, did I wake you?" a croaky voice said.

"Who is this?"

"I knew it. Working late as usual. How's the ol' boss?"

"Byron, for Christ's sake. I see you're still an insomniac. How the hell are you? How's Gracie?"

"She's fine. We're great, staying on for an extra while up here in Maine. Sailing's been good. Couple more weeks left."

They chatted briefly and eventually Byron got to the reason he was calling.

"I need to ask a favor, Billy."

"Shoot."

"I'd like you to send me some of my research papers from my

office." As the most prominent inventor in ICP's history, Byron was granted lifelong privileges in the company, including an office suite that was cleaned every day in case he should ever decide to drop in and roll up his sleeves again.

"Sure thing. Which documents?" William smiled to himself. The esteemed founder's son was apparently experiencing a flare-up of postretirement blues. Perhaps he just wanted to reacquaint himself with his past accomplishments. He was, after all, getting up there in years. Harrell still considered him his closest business ally and friend. He grabbed a pen and slid his notepad closer.

"On the shelf right behind my desk, there's a fat binder called 'Advanced Intelligent Agent Design.'"

"Got it. Can I have Barbara send along anything else?"

"No. I mean, I don't want her to send it to me. It's going to a friend."

"Fine. Let's have it." He heard papers shuffling on the other end.

"Here it is: Forty-two Inlet Drive. Camden, Maine. Zero four two eight eight."

"You got it, Byron. I'll have Barbara express it out tomorrow and you'll get it the next day. Oh, wait a second. Who's the addressee?"

"Peter Jones."

William's eyes shot to the framed photograph of his deceased wife, Martha, a serene smile on her lovely face. He blinked a few times and his mouth was dry when he spoke. "You know Peter Jones?"

"Yep, new buddy of mine. I know you know who he is, Billy."

"Of course," William said, staring at his At Hand PC Plus. He made an effort to sound matter-of-fact. "What's he up to these days?"

"Oh, a little of this and that. We're kicking around some ideas."

"Interesting. Something you can tell me about?"

"Hell, I don't know. It may be nothing. But it may be something, too. Listen, I don't want to talk your ear off. It's late, and you've got a real job to go to tomorrow."

"No, I'm wide awake. I was just reading, actually."

"Well, if you've got a few minutes."

"I do for you," William said, seating himself in his desk chair. He reached over and straightened Martha's photo.

And for the next forty-five minutes he listened, not once interrupting his old friend and business partner as he excitedly described what he and Peter Jones were getting themselves into.

# PART III

Four months after Matthew Locke handed over his strategic-alliance binder to William Harrell, the two men were meeting again in Manhattan, this time backstage at Lincoln Center to announce the real thing.

Seated in the audience were executives from both companies, industry partners, analysts, customers, and the press. The two executives shook hands, and Harrell wished Matthew luck before leaving to find his front-row seat.

Waving away the makeup attendant, Matthew listened to a few last-minute pointers from Laurence Merrill. "Make sure you remember to smile," she said, trailing behind him as he made his way through the rear hallway. He waited at the curtain's edge, and Laurence flicked a lock of hair from his brow.

A production assistant wearing a microphone headset informed Matthew that he was on in one minute. Laurence wished him good luck and then hurried backstage.

The music dissolved and an announcer's voice greeted the audience as an enormous screen descended from the ceiling. The

colorful Via logo filled the screen, and the announcer boomed: "Please welcome the chairman and chief executive officer of Via, Incorporated, Matthew Locke."

Applause sounded as Matthew Locke strode onto the stage, traversing the distance to the podium with clear composure and self-assuredness. He graced the audience with a sweeping smile, then focused his attention on the center of the auditorium, just like Lauri had suggested. He felt incredibly at ease and confident, energized by the thousands of faces awaiting his announcement.

He wished the audience a good morning, then went immediately into his presentation. "As you know, Via is synonymous with empowering individuals with powerful handheld computer technology," he began.

After his first minute into it, numerous attendees throughout the audience leaned to one side to comment on his style. Or more correctly, his lack of style, nothing at all like that of the charismatic Peter Jones, who was notably absent. Today's announcement marked Locke's first major public appearance at the company's helm. He was a dry speaker, but the audience listened patiently as he continued, giving him the benefit of the doubt. The At Hand PC Plus had sold well through the last quarter, and analysts were once again giving Via a thumbs-up.

"Many of you today are in fact stowing a Via handheld in your pack or briefcase. But not as many of you as we would like. It would be naïve of me not to acknowledge that many more of you are carrying a competitive PCSoft-compatible portable, running on a Future Processing–equipped clone."

In response to this last, an informally attired band of rowdy Via loyalists shouted boos, and both the audience and Matthew chuckled good-naturedly before he went on. His voice rose, and his expression turned serious.

"We'd like to turn those numbers around, so that by this time next year, Via's popularity in the handheld market will find us well

on our way to surpassing the installed base of PCSoft-compatible devices."

The Via logo shrunk in half and slid to the left of the screen, making room for ICP's logo. The audience stirred, just the sort of reaction Matthew had hoped for. He smiled broadly and gave them the news they had come for.

"Today, it gives me enormous pleasure to announce that Via has entered into a strategic alliance with the world's largest computer maker, International Computer Products."

The crowd was dead silent for a few beats, and then suddenly a burst of applause erupted throughout the room. Matthew Locke was overcome by a sudden wave of heat, a head-to-toe sensation of absolute power. The first stage of the deal was out in the open now, and the audience's reaction was overwhelmingly positive, even though he had yet to spell out the details. After a full minute of applause he lifted his palms in a gesture for silence. The room quieted and he pressed on.

"Now, rather than me stand up here and describe what our new strategic alliance is made of, we've decided to let some of Via's and ICP's largest and most enthusiastic customers tell you in their own words, in the following short film. Thank you." He moved to one side of the stage, where he would have a clear view of the presentation as well.

The houselights dimmed and the pair of logos faded to black. A moment later the screen came to life again, as an attractive woman from a large insurance firm described how the new Via and ICP SoftLink program would enable the At Hand PC Plus to integrate with her firm's installed base of ten thousand PCSoft desktop systems. Cut into her explanation of her company's business and handheld computing needs were various animated graphics illustrating her points. A PCSoft spreadsheet document zipped across a LAN to an adjoining At Hand PC Plus, where moments later the same work sheet appeared, with all of its formulas, styles,

and fonts intact. She ended by saying her firm had placed an order for three thousand brand-new At Hand PC Plus handhelds for the company's field agents. She held one up and the camera zoomed in on the left cover of the device to highlight the new "Via/ICP SoftLink" logo decal. The audience applauded enthusiastically.

The film continued to roll, and so did Matthew's charged-up feeling. Letting some of the two companies' most loyal customers in on the announcement last month had been risky, requiring them to sign nondisclosure agreements that attempted to keep the cat in the bag until today's announcement. Miraculously, not a single leak had slipped to the press. He stole a quick glance offstage and smiled when he caught Laurence's thumbs-up gesture, then returned his attention to the screen.

The presentation highlighted three other companies and their intended uses for At Hand PC Plus and PCSoft integration. At the sound of crashing cymbals, Matthew returned to his position at the podium to applause. He let the praise go on and on, making no move to stop it this time. He nodded his gratitude, gushing with pride and satisfaction.

When the audience quieted down he thanked them for their enthusiasm, then provided additional details not described in the film. "ICP will begin immediately co-selling At Hand PC Plus computers loaded with the new SoftLink compatibility software. For the first time in history, two former rival groups—Via salespeople and ICP salespeople—will share and support the same customers.

"It is important to point out that this is a nonfinancial agreement, and represents the first-ever strategic alliance between our companies, making it possible for Via to continue to develop the world's most advanced handheld devices while enjoying a new role as ICP's desktop companion of choice, ahead even of its own PC Soft-compatible handheld computer."

His presentation went on for another ten minutes, and ended with more spirited audience approval. With a final word of thanks,

he went backstage, where he joined William Harrell and Laurence. Together, they headed to one of the theater's private meeting rooms to participate in a press conference, where they would answer questions posed by an invited group of journalists.

Inside, Matthew Locke was greeted by Janice Lane, whom he'd chosen to coauthor his book. She'd recently begun the early chapters, describing Locke's youth, his college years, and his first job as a summer intern at International Foods. Matthew was pleased with his choice of coauthor. The whole business of "writing" his autobiography was less complicated than he would have guessed. It seemed like every high-profile executive was doing it these days, and the only part he disliked was the long interviews Lane conducted with him, recording his every memory and opinion. Still, it beat the time-consuming task of writing it himself, that was for sure. And the advance had been worth it: a million for him, and three hundred thousand for her. His esteemed publisher had had a string of best-selling business biographies, and it was doing everything possible to make his name a household word by the time the book appeared in stores next year with an enormous first printing. All parties concerned were hoping for another *Iacocca*, the best-selling business bio in history. It was a gamble, but today's announcement would go a long way toward achieving that goal.

Matthew and William took turns answering questions from the group of well-known business and high-tech reporters. Having dealt with most of them in the past, both men addressed by first name those journalists who had been benevolent or even-handed in their portrayals of them in the press. It was not until they took their first question via satellite that the gathering turned unpleasant for Matthew.

Via usually announced new products in San Francisco's Moscone Center. However, both companies had agreed that today's announcement would be best served closer to Wall Street, on ICP's broader turf. To accommodate its West Coast loyalists, Via rented

the Moscone auditorium for the occasion, beaming today's live presentation to the packed audience via satellite. Afterward, a small faction of California-based journalists was invited to participate in the press event.

Laurence acted as the go-between, seated between Matthew and William. A large-screen television was set to one side of the table, enabling the men to address the West Coast reporters.

First up was Joshua Ellis.

"Good afternoon, gentlemen," Ellis said, wearing a skeptical look. "My question is for Mr. Locke. Hello, Matthew."

Matthew was momentarily caught off guard. For the life of him he could not remember the reporter's name. Noticing his pause, Laurence covered the tabletop microphone with her palm and leaned over to whisper the journalist's name. It was obvious to everyone seated in the room that Locke didn't recognize the reporter, and a few chuckles made their way to the microphone.

On the screen, it was also obvious that Joshua Ellis had heard the laughter. His expression tightened and his cheeks reddened.

"Joshua, of course," Matthew Locke said, trying for an amiable tone. "I'm sorry, I didn't recognize you at first with your goatee. Welcome. Who are you here for?"

Ellis seemed no less at ease. "*Wired* magazine, thank you." More soft laughter arose from the seasoned East Coast newspapermen and -women. Matthew kept a straight face as Laurence prompted the tan and youthful Joshua Ellis to ask his question.

"Would you confirm that today's strategic-alliance announcement is only the first stage in a larger move that will occur by this time next year."

Locke's heart speeded, but his face betrayed no emotion. He nodded firmly to acknowledge the question, and leaned in to the microphone.

"I'm not sure I understand what you're getting at, Joshua." His tone was agilely patronizing, prompting more laughter in the room.

Ellis fumed. "On the contrary, Mr. Locke. I should ask you what you are getting at. Quite literally. A source extremely close to the company has informed me that you intend to sell Via to ICP in the not-too-distant future. Is Peter Jones just going to sit on the sidelines and watch his company go to the highest bidder? And while we're at it, where is Jones today? You didn't mention him once in your presentation. Pretty odd, considering he's still one of the company's largest shareholders. What's really going on, Mr. Locke?" He put a particularly bitter inflection on Matthew's surname.

Matthew's immediate reaction to Ellis's accusation was an amused, showy glance to William, as though they shared some private joke. As though the suggestion were so absurd it was laughable. Out of this world. Insane.

In fact Matthew was stalling, searching for the right words. Inside, his pulse was racing, his mind reeling. Ellis was of course dead-on in his accusation, and both Matthew and William knew it. And at the same time, both knew with absolute certainty that they were the only men privy to this fact. Yet Ellis had nailed it. But how? It was very possible that Ellis had posed the same question to a member of either company's executive staff, whose sloppily worded response he then construed to imply what he had suggested.

But whether Ellis was merely posturing before his peers or was somehow actually onto the secret plan, Matthew knew he had to be very careful in his response. And credible. If the other journalists remotely suspected there might be some truth to Ellis's question, then the deal would be in serious danger. Christ, Ellis was even correct in his estimated timeline. Indeed, the next year would be absolutely crucial to the deal's eventual fulfillment.

And then the correct response occurred to him. In those few seconds between the question and his answer, his whole worldview turned inside out with blazing clarity.

Yes, he knew what to say, and just how to say it. Hearing the words in his own head nearly caused him to burst out laughing at the pure irony of what he was about to proclaim. It would be lost on everyone—and William Harrell in particular. It was a completely unexpected turn, but he knew once he said it he would be able to pull it off.

He looked straight into the camera and gave his reply.

"Joshua, what you've suggested is absolutely, one hundred percent untrue. I can assure you, right here, right now, that Via would never put itself in a position of being sold to ICP, or to any other company. I give you my word."

His delivery was pitch perfect, his eyes unwavering through the entire response. Joshua Ellis's own gaze burned.

From the corner of his eye he sensed the other journalists nodding in agreement, or shaking their heads in pity at Ellis's farcical theory. Indeed, they believed what Matthew had said. And he was not in the least bit surprised by their reactions, because he believed it himself. Completely. Because Matthew Locke had told the truth.

And no one was more surprised by this fact than Matthew himself.

The second person most surprised by the day's business develop-ments was Peter Jones, but for a different reason.

"That's right, as much of it as I can sell," Peter said into the telephone. His voice was highly agitated. "FedEx already left with my resignation. Locke and the board will get it first thing in the morning. Okay, Ben. Thanks. And take care of yourself." He hung up and looked at Byron with a mildly disbelieving expression.

"You sure you want to do that?" The older man sat before a large worktable, turning his coffee mug in his palm. He was wor-ried about Peter.

"Absolutely. For Christ's sake, Byron, they're in bed with ICP now." He batted his hand at a copy of the *Wall Street Journal*, which featured a headline announcing the unexpected Via and ICP alliance.

"Hey, don't forget that's where this old-timer got his start."

Peter ran a hand through his newly close-cropped hair. "I know, I know. I'm sorry. I don't mean to disparage you or where

you're from. You know that. I'm just astonished that Locke actually went through with what I would never agree to. To sell out."

Byron scoffed in a friendly way. "That's not what I'd call it. The way I see it, he's upping Via's market. He'll probably triple it by the end of the year. From an outsider's point of view, it's a damn clever maneuver."

Peter crossed his arms. "Yeah, well, good for him. That's all the more reason why it's time for me to say adios and cash in my stake. Besides, it looks better to investors if I match their potential investments with my own money. You know, I'm in the mood for a little shopping spree. I've decided to move ahead with those acquisitions we talked about, the Web browser, the compression routines, and that awesome little LCD display we saw last week in Boston. And definitely that knockout handwriting-recognition kernel. It's way better than what we had at Via. Let's see, those couple goods should cost me, what, about sixteen million? Yes sir, I'd say it's a good time to sell."

Byron tried to maintain a stern look, but it was impossible. "Well, I guess that's settled, then. So wipe that snarl off your face and let's get back to work." His fondness for Peter was strong, and they had become close in the few short months they'd been working together.

They'd turned the Holmeses' basement into a lab and workroom. Scattered all around were diagrams and circuit boards, tools, and foam models sculpted to depict different handheld computer designs.

Peter went over to the models and picked one up. It was about the size of a man's folded wallet, only thicker. He seated himself at the huge worktable and turned the model over in his hand.

"That one still bothering you?" Byron said.

"Yeah. I'm just not sure why." Peter tossed the foam mock-up onto the table and picked up another, this one no larger than a checkbook. He flipped it open and pretended to type on the tiny

keyboard. "Very cramped." He picked up a pencil and pretended to scribble on the model's "screen." "And really hard to write on it this way." He tossed it aside and went back to the first model. "I sure like the way this one feels. But with no keyboard, it's got to depend wholly on the handwriting recognition. I'm not sure people will go for that as their only option. What do you think?"

Byron fished his tobacco pouch from his shirt pocket and slowly went about packing his pipe. He sucked a few glowing tokes, then shook out his match and turned his head and exhaled a plume of smoke. He clamped down on the pipe to free his hands, and slid a blank index card front and center. He drew a few rows of circles along the length of the card, filled in some letters of the alphabet.

He gestured for the smaller model, and Peter handed it over. He turned it lengthwise in his palm, then held the index card along the bottom edge.

"How about something like this? Lid acts as a keyboard. Granted that handwriting software you're buying is so good they'll probably never use it. But it's there, for the holdouts." He folded it over and turned it around in his hand. "Plus, it doubles as a lid to protect the display, so you really could put it in your pocket, just like a wallet."

Peter nodded. "Yeah, that's good. With a rotation routine, you could reorient the screen this way," Peter said, snatching the model out of Byron's hand. "Face up, like this. And I bet that's how most people would use it. We could even hinge the lid so that it flips all the way around."

Byron plucked the model from Peter and picked up the index card again. "Like so."

"Exactly."

"And then hit the Reorient button again," Byron said, turning the mock-up lengthwise in his palm, "and you get the wider display for the baby Web browser she'll have in her."

Peter nodded his agreement. "But there's still something, I don't know, missing. I mean, most handhelds have keyboards, or the option to attach one. And a stylus, like ours here. So we're doing what everyone else is doing. Which is fine if we can pull off everything else we think we're going to do. Especially the no-brainer synchronization routines. But is that enough? Are we missing some obvious idea, some new way to use these things that no one else has thought of?"

He stood up and casually settled his hands on his hips, frowning at the make-believe devices scattered over the table. "That's what's bugging me. That we're not thinking differently enough from everyone else."

"A new paradigm," Byron said, deep in thought.

"Or whatever you want to call it. I mean, sure, these are good," Peter said, waving a hand at the table. "But good enough? Good enough to really challenge the way everyone thinks of handhelds? Enough to make them buy one of these instead? I'm not so sure." He gave a frustrated shake of his head. "There's something missing. And we've got to think really hard about what it might be."

At the sound of footsteps both men turned to watch Grace coming down the steps carrying a lunch tray. "Time for a break, boys."

"Ah, relief." Byron stood up and rubbed his hands together. "Honey, we got any vinegar for those fries?"

"Coming right up." Grace set the tray on the table and started up the stairs.

Byron picked up a hot French fry and shook it at Peter. "Now, give it a rest and eat, and I promise while your stomach is working your brain'll take care of the background processing."

"Do you always think with your belly?" Peter laughed, picking up a sandwich.

The telephone rang.

"I'll get it," Grace said, coming back down with the condiments. Byron gestured for the bottle of vinegar.

"I got it," Peter said, going to the wall phone. "Holmes residence." He wiped his lips on his sleeve. "Hey, Ben. What's up? Wait, let me guess, the market crashed and my stock's worth squat." He looked at Byron and Grace and rolled his eyes.

"His secretary," Byron whispered to his wife, identifying the caller. "Or former secretary I should say, as of tomorrow. Our boy here has just resigned from his own company."

The couple abruptly started at Peter's surprised shout.

"What?" His eyes were wide with panic. He gave Byron a stricken look and the older man put down his sandwich.

At the same time, Kate's voice called out from upstairs. "Anyone home?" Peter had been expecting her to arrive in town today.

Grace started up the stairs and met Kate just as she was coming down. Seeing Grace's concerned look, Kate asked if everything was all right. "I think it's something with Via," Grace whispered.

Kate silently mouthed hello to Peter, and he gave her a weak smile. Whatever it was, it didn't look good.

"All right," Peter said into the phone. "I'll get there as soon as I can." He returned the handset to its cradle and stood facing the wall.

Kate moved to him and put a hand on his arm. "Petey, what is it?"

He turned around, his face slack. He stuck both hands on his head and averted his eyes, looking at the table with its scattering of notes and models.

Byron stood up. "Son, is everything all right?"

"Peter?" Kate said. "What's the matter?"

Peter let his hands fall heavily to his sides. "It's something back home."

"Your stock sale?" Byron said.

Kate looked from Peter to Byron. "What stock sale?"

Peter shook his head. "No."

"You're going to do it, babe? Sell your stock?"

Peter nodded.

"That's great," Kate said, taking his hands in hers. She felt the smallest flinch in his fingertips. "So what's the matter?"

Unable to look her in the eye, he focused on their joined hands. "Something happened back home. I have to go back. Right now." He forced himself to look at her. An old line went through his head, like the lyrics from some downhearted song. But this was a line of his own making, not from any of Kate's music. He let go of her hands and turned to Byron. "I have to get to the airport. Right away. Will you take me?"

"I'll go back with you," Kate said. "Let's go."

Peter didn't move. "No, Kate. I have to go alone." A voice in his head screamed for him to take her by the hand, go upstairs, and sit her down on the sofa and tell her the truth. What had happened those few months ago. How it happened. Why it happened. And what it had, or hadn't, meant. Until now.

He squeezed her hand tightly, but that was all. Once again he couldn't bring himself to tell her. Not yet. He knew this time there was no getting around it, he'd have to tell her before it all came out, but this wasn't the time or place. He had to leave, right this minute, and after the immediate crisis was dealt with he would tell her everything. "Kate, I have to do this alone. I'll explain everything when I get back. Please, you have to trust me on this."

Kate met his conflicted eyes with suspicion. He'd never done anything like this before; they'd always been so open and honest with each other. And now, for the first time in all their years together, he saw doubt in her eyes. Mistrust.

Grace discreetly nudged her husband to intervene.

"Okay," Byron said, setting his gentle hands on the couple's

shoulders. "Go get your coat, son. I'll take you." He gave Kate a re-assuring wink.

"Don't you want to pack some things?" Kate said.

"There isn't time." He looked at her once more with distressed eyes. "I'll call as soon as I can." And then he turned and headed up-stairs, leaving Kate to stand there in utter confusion.

"Back in a bit," Byron said. "Don't eat all my fries." He kissed his wife on the cheek, then turned and put an arm over Kate's shoulder. "Whatever it is, it's going to be okay."

He said good-bye and went after Peter, who had quietly sta-tioned himself at the top of the stairs, one ear turned toward the basement. The distant line danced again in his head, threatening to upset the recovery he'd achieved since that foreboding night and the day that followed it.

Heading for the airport he was silent, and Byron did not press him for details.

On the plane he could do nothing but stare out the window and listen to the reproachful voice in his head as it repeated the lame excuse over and over.

He'd prayed he would never have to say it aloud.

*It was the wine.*

Greta Locke was riding high. She raised herself from the exer-cise bike's seat and pedaled harder, faster, glancing at her white-knuckled fists. Since her intimate online rendezvous with Gregor, she had held firm in her decision to give up the gloves. Admiring Gregor's body as she did, she threw herself into a daily workout routine. He was younger than she and reasonably attractive, from what she could tell. The exercise bike had firmed her formerly limp thighs and tightened her rear and her upper arms. Though they had not yet met in person—or "F2F," as Gregor liked to say—

their special affair, as she had come to think of it, had turned serious.

They got together online every morning, and Greta no longer hid her video camera device from Matthew. When he asked her about it one day, she said she liked to take snapshots of herself to include in the letters she sent back home. He'd smiled at that and then went back to his own office, satisfied. She knew Matthew had sensed the change in her. She didn't believe he knew she was having an affair, and an unusual one at that. Nor did she feel guilt anymore about her online liaison with Gregor. But that was only because they hadn't met in person to consummate their feelings for each other. And that was just the way she wanted it, until she was sure about a few things.

She saw by the bike's timer that she had two more minutes. She pressed harder, her breathing heavy but controlled, her heart rate registering right where it should. A light breeze from the open window cooled her sweating face and torso. Her coppery hair was pulled back into a ponytail. She glanced at her At Hand PC Plus on the secretary desk. Matthew had since brought her a printer, monitor, mouse, and keyboard. She had turned the guest room into her combination exercise space and home office. And, she thought pleasantly, her secret love nest of sorts.

The timer beeped and she let out a great, energized shout. She maintained a slow pace for another minute to cool down, then hopped off the unit. She admired her physique in the full-length mirror mounted on the closet door. Not bad. Another month or two and she'd look like one of those sprightly TV fitness chicks she stretched out with every morning. Dabbing her face with a towel, she clicked the At Hand's mouse and connected to World Online.

Still no Gregor. He'd mentioned last night that he would be busy in the morning, and probably not online until noon or so. She looked at the clock: eleven-fifteen. She disconnected from World

Online, snatched her water bottle, and headed into the master suite to shower. Seeing the king-size bed stirred little feeling in her. Since the "first night" with Gregor, she'd been sleeping in her own room. Like the rest of her changes, Matthew had not objected. If anything, he was probably glad, she thought. Which was just as well. This way, he would be better prepared for what she was going to hit him with.

She wasn't sure if she would really go through with it, and she would have a better idea in a little while, when she made the call she had promised Gregor she would make.

She jumped into the shower, picturing Gregor in her mind as she soaped her body. God, he made her feel so good, so wanted. It was torture not being with him. But no matter how out of hand her marriage had become, she wouldn't let herself be unfaithful to Matthew until she was absolutely certain.

Drying off, she looked at the clock and wondered if Gregor had come online yet. She hurriedly threw on a pair of cotton slacks and a light silk blouse. She generally skipped the bra when she was expecting to see Gregor. Unless of course he asked her to wear one, in order to see her remove it. He'd asked her to do a number of things she'd never before imagined.

Stationed at her computer, she took a moment to study her left hand. It really wasn't so awful after all, but she would never have thought that if it weren't for Gregor. It gave her much pleasure to traipse about without gloves in front of Matthew. She especially liked to do little things that encroached on his comfort level, like offer to refill his empty coffee cup, or waggle her four fingers good-bye when he left for work. He would inevitably avert his eyes, but this no longer hurt her the way it once had. Gregor, on the other hand, never averted his eyes. Like now.

"Well good morning," Greta said to his slightly grainy video image.

"Hey."

"Just hey? Why so glum? Are you all right?"

"Yeah, sure. I'm just pissed off. I got fired off this feature story I was working up for a magazine. Said if I couldn't substanti-ate my premise then I've got no story. Jesus, Gret. I hate this fuck-ing work anyway. I wish I could just write my novel." He let out an exhausted sigh and massaged his neck.

"Poor baby. I wish I could be there to do that for you."

"Yeah, me too," Gregor said, without his usual enthusiasm.

Greta had never seen him so down. "Gregor, what can I do to help? Tell me."

He managed a small smile. "You make that call yet?"

She shook her head. "Not yet. I was waiting for you. I got an idea. With the two phone lines in my room here, I can call him while you're here. I need the moral support. Okay?"

"I guess, yeah. I still feel kind of funny, though. Like, I don't know, maybe you think I'm some sort of gigolo or something."

She laughed. "Hardly, darling. We've already gone over this. Think of it as an arts grant, like the universities and foundations give away. You're an artist, Gregor. And you need to be able to work on your novel instead of suffering through these articles you don't even want to write. Right?"

He nodded. "Gret, you're so nice to me."

"Ditto. Now let's make the call. You ready?"

He moved closer to his screen, suddenly very interested. "Do it." He watched her pick up the handset and dial. "Hey, open one button there, would you?"

She waved a hand at him in mock surprise, then undid the top two buttons of her blouse. She blew him a kiss and turned her attention to her phone call.

"Yes, this is Greta Locke. I'd like to speak with Mitchell, please." She glanced at Gregor. He'd taken off his shirt and tie, giv-ing her a nice view of his impressive pecs and abs. They both knew

this was a serious call, yet they were behaving like love-struck teens. She looked away when the attorney came on the line.

"Mitchell, hello. You too. Fine. Yes, he's fine, thank you." She hesitated. "Actually, Mitchell, things aren't exactly fine."

She glanced at Gregor framed in the little window on her At Hand's display. He'd quit playing around, and was listening intently to her side of the conversation.

"I'd like to ask you a few questions," Greta said. And for the next few minutes she spoke without pause. When she finished, the attorney asked her to clarify a few points.

"No," she said, "I don't know if it's what Matthew wants. We're going to discuss it. But I think it's what I want, which is why I need to understand certain aspects now, before I talk to him about it."

She listened some more, tipped her head into her free hand as she nodded to what the lawyer was telling her. "I see. Okay, then. No, I can't think of anything else right now, just those few—"

"Pssst."

She looked up.

Gregor was waving for her attention.

"Mitchell, can you hold on a moment? Thanks." She cupped her hand over the mouthpiece and held the handset away as she leaned close to the At Hand's built-in microphone, mounted in the upper lid. "What is it?" she whispered, a bit testy.

"You didn't ask him about the main thing."

She registered surprise at having forgotten to cover this point with the lawyer. She moved the handset to her ear again. "Hi, Mitchell. One more thing, about the half-of-everything law. I'm vaguely familiar with it. I don't mean to sound, well, presumptuous. But it is important for me to know where I may stand, should we decide to move ahead with this."

She listened, and as the attorney explained she looked at Gregor, who appeared to be holding his breath. She nodded slowly. "I see," she said, her voice barely audible. "Thank you, Mitchell. Yes, I will. We will. You too. Bye."

She hung up the phone and dropped back in her ergonomic office chair until she was staring straight up at the ceiling, her mind suddenly blank. The attorney's words had overwhelmed her, and for the briefest instant she forgot that she wasn't alone in this.

"Greta?" Gregor said, rousing her attention. "What did he say?"

She straightened in the chair and met the camera's indifferent eye with her own vacant gaze.

"He said it's the law," she whispered in disbelief. "Half of everything."

The following morning William Harrell scanned the important newspapers on his limousine ride to work. All reports on yesterday's strategic-alliance announcement were positive, and Harrell was pleased to see that no one had pursued the disheveled West Coast reporter's legitimate accusation of an impending merger between the two companies.

He stared out the window as they rolled through Central Park, fondly recalling when he'd first devised the deal. At the same time, his mind wandered to the late-night conversation he'd had with his old friend Byron Holmes four months ago. William had been troubled when Byron had mentioned Peter Jones's name, but by the time he'd hung up he'd felt better. Jones remained an enigma to William. A creative curiosity. He made a mental note to check in with Byron in a few months to see how the pair were coming along with their project.

Right now he had other things to think about, like the impending merger. After yesterday's announcement he'd called together his senior staff and revealed his intention to acquire Via. His senior

counsel foresaw no FTC objection, since ICP's current portable devices were merely clones running PCSoft's OS. This fact excited William's highly competitive nature. What was so attractive about Via was its proprietary operating system software. It was theirs, and theirs alone. And soon it would be his.

And eventually, when Via was firmly ensconced in ICP's organization, he intended to license Via's operating system to clone makers, just as PCSoft had done. But this time he would be on the receiving end of all those royalties. It was all supposition, of course, but after yesterday's successful announcement and flood of advance orders, his dream was closer than ever to becoming a reality.

The limousine abruptly halted in a knot of traffic. Craning his neck to see up the block, William spotted a long string of trailers, and lots of official-looking men and women running around with walkie-talkies, clipboards, and anxious faces. He'd seen this sort of thing enough to know it was a film production, which New Yorkers looked upon with a mixture of admiration and frustration. His driver announced that he would attempt to get him to work another way, and William told him there was no hurry.

He opened his briefcase and withdrew his At Hand PC Plus. He set it on his lap and popped in the cellular modem card. The configuration had proven useful for weekend jaunts to his quiet retreat in the Adirondack Mountains, making it possible for him to get work done during the chauffeured ride there and back. He launched his E-mail program, and a few moments later he was connected to the company's server. Having already checked and dealt with the brunt of his E-mail over breakfast, it came as no surprise that there were only a few new messages, including one from Matthew Locke. He selected it, and while the message downloaded he plucked a tissue from the armrest dispenser to dust his screen. Drawing the tissue away he scanned the E-mail message—and froze.

His chest tightened and he experienced a strange tingling

sensation in his left arm, the kind of feeling he'd heard other men say occurs just moments before suffering a heart attack.

He gripped the armrest tightly and struggled to catch his breath as he read the message.

TO: wharrell@icp.com
SUBJECT: JONES RESIGNATION & THE DEAL

william, i'll get right to the point: yesterday's unveiling of the softlink program and our strategic alliance opened my eyes to the fact that what we announced is exactly the right thing for via and icp.

as such, i am asking that you honor my response to the press, and we do not move forward with the final merger stage of the deal. instead, via and icp shall proceed as described yesterday, in a strategic-alliance pact.

furthermore, peter jones today officially resigned from the company, and sold off more than two-thirds of his shares. his decision assures my position at via's helm, which i have come to appreciate.

as far as i am concerned, the deal is done. while the outcome isn't exactly as we'd originally planned, we both emerge victorious.

i look forward to our two companies working together.

—matthew

William let his At Hand fall to the floor as he slumped into the seat back. His breathing was coming in short gasps, startling his

driver enough to pull over and stop the car. He asked his chief if he was all right; he was ready to dial 911. William waved the tissue at him and asked him to go on, that he would be fine in a moment. The driver did as he was told, keeping a worried eye on William in the rearview mirror.

But William was anything but fine. He was utterly shocked and infuriated by Matthew Locke's message. In one fell swoop the son of a bitch had torpedoed the deal. Harrell looked out the window and shook his head in stunned amazement. His driver had backtracked through Central Park to break from the film traffic, and a nauseating sense of déjà vu set in when William realized here he was again, zipping along the same tree-lined course that had given root to the deal in the first place. Fucking Locke.

His mind immediately shifted into a defensive position. He considered the full weight of Matthew's selfish turn. Yes, both companies would benefit from yesterday's announcement, Via more than ICP. The real win for ICP, and for William personally, was in the merger that would have enabled him to retire with the satisfaction of having stuck it to PCSoft and Future Processing.

He considered his company's current line of portable computers and their dependence on the world's leading processor and software companies. Lessening that dependence was what had motivated him to pursue Via, which six months earlier couldn't possibly have competed against the dynamic duo. But yesterday's strategic alliance with ICP gave Matthew and Via just the fighting chance they needed, and William knew he would look like a fool if he were suddenly to pull the plug on the alliance.

More than once there had been rumors of a PCSoft/Future Processing merger. Both companies had at various times over the last decade entered into very brief discussions with William about working more closely together, each unsubtle in its genuine interests. Acquiring one company or the other was an option, but the price for either would be extraordinary. And a merger? Certainly

not on William Harrell's watch. Both companies were enormously successful, and headed by extremely capable chiefs. No, William was not about to join forces with either of them.

He supposed his only option now would be to approve the accelerated development of his company's long-delayed BPX computer. Despite the assurances of his technology adviser, the BPX wasn't nearly as compelling as Via's At Hand PC, especially now that the Plus was rapidly gaining market share. Damnable Locke. William had underestimated him. How could he have missed the double cross? Had there been any hint of it?

He recalled their meeting of four months ago, when Locke had brought him the detailed strategy report. He thought about how perturbed Matthew had become when the conversation had turned to Peter Jones. For Christ's sake, William had been so worried about Jones and his next move, he'd never once considered the sort of reversal Matthew had just pulled. The audacity of it. The unabashed ego. Did Locke suddenly fancy himself of Jones's caliber? Of his, William Harrell's, caliber? And who was he kidding? Hadn't his own bruised ego, for fucking up by not buying PCSoft when he'd the chance, fueled his revenge? Motivated him to concoct the deal in the first place?

He swore loudly in disgust and stamped his shoe onto the open At Hand PC Plus on the floor, cracking the screen and keyboard. It was a childish act, but it felt good all the same. His chauffeur cautiously asked if he would perhaps like to go to the doctor or back home. William apologized for the outburst and asked the chauffeur to circle the park a while longer. He wasn't ready to go to the office just yet.

Feeling a little less bombastic, he looked at the smashed At Hand on the floor and sighed. He picked it up and turned it over. A couple of keys fell out like broken teeth. The trackpad dangled and swayed by its slender ribbon cable, a hypnotist's watch. He angrily flicked it with his finger but it didn't break off. He flicked it again,

harder, but it still held fast. He laughed in spite of himself, and dropped the whole mess onto the seat beside him, looking once more at the trackpad.

He stared out the window and worked through the possibilities. A minute later he turned back to the smashed At Hand PC Plus. He picked it up in one hand and wrapped his other hand around the hanging trackpad. He gave a hard yank, and the flat device ripped free. He tossed the computer aside and turned the trackpad over in his palm.

And then it occurred to him—a possibility so obvious he'd nearly missed it.

Dialing his secretary on his mobile phone, he had a moment to remember a question he had once posed to himself: Without Jones, could Via manage to hold on to its prized disposition? The answer to that question was still beyond him, but maybe not for long.

When his secretary answered he explained that his computer was on the blink, and asked her to look up a phone number for him. He wrote down the number, thanked her, said he would be in a little later than usual, then hung up. He assured his driver that he was feeling better now, and asked him to keep driving around the park.

He observed the trackpad in his palm once more before closing his hand around it. He gave it a little shake for good luck, then dialed up his oldest friend in the business.

Peter stared absently at the clock on the yellow cinder-block wall. The red second hand crept slowly around the face, and it was the only thing he could concentrate on. The smell of the place made him feel ill, and he wasn't interested in any of the worn-out magazines piled on the end table beside his hard orange plastic chair.

He shifted his weight, tried to find a more comfortable position. It was impossible. He'd been sitting here for hours, dozing on

and off, staring at the clock. The red hand continued its agonizing clockwise passage, and he prayed for it to go even slower. Time itself had never seemed so precious. Each second offered more hope, a greater chance of survival for his unborn baby.

His baby.

At first he had refused to believe the doctor, insisting there'd been a mistake, a mix-up, that he and Ivy Green were merely acquaintances, nothing more. They double-checked Ivy's admission form and explained what she had put down. That he was the only man she'd been with in more than a year, and afterward there hadn't been any others. The doctor offered to conduct a simple blood test that would settle the matter, but Peter declined.

It was his baby, and he prayed she wouldn't deliver it. Not just yet. It needed more time. Weeks, if possible. The physician told him the survival rate for a twenty-eight-week infant was roughly ninety-five percent. He assured Peter that even if she were to deliver prematurely, the baby would most likely come out fine. Still, the longer she could hold off, the better.

Sitting there watching the clock, he thought back to their night together. She'd been so desperate and edgy. He remembered the white powdery circles around her nostrils. When he inquired about her state of mind and general health, the doctor said she was weak and had admitted to using drugs during the pregnancy. They'd administered medication that was supposed to postpone labor, to try to keep the baby in the womb for as long as possible. With her weakened condition working against them, the chances of the drugs doing the job were slim. They could only wait and see.

And so he sat waiting in the uncomfortable sitting area away from the general maternity ward, where anxious relatives talked nervously among themselves as they sweated through the hours. Peter was the only person seated here, in the neonatal care ward. He stared at the clock once more, wondered what he would do

if the baby was born today. Or next week. Or whenever, for that matter.

Even if they were successful in postponing the birth, there was no running from the fact that he was about to become a father. What the hell would he do? And Ivy? Would she expect him to marry her? Naturally his thoughts drifted to Kate.

He thought about their talk a few months ago, the evening they'd dined with the Holmeses for the first time. Asking if she was ready to think about marriage. About adopting a baby of their own. Christ almighty.

At around noon, another doctor introduced himself and sat down to speak with Peter.

"How's she doing?" Peter asked, but by the doctor's expression he could tell something was wrong.

"Not like we hoped. The medications slowed her contractions, but she broke water and we're going to have to induce labor now. You need to sign some authorization forms."

He nodded, too fatigued to ask any questions. The doctor promised they'd do their very best and then hurried through the metal double doors at the end of the hall.

A nurse returned with a clipboard and a stack of paper. She flipped through the documents, pointed out where he was to sign. She offered to bring him a soda or coffee, but he declined.

With nothing left to do but wait, he returned to his hard seat, stared at the clock, and wondered about the unexpected new life that was about to enter his own.

Grace Holmes answered on the second ring and greeted William warmly. He asked if Byron was in, and a moment later Byron was on the line shouting a hearty greeting. They chatted briefly, and Byron commented on yesterday's big announcement. "Quite a shocker."

"Indeed," William agreed. "And how are things coming along up there?"

"Oh, not bad. You know, too cold to fish or swim, so we mostly sit around the house and play poker, eat our strained veggies."

William laughed politely, but it was evident he had something on his mind, and Byron called him on it.

"You're right. I'm actually checking up on your hobby, as you called it."

"Well now, that's more like it. Got your curiosity aroused, does it?"

"Yes. Very much so."

"It's good stuff, Billy. Though we've hit a bit of a snag."

"How so?"

"Peter had to go back to California. Had some business to deal with."

"His resignation?"

Byron scoffed. "That's not even out to the press yet. How the hell did you hear already?"

"Inside source."

"Well, it's true. He's dumping most of his stock, putting a big chunk into our project. I'm matching him dollar to dollar, of course."

"So you guys are serious?"

"Oh yes. More than ever, after yesterday. Peter was damn upset about the deal you guys announced. Nothing personal, you understand. It's Locke. A lot of sore feelings on that front."

William couldn't agree more; however, he kept his own disappointment in Locke to himself. Instead, he stuck to his real interest. "Listen, I'd like to ask a favor."

"Anything."

"Let me have a look."

Byron whistled into the phone. "I don't know, Billy. I mean, far as I'm concerned you're always welcome. But I can't say Peter will feel the same way."

"I can respect that. However, I can and do respect him, too. I assure you we wouldn't have done yesterday's deal if it weren't for Jones's past efforts and vision. It was all because of his genius. Tell him that."

Byron thought for a moment. "Let me talk to him, Billy. I can't promise anything."

"That's all I'm asking, my friend. When does he get back?"

"That I don't know. He's got some personal business to sort out. Could be days, could be weeks. Months, even. I'm waiting to hear from him myself so I better get off the line."

"Fair enough," William said. He thanked his friend and hung up the phone.

His chauffeur smiled at him in the rearview mirror and commented that he was looking better, more like his old self.

William smiled agreeably and told the driver he'd had enough of Central Park for one morning. "Time for me to get back to work."

## >CHAPTER 15

Matthew returned from the Manhattan alliance announcement in high spirits. He bounded in from the garage entrance with his garment bag and briefcase in tow. He dropped both just inside the door and warmly greeted his wife, who was sitting down to a lunch of fruit salad and cottage cheese.

That she didn't return the greeting with the same enthusiasm went by unnoticed. Their housekeeper, Dolores, said hello as she passed by with a load of laundry, and Matthew stopped her with an uncharacteristic hug and kissed her cheek.

Dolores pulled back in astonishment at her boss's behavior.

"Lucky you, Dolores," Greta said dryly. "He stopped treating me like that years ago."

Matthew let go of the housekeeper and gave Greta a look. "Oh yeah?" He came over to her and planted a kiss on her cheek. Dolores vanished out the same door Matthew had just come through as Greta groaned and waved him off.

He went into the kitchen and poured himself a glass of juice

and drank it down in one gulp. Peeling the wrapper from a blueberry muffin, he fished through the newspapers Greta had put down the moment she'd heard his car pulling into the garage.

She'd gone over what she wanted to say in her head all night. However, now that he was home, she didn't know how to begin.

He hummed a little tune to himself as he flipped through the *Times*, the *Chronicle*, and the *Wall Street Journal*.

She cleared her throat and said his name.

He didn't look up from the papers. "Hmm?"

"There's something we need to discuss."

"Sure," he said, tossing aside one section of the paper and picking up another. "Hey, do we have yesterday's *Examiner* somewhere?"

She was momentarily thrown off by his question. "Over there, next to the sofa."

He got up and moved across the room, dropped down onto the sofa and started pushing apart the papers on the floor. "What were you saying, Greta? Ah, here it is. Wow, that's quite a shot they put in."

He turned the front page of the business section around for her to see the large color photo of him standing at the podium at Lincoln Center with the huge Via and ICP logos looming over his head. "Pretty big, huh?"

"Enormous," Greta said.

Seeing him like this, behaving as usual, half aware of her presence no matter what the situation, had an interesting effect on her. Any feelings of guilt that had seeped in turned once more to anger, frustration. In some ways it was fascinating, to see such a successful man act so giddy over his own photograph in the paper. And it was sad too, the way he beamed at the picture as though it were a wedding engagement announcement rather than his own earnest face. And that, she reminded herself, was the

crux of it—his marriage to his work, versus the life they lived under the same roof.

She tried to get his attention again, and he once more acknowledged her with a sound but didn't bother to look up from the papers. She uttered a disbelieving laugh and stood up, picked up her plate and glass, and on her way into the kitchen casually said, "I'd like a divorce."

Now he was listening. Before she even reached the sink he was calling her back. She set the things on the countertop and strolled to the recreation room. He was standing with his hands in his pockets, the newspapers fallen all around him. He looked hurt, but she knew him so well. He wasn't hurt by what she'd said. No, he was hurt that she could upset his sunny, self-satisfied mood.

"What do you mean a divorce?"

"Shall I get you a dictionary?"

"Don't, Greta. Don't drop a line like that, then fuck with me."

She looked at him with genuine surprise. "Fuck with you? Darling, if that were the case I don't think I'd be asking you for this. One day in New York and you come back speaking the language. Charming."

"You're jealous, is that it? About all this." He picked up one of the newspapers with his picture and shook it at her. "You're actually jealous."

"My, the papers are right. You are a smart one. Yes, Matthew. How nice of you to finally notice. Yes, I'm jealous. I have been for years. But not because I have a choice. Because it's true. You know it's true. You care more about your work than me, or anything else in the world. And I'm sick of it."

"You're sick of it? You're sick of Tiffany and Chanel and Mercedes?"

"For God's sake, you sound like you're talking about children. But Lord knows you wouldn't even give me those. I'm sick of all of it. What good is any of it without what matters most?"

"Let me guess—true love."

"Always the cynic." Her voice was on the rise.

"Greta, for crying out loud, we go through this what, at least once a year?"

"You're wrong. I've never asked you for a divorce."

"Yeah, well you'll never get one, so you can stop asking."

"Won't I?"

He dismissed her with an annoyed wave.

She charged closer and poked him with her left index finger. "Don't you wave me off anymore. I said I want a divorce, and I mean it."

He gave her a warning look. Though he had never struck her, he looked awfully capable of it now. "Don't push it, Gret. I've given you every fucking thing you've ever asked for."

"And you're going to be giving a lot more before I'm through with you."

"Don't count on it."

"If you don't believe me just call your lawyer and ask him."

He suddenly spun on her, his fists clenching at his sides. "You called Mitchell? You called my goddamn lawyer and said we wanted a divorce?"

She stood up to him. "Go ahead, Matthew. Lay one on me. I'll get you for that, too."

He was unable to speak, struggling to keep himself from grabbing her and shaking her. He looked up at the ceiling and forced himself to count to ten.

She held her breath, and when he looked at her again the violent flash in his eyes was gone. In its place, his analytical look. He scrutinized her from head to toe, shrugged his shoulders, carefully stepped around her, and began pacing the room.

"You're serious about this, then?"

"Dead serious."

"Please, Greta, don't tease. That would be too perfect."

"Fuck you, Matthew."

He clucked his tongue. "Now who's the vulgar one."

"I know what you're thinking."

"Do you?"

"Oh yes. You don't live with someone like you this long and not know what's going on in that calculating head."

"And?"

"Look at you. I see the way you're looking at everything, rolling through the numbers. The formula is easy. Just divide by two. That's right, darling. Half. Half of everything. California law."

He quit pacing and glared at her from across the room. "This is bullshit, Greta. You're pissed off. Look, I'm not happy either. But a divorce isn't the answer. We both just need to take a break and think things through."

"Too late. I've thought about it plenty. There's no thinking about it. No fixing things. We're through already. I've known it for years, and so have you."

His patience was beginning to falter. He tried another approach. "Don't challenge me on this, Greta."

"I've made up my mind."

"You're crazy."

At this she cackled. "Now we're getting somewhere. Why, yes, darling. That's exactly what I am. Crazy. Driven mad by Mr. Chips. And that's just what I'll tell the court if I decide I'd like more than half. And don't think they won't take my side. In fact, I think I may even be feeling a wee bit suicidal again, Matthew. All the stress I've been under ever since this happened." She waggled her four-fingered left hand in his face.

He shoved it aside with a grimace. "I'll fight you on this."

"Go ahead and try. You'll only make matters worse for yourself." She kicked at the pile of newspapers on the floor. "It doesn't matter what they might say about me in the papers. But you? Oh,

the stories I could tell, Matthew. That's right. So you better think twice before you make your next move, sweetheart."

What she said was true, and he knew it. The press could turn this sort of thing into a circus. The publicity would be horrible for Via, and after yesterday's change of heart he couldn't afford the risk. Her wish for a divorce was completely unexpected, and he needed time to consider his options, figure out how to minimize his vulnerability. If he could get her to hold off, even if only for a little while, he could investigate ways to make certain assets disappear, hide them in offshore accounts or wherever it was people hid money they didn't want anyone to find.

He knew it was possible, but he knew nothing of the details. Let her think of the house as hers, the cars, the things that didn't really matter to him. All of it could be replaced. His eventual fortune in Via stock options couldn't, however. His vesting schedule, which stated when and how many of his options he could sell at specific intervals, was spread out over the next eight years. If they divorced she would continue to get half of that until the very last option was sold. No, there had to be another way.

"All right, Greta. I'm not going to fight with you anymore. But you have to give me a little time to come to grips with this. A trial period, and then we'll work out a settlement that we can both agree on. You're right about me and my work. I doubt you care, but yesterday I pulled the plug on the deal with William. There won't be a merger."

With this concession, her temper fizzled away almost immediately. No matter how much she despised him now, she still loved Matthew. Seeing him defeated like this gave her none of the satisfaction she had anticipated and hoped for.

"You're right, Matthew. It is of no interest to me. That's what's been wrong all along. You've never been able to separate the two. And so we must."

He raised his palms in a helpless gesture. "I'm sorry, Gret. I

really mean it. If there were some way to change it I would. I just don't want us to do anything rash. We're adults, and we'll deal with this as such. In the meantime, I'll leave you alone. And as always, you may have whatever you like. If you want to travel while we sort this out, I'll understand. Just please give me some breathing room to get through this rough spot with Via; then we'll take care of everything nice and neat."

Greta nodded her silent agreement and started out of the room.

"And Gret?"

She turned around to look at him, her heart playing some unjust trick on her, making her feel pity for the way he stood there, a little slouched, looking genuinely dismayed by the whole ordeal.

"No matter how much I may have let you down, I've loved you the best I can."

She said nothing as he picked up his briefcase and left the same way he'd come in. The door closed, and he was on his way back to work again. It was as though nothing and everything had changed at the same time. At least the worst was finally over.

She turned and ran upstairs, desperate to rendezvous with her virtual lover.

"Mr. Jones," the doctor said, lightly shaking Peter awake. He'd dozed off in the waiting room, and it took him a moment to remember where he was.

"It's a girl, Mr. Jones," the doctor reported as he led Peter down the corridor. "And you can see Ms. Green now."

Peter stopped in his tracks, his face flushing. He'd fallen asleep, and awakened a father. It was a heavy change to deal with and he needed to pull himself together. "Is the baby all right? Ivy? Are they both okay?"

The doctor motioned for Peter to step out of the busy corridor traffic. "Not entirely," he said. "There were complications. Both are quite fragile at this stage. The baby weighs three and a quarter pounds. She's in neonatal care right now, hooked up to support equipment."

"But she's alive," Peter said, for his own peace of mind.

"Yes," the doctor said. "And the outlook is fair, but we don't know yet if there may be latent complications. Possible damage that we can't see yet, from the drugs."

Peter felt an abrupt wave of nausea in his stomach. Images of strangely twisted limbs and gnarled faces flashed in his mind. His expression was suddenly grave, and he forced himself to ask the horrible question that suddenly entered his mind.

"Is she retarded?"

"There's no disfiguration, Mr. Jones. But it's just too early to judge her overall condition. She appears to be a normal, if premature, baby."

Peter allowed himself a tight, hopeful smile.

They ambled down the hall and stopped before a patient room, the door closed. "Ivy's been through a strenuous ordeal, Mr. Jones. She needs lots of rest. However, she insisted she see you now. She's very weak, so I'm afraid we can only give you a few minutes together."

Peter nodded. "And then can I see . . . ?" He paused, wondering what Ivy had named the baby.

"Then you can see the baby. And that'll have to be brief, too."

Peter agreed and reached for the door latch.

"Wait," the doctor said, stopping Peter's arm. "I want you to understand before you see her that her condition is unstable, physically and mentally. Be careful not to upset her. Keep things light. She needs encouragement. From what we can tell she wasn't what we would call a serious addict, but there is evidence of substance abuse." The doctor paused, uncomfortable with the next part of what he had to say. "I don't know your situation, or what your plans are, but try to reinforce her with positive thoughts. It'll help her recovery."

Peter took a deep breath, turned the latch, and went inside. The shades were partially drawn and electronic sounds emanated from monitoring equipment stationed beside her bed. He went to her.

A dim lamp spread yellow light over the bed, and through the blanket covering he could see she was very thin. Her head was

turned toward the window, and her closed eyelids were bluish in color. The skin of her face was drawn tight and blemished. She was very pale, and so different from the sunny Ivy he remembered, a woman so lively, so animated. He felt horribly responsible for the way she now looked. He made a private vow then and there to set things right, to take care of her in whatever way she wanted.

And Kate? No, he couldn't let himself think about Kate or what would happen between them. Right now he had to think of his unexpected baby, and of Ivy. He had to assure her that he would take responsibility for his actions. He whispered her name and she stirred, eyelids fluttering open.

Her gaze widened when she realized who it was, and a thin smile touched her lips. A moment later she began blinking rapidly, overwhelmed with emotion, tears suddenly forming in her eyes. Her voice was a sore whisper. "I told myself I wouldn't get like this when I saw you."

"Hey," he said, touching her cheek.

She pulled her hand from beneath the blankets and wrapped her thin fingers around his. His body tensed at her chilly touch, stirring pity and fear in his heart. He was afraid for her life. She looked so weak and vulnerable, like she'd been through hell. Just what has she done to herself? he wondered. And the baby? He wanted to hold her, tell her it was all right now, that all was forgiven, yet at the same time he thought he was the one who should be begging for forgiveness, for unwittingly letting her get like this. It was all so twisted.

She brushed his hand away. "This is so bizarre, you know? I mean, wow. The baby. And here you are. I don't know what to think or say now."

He told her to stay quiet, to rest. "It's going to be fine."

"Fine. Yeah." She licked her dry lips. "It's funny, but I don't know what's more upsetting. Me or you."

"Don't think about any of that right now."

She ignored him, as though he weren't in the room and she were talking to herself. She didn't look at him. "God, I wanted him. And I got him. And then wham, he tosses me away."

Her speech was slurred, and glancing at her intravenous tube he wondered what kind of mix they were feeding her. Tranquilizers and painkillers, he suspected.

"I couldn't deal, I guess, so I threw myself away," she went on. "And maybe wanted to throw the baby away, too. A little of this, a little of that, sort of a slow poisoning." She looked at him. "I'm sick, Peter. I know it. I have to get all this poison out of me."

"Ivy, don't talk this way. I'm sorry. You're sorry. We're both sorry for the mistake we made. But we'll deal with it. I'll take care of you. It's my responsibility, too."

She winced. "Now you've come to my rescue." It was hard to follow her abruptly shifting mood. She was struggling with her emotions, with whatever chemical imbalances past and present were making it so hard for her to understand what was happening. "I'm sorry. I don't want to be like this. I just feel like I hate you right now, and love you too. It's crazy. I keep thinking about that ride up here."

She was making little sense, apparently caught in some free-association loop, uttering whatever entered her mind. He smoothed her hair around the pillow. It had lost its original white-blond luster, and felt brassy and rough to his touch. He spoke softly, soothingly.

"What ride, Ivy?"

"My big trip to San Francisco. To see Kate McGreggor. She was the one I wanted to meet, you know. More than you, that's for sure. I wanted to be like her. Sing, make music. I'd had voice lessons when I was young, I guess that's how I somehow ended up so into speech. Her guards or whatever wouldn't let me meet her at this concert she gave in Golden Gate Park. I tried to find out all about her, where she lived and all. I wasn't stalking her or anything, just

curious, really interested. Like a role model. That's when I read about you. All you'd done. Then, I don't know, I guess I changed my mind. I wanted to meet you instead. I hated her then. I didn't want to be a musician anymore. I wanted to be a techno-artist or whatever. I don't know, blame it on my parents. They're here, somewhere. Probably out back getting stoned."

This made her laugh, so hard that she started coughing. She gripped the handrails and sat up until she stopped.

He gently rubbed her back and encouraged her to calm down. "You have to rest now, and I'm going to see the baby." He remembered wondering about her name. "What did you name her?"

"No name," Ivy said, dropping back on the pillow. "I can't. I don't know. You do it, Peter. I got her this far, now it's your turn."

He nodded his assurance and decided that now wasn't the best time to talk about it. Or anything else, until she had a chance to rest and let the strong narcotics clear out of her system. He told her he would come in to see her again in a while, after she rested.

"Wait. We're not done." She sat up a little. "We're gonna make a deal, Peter, then I want you to go. Don't come back. I don't want to see you for a while." She was talking crazy again and he assured her that he would do whatever she asked.

"The baby's yours to take care of, Peter. I can't do it. Not right now. I can't name her, they won't let me feed her. I can't do anything. Or my work. I told you I did it all for you, and that was the truth. You have to take that, too. Do what you once said you might, help me make it really happen."

He didn't know what she was talking about. "What work, Ivy?"

"That stuff I started at your place." She waved a hand and scratched her fingers through her hair, suddenly more lucid. "The speech and language software." She gestured to the corner of the room. "It's in that cabinet, in my pack. Get it."

He did as she said, retrieving the same well-worn backpack

she'd brought with her when she'd stayed with him. He held it out to her and she pushed it away.

"You open it."

He expected to find her At Hand PC, but instead he found only notebooks, pens, and books.

"The disks," she said.

He found them at the very bottom of the bag, six Zip disks bound together with a rubber band.

"What is it?" he said.

"Read the label."

"ISLE."

"That's what it is."

He wanted to ask more, but then decided it wasn't the right time. They could deal with her work and everything else in a few days, when she was feeling better. "Listen, how about we talk about this later."

She gave him an impatient look. "No. You're not listening. I meant what I said. I don't want to see you after today, not for a while. Take those. Take the baby. Take care of both."

He turned over the pile of disks in his hand. "What do I do with it?"

She explained. "After I decided I wanted to meet you, I got this idea. It happened because of that old song, 'Teach the Children.' You know the one. I thought, yeah, teach them well, and do it with computers. In their own language, their own words. So I switched studies, started researching it. And somehow my hormones or whatever else was going on in me complicated everything. Beyond just the program. To be with you. So I waited until it was the right time of the month to make you that dinner I made, so we'd, you know, do it."

Peter stared at her in disbelief. "You did this on purpose? The baby?"

She closed her eyes tightly and nodded. "I thought it would

turn out different. I thought you really liked me. But we're talking about the work now, not her."

"What the hell do these have to do with any of it?"

She looked at the disks. "Take them home and see. It stands for 'Intelligent Speech and Language Environment.' But it's not just for kids anymore, or just learning. It's more than that. Whatever you want it to be. You'll see. Go ahead. Take them, the notes and code charts, it's all in there. Figure out what it's worth to you. Hell knows I'm gonna have a shitload of bills when I'm through this rinse cycle."

She'd laid so much on him he was at a loss for words. Thankfully he wouldn't have to say more, as the door opened and in came the doctor and a nurse. The doctor put on an easygoing smile and asked Peter to let her rest now.

"We'll figure this all out, Ivy. I promise," Peter said, and went to put the knapsack at the foot of the bed.

"No, Peter. Take it, please. Take it and go."

The doctor gave him a meaningful nod, encouraging him to do as she asked.

He slung the sack over his shoulder and laid a hand over Ivy's. "All right. Get better."

"I'll try," she said, with none of her early bitterness. Tears were building in her eyes again and she looked away. "Make me proud."

The nurse gently urged him away as the doctor went about checking the girl's vital signs. Peter backed up a few steps and looked at her again, but she wouldn't look his way. He turned and left, the door quietly swinging closed behind him.

He stood in the hallway unsure of which way to turn. The events of the last forty-eight hours had taken their toll. He'd resigned from his company, sold a great portion of his stock, and become a father. The baby. He had to see her.

A floor nurse directed him to the neonatal care unit. He

tramped down the corridor, rounded the corner, and pushed through a set of double doors. He announced himself to the head nurse, who promptly led him into a clean room, where he was instructed to put on a sterile gown and face mask.

Dressed in the sanitary outfit, he followed the nurse into a brightly lit room containing a row of bubblelike incubators. It was a strange and surreal environment, like a set in a science fiction movie.

"Here she is," the nurse said, leading him to the last incubator.

There, encased in the hygienic shell, lay his baby girl.

She was impossibly tiny, and he was taken aback by the size and shape of her head. It looked so huge and unnatural that he audibly gasped.

The nurse interpreted his reaction and calmly explained it was normal. "Don't worry. The head develops a little faster at this stage. All the rest of her will catch up in the next couple of weeks. It's perfectly ordinary."

He breathed a sigh of relief and took a minute to ponder the assortment of tubes and wires and probes taped to her impossibly little body. He turned to the nurse. "How is she?"

"We're keeping a close eye on her. It was a difficult birth, but she looks like a real fighter."

Peter smiled and shook his head as the first sensation of fatherly pride gushed through his heart.

The nurse explained that despite their sterile protection they had to be careful about exposure. Peter understood that he would have to leave already. He wanted to take her in his arms and kiss her good-bye, but he knew that wasn't possible yet. Instead, he pressed his gloved fingertips to his masked lips, then touched the top of the incubator in front of the baby's sleeping face.

Back in the anteroom he discarded the green scrub outfit, collected the knapsack he'd left on a chair, and thanked the nurse. He took one last look at his baby through the observation window, then

turned and pressed through the double doors, back into the busy corridor.

And into Kate's arms.

She had been waiting just outside the unit, and he nearly fell over when he saw her. She caught him and stiffly helped him regain his footing, guiding him to one of the hard plastic chairs.

"Jesus, Kate. How did you find me?"

"Byron wouldn't tell me. So I called Ben, at your office. He told me he'd gotten the call they were trying to find you."

Peter looked at the double doors. "She's so tiny."

"I heard," Kate said with anguished eyes. "Why didn't you tell me, Peter?"

He was completely exhausted and unprepared for this conversation. He made a helpless gesture. "Kate, I swear I never thought this would happen, or—" He didn't complete the thought.

"Or what? You would have told me? Wasn't that our agreement no matter what, Peter? That if you or I ever met someone, even casually, we'd tell the other? Wasn't that it? No rules, except honesty?"

"But this was different."

"Different." She shook her head sadly. "And how many others were there, Peter? Different ones, I mean."

"None, Kate. Just this once. I swear."

She looked unconvinced.

"Kate, I'm telling the truth. It was the night before Via dumped me. She was just a guest, like any of the other students. I didn't plan for it to happen."

"And she did?"

"Actually, yes. She did. We had dinner. I guess I had too much to drink. I don't know, she was desperate. I didn't want to do it. I wasn't myself, and it just happened. But it wasn't my fault. It was the wine—"

She slapped him across the face, and he wobbled in his seat, stunned. He reached up and touched his cheek and looked at her. Her lips were tight and trembling and he knew he had hurt her far more than she had hurt him with her strike. "How dare you offer an excuse so foolish."

His voice was a broken whisper. "God, Kate, if I could undo the whole thing I would. It meant nothing to me. It was a terrible mistake, and now I have to face up to it. But you have to believe me. Kate, I need you."

She was about to respond just as the doctor pushed through the doors. He saw at once that the couple were in the middle of a sensitive discussion. He acknowledged Kate and asked to speak privately with Peter for a moment.

Peter turned to Kate. "Wait. I'll be right back." He sought her hand for assurance, but she pulled away and crossed her arms, unable to look at him.

He followed the doctor around the corner and they seated themselves in a pair of waiting chairs. It occurred to Peter that he was still carrying Ivy's backpack over his shoulder. He was operating on autopilot now.

"We need a name, Mr. Jones. Have you chosen one?"

A name, Peter thought. Such a simple question, yet his mind was blank. Ivy had asked him to name her, and he hadn't really let himself acknowledge the importance of this small but significant responsibility. The reality finally set it, and he felt the last ounce of energy drain out of him. He gave a helpless shrug, and the knapsack slipped off his shoulder and fell to the floor, spilling the contents all over the place.

The doctor repeated his question.

"Wait," Peter said, and hopped up, leaving the spilled knapsack on the floor. He trotted around the corner to seek Kate's support.

But she was gone.

He let out a frustrated sound and trudged back to the doctor, who was collecting the knapsack's spilled contents.

Peter knelt down to take over, raking the pens and notebooks and disks into a pile.

And there he saw it, and for a moment he couldn't move. He reached out for the adjacent chair to steady himself, and the doctor asked if he was all right.

Ignoring him, Peter leaned over and picked up the bundle of Zip disks.

In Ivy's own hand was the name he was searching for. He read the word written on the label of the topmost disk.

"Isle," he whispered.

"I'm sorry?" the doctor said, not sure he'd heard correctly.

"I said Isle," Peter declared. "Her name is Isle."

# PART IV

Strolling into the bank, Greta sneered when she saw the long line of waiting customers. She settled her sunglasses in her hair and sighed loudly as she joined everyone else in line, fishing through her purse for a stray form left over from a previous visit.

Finding none, she decided it didn't matter. She had no idea what kind of form she would have to fill out for the kind of transaction she was here to complete. She looked impatiently at her watch, eager to get the whole business over with.

Glancing around, she spotted the branch manager on his way through the lobby, hands full with paperwork. She managed to catch his eye, and the smartly dressed middle-aged man approached with a smile.

"Julian, how are you?" She touched him lightly on the arm.

"Well, hello, Mrs. Locke. How are you?"

She leaned close to his ear. "I was fine until I walked into this. It's becoming so difficult to bank these days." Taking advantage of her impairment, she fluttered her left hand in the air. "Oh well."

The manager's eyes widened for the briefest instant, startled

by her hand. He'd never noticed it before. Until Gregor, she never would have left the house without her gloves. But all that had changed. And to her surprise, she discovered she could sometimes work her impairment to her advantage. Like now. The manager silently gestured for her to follow him.

She knew what was going through his head. That she was Mrs. Matthew Locke, whose accounts and balances were significant, and so she deserved special treatment. He led her to one of the desks near the front of the bank and asked her to make herself comfortable, then excused himself for a moment. She smiled gratefully and busied herself by cleaning out her purse, picking through discarded chewing gum wrappers and old receipts.

A few minutes later the manager returned and seated himself behind the desk. He gathered up the small pile of litter she'd collected and tossed it into the wastebasket. Clasping his hands atop the desk blotter, he asked how he could help her.

She laid her checkbook on the desk and opened it. "I'd like to transfer some funds into a friend's account."

His expression flattened a little, as though he'd been expecting a large deposit instead of a withdrawal. "Of course. How much would you like to transfer."

"Fifty thousand."

"Very well." He twisted sideways to access his computer terminal. "And from which account?"

She slid the checkbook across the desk. "This one." She withdrew a Post-it note from her purse and placed it beside the checkbook. "Into this one."

He tapped the keyboard and a moment later the account information appeared. "Oh," he said with a frown. "Mrs. Locke, this is a joint account."

"Right. And I'm the other half of the bargain."

"Correct," he said politely. "However, it appears Mr. Locke,

who is actually the account's primary holder, recently put a limit on the amount you may withdraw."

"That son of a bitch," she said, loudly enough to draw a few stares.

The manager lowered his voice. "I'm afraid you can withdraw only up to five thousand dollars, Mrs. Locke."

She clucked her tongue in frustration. Then she got a bright idea: "Wait. How about I write ten checks?"

He smiled apologetically. "I'm afraid the amount is absolute, versus per transaction. The maximum is set to a per-month schedule."

"Meaning?"

"Meaning that you may withdraw up to five thousand dollars each month, but no more." He slid the checkbook back to her side of the desk. "I'm sorry, Mrs. Locke. Would you like to transfer that amount, then?"

She tapped her fingernail against her lips. "There's no other way?"

He lifted a finger. "There is." He opened one of the drawers and tore a small slip from a pad and set it down on top of her checkbook. "With this you can withdraw the entire amount."

"Wonderful," she said brightly, without bothering to interpret the title. She started filling in the amount line.

"Yes, but Mrs. Locke, you see here"—he leaned over the desk and traced the bottom line with his pen—"two signatures are required. Yours, and Mr. Locke's, authorizing the amount."

"Oh." She blew out a defeated sigh. "And that's the only way?"

"I'm afraid so. In fact, Mrs. Locke, the bank normally requires that both parties are present for this sort of thing." His tone betrayed a subtle air of unpleasant familiarity with accounts and arrangements such as these. He lowered his voice. "But I'm willing to pardon that policy for you, Mrs. Locke. Just have him sign this,

and if you can get back here before three we put the transaction through today."

She rose and dropped the form into her purse, thanked the manager, and promised to return before three. To do so, she'd have to drive all the way down to Via to get Matthew to sign the form. But not before she gave him an earful, of course. How dare he put a limit on her spending.

Climbing into her burgundy Mercedes SLK230, she checked the clock. Providing she caught Matthew during lunch, she'd have just enough time to make it back to the bank. Tearing out of the parking lot for the highway, she pictured the reaction her surprise visit would elicit.

She was raring for a good scene.

"That's a good girl," Peter said, cradling the tiny Isle in his arms. He checked her bottle. "Almost done."

Today marked her third month in the world. She had been home with Peter for half that time, deemed healthy enough to leave the hospital. She weighed a scant six and a quarter pounds. Her eyes were curious and alert, the same sapphire color as her mother's. The satiny whorls of hair growing in were so bright blond they were almost white, just like both her parents'.

Sitting with his baby daughter in his lap, Peter considered everything that had happened since her birth. He reflected on how after the breakup with Via he'd felt like an infant, weak, helpless, so vulnerable to the vast forces of the big world around him. When he'd needed taking care of, Kate had been there for him. Now she was gone, and here he was taking care of Isle, and she, to his surprise and thankfulness, was taking care of him too, like an angel descended, put on this earth to draw him out of his previously selfish ways to focus on the needs of another, one small life totally dependent on him.

Grace padded into the living room to check on father and daughter. She took one of Isle's wee hands into her own. "Go ahead, Peter, I'll finish up with her. Your demanding partner is growling for you."

"Okay, shrimp, over you go." He gingerly passed the bundled infant to Grace and planted a light kiss on both their foreheads. "You're both angels."

From the back of the house they heard Byron shouting for him. Peter shared a laugh with Grace, then headed back to work.

The Holmeses had been a godsend since Isle's birth. They came out to California without hesitation, and he set them up comfortably in one of the upstairs guest rooms. Grace was all too happy to help with Isle, while Byron and Peter had resumed their project. Peter hadn't seen or heard from Ivy, and she refused his calls at the detoxification clinic where she was recovering from substance abuse.

Byron and Peter and their small team worked around the clock on the design they'd settled on. Isle's arrival had brought with it a second surprise, in the form of Ivy's ingenious software. Indeed, her ISLE program had provided the missing link, giving Peter and Byron the distinct difference they'd been searching for.

Peter wound his way to the back of the house and Byron eagerly waved him over. He held a large device, the latest version of their as-yet-unnamed invention. It was rough and unfinished, an unattractive box and touch-sensitive liquid-crystal screen, with wires and components dangling from every corner.

"Get a look at this." Byron turned the device to show the top edge. "John just got the microphone squeezed in. Go on, tell it you want to make a date."

Peter cleared his throat. "Computer," he said, saying the keyword the ISLE speech recognizer listened for to carry out spoken commands. "Lunch with Byron on Friday."

As Peter spoke, a small ear icon flashed at the top of the display to indicate the device was listening.

The screen came to life, revealing a month-view calendar that quickly zoomed in on the upcoming Friday. In the 12:00 slot a line of text appeared: "Byron Holmes/Lunch."

The device's tiny speaker sounded: *"Lunch with Byron Holmes, confirmed. Is there an agenda?"*

Peter gave Byron a quizzical look.

"A little bonus Rick threw in this morning. We figured most people might want to add a description or reminder to dates or meetings."

Peter gave an appreciative nod, then answered the device. "Yes. Discuss computer enhancements and—"

The device interrupted. *"Computer,"* it said, *"is unrecognized."*

Peter was puzzled. "What happened?"

Byron scratched his head and chuckled. "Well what do you know. We never considered that."

Peter didn't follow, and said so.

"Just that, what happened. If we call the computer 'computer,' then we can't use that word when it's listening to whatever you tell it."

"Ah," Peter said. "Right." He thought about the problem for a moment, then sat down to the keyboard and modified the device's preference settings.

The device was connected to a nearby At Hand PC Plus computer, which handled the processing. Eventually the code would be transferred onto the solid-state chips used in the final product. However, at this stage all of the coding was done on the At Hand.

Peter finished typing and sent the code to the device in Byron's hand.

"What'd you do?" Byron said.

"Changed its name. Since the word 'computer' won't com-

pute, I've given it a unique name that is unlikely to come up in an everyday context."

"Gotcha," the older man said. "Ready?"

Peter nodded.

Byron touched a stylus to the screen and selected a command. A moment later the device said, *"Please name me."*

"Pip," Peter said, loud and clear.

A moment later, it said, *"Hello, this is Pip, at your service."*

Byron looked at Peter. "Pip?"

"From Dickens's *Great Expectations*. One of my all-time favorites."

"Then Pip it is." Byron laughed. "Let's give it a try."

They repeated the scheduling test and "Pip" pulled it off without a hitch.

"Hey, you guys," Peter called over the room's partition, "great job."

John Dulin and Rick Caruso stood up from their workstations to look over the temporary office partitions dividing the room. Both young men wore tired but appreciative expressions. They were Peter's two favorite engineers. Both resigned from Via the moment Peter invited them to join him and Byron.

Byron asked the engineers if everything was set for the demonstration, and they assured him they were ready. The older man rubbed his hands together. "We're gonna knock his socks off."

"We'll see," Peter said, unable to mask the skepticism in his voice. It wasn't the device he was concerned about; ICP was the last company he had ever imagined he'd meet with to discuss a potential business relationship. Byron argued that Via had become more profitable since aligning itself with ICP, and Peter grudgingly agreed. But the real source for his change of heart was rooted in the prospect, however remote, of outdealing the man he'd come to think of as his nemesis, Matthew Locke.

"Can you do anything about that sour face?" Byron said

jovially. "Don't forget this man is first and foremost a friend. And a smart guy. You'll like him, I promise."

"We'll see," Peter repeated. "And since he's due here in ten minutes, I'm going to check on Isle real quick."

He headed back to the front of the house to find Grace sitting on the sofa reading a book. Isle lay sound asleep at her side.

"Any calls?" Peter whispered.

Grace looked at him with a tight smile and shook her head, knowing whom he was hoping to hear from. They were all waiting to hear from Kate. But she, like Ivy, had not taken or returned Peter's calls since that day at the hospital. He knelt before Isle to watch her sleep, relishing the beauty of her serene face.

Grace set down her book. "Petey, you know you can call her."

He shrugged. "I've tried. She won't call me back. One of her assistants asked me to please stop calling. I sent her flowers with a letter asking her to just come up for a visit. I tried to explain everything, but I don't think she wants to hear it. I think I've lost her for good, Grace."

She placed a warm palm on his shoulder. "I wouldn't be so sure," she whispered. "You know, after Byron had his heart attack, I almost left him."

Peter looked up, surprised. "How come?"

"His pride," she said with a purposeful nod of her head. "I don't have to tell you how stubborn he is. And afterward, he felt so incapacitated by the fact that he couldn't do anything for himself. He was coming up on his retirement when it happened, which was already enough for a man like him to face. Anyway, it was as though he had turned against me. He was bedridden, so he needed me, but he resented me just the same, because he was so absolutely dependent on me. I'd set up his room with all his favorite things, maps and model ships, books he loved. But all he could do was quietly hurt me."

Peter thought about this for a moment. "But it's not the same."

"Isn't it? Didn't what happened between you and Ivy happen because you knew in your heart that you were going to lose control of Via?"

It had never actually occurred to him quite like that, yet it only took an instant to realize it was true. He stared at her, startled by the acute appraisal.

"And maybe, Peter, you thought in the back of your mind that you would somehow lose Kate, too. Both of the things you loved."

Peter gently brushed his fingertips across Isle's soft hair. What Grace said made total sense, yet it wouldn't bring Kate back to him now.

"Listen, I know my husband better than anyone. And I know when I see someone who's like him." She lifted Peter's chin to make him look at her. "I made a decision many, many years ago to stand by him, till death do us part. We came close to breaking that promise, but then he told me one simple thing."

Peter made a face, like tasting something bitter. "I have a feeling I know what he said."

"Then why don't you say it yourself?"

He hesitated. "I'm scared."

"And so was he. But when he told me, when he came right out and said it, I understood. Yes, it's different. Infidelity is difficult to forgive. But if you tell her the truth, the way you just told me, she just might give you a second chance."

Peter looked at Isle. "I don't know, Grace. It's so mixed up. The baby and the project, our visitor today. I'm not sure now is the right time. Everything is so up in the air."

Grace gave him a skeptical look. "And if she were back in your life, wouldn't all those things seem a little more tolerable?"

They would. But if he'd learned anything these past few months, it was that he'd been an extremely selfish person who'd always gotten what he wanted. Sure, most of it came from hard

work, a keen vision, perseverance. But he'd be kidding himself if he didn't acknowledge the orphan in him that he'd never really grown out of, and maybe never would. The child dropped down in an unfair world, an unloving world, wanting only what most everyone else had, a chance at a life with loving parents, a real home. Since he could never have those things, he determined early on to always get the things that were in his power to get. But to think of Kate that way, as a thing he could just reach out and take, the way he'd gotten so much else, wasn't fair. She meant everything to him, and he couldn't honestly say he deserved her anymore. Yet even these reasons were minor when he considered what was really stopping him from calling Kate.

The possibility of rejection, that she wouldn't want him back.

As though reading his mind, Grace clasped Peter's hand in her own and gave a bracing squeeze. "Isn't she worth fighting for, Peter?"

He nodded. "You're right, Grace. I'll do it. I'll call her later today."

"Matthew, it's all so positive," Laurence Merrill said with smiling allegiance as she closed the copy of the *Wall Street Journal* on his worktable. "You've got the press in the palm of your hand."

Matthew appreciated the way that sounded. The *Journal* had run a profile on him, highlighting how his strategic alliance with ICP had dramatically improved Via's market position in so little time. He ignored the part where they pointed out it was actually Peter who'd invented the company's breakthrough product, the At Hand. What mattered most to him were sales, and they were way up. As for his other biggest concern, he and his coauthor were almost finished with the first draft of his autobiography.

The only disturbance in his life right now was the unpleasant business with Greta. Well, at least they'd managed to reach a sort of peaceful coexistence at home, going about their own business without upsetting each other. As far as he was concerned, he could live like that for a long time and be reasonably happy.

He smiled gratefully at Laurence, and not only for her compliment. There was more to his evident self-satisfaction than her

kind words and undying loyalty. She'd been his constant companion through some of his career's most challenging events, lining him up with just the right publications and speaking engagements, and landing him favorable coverage such as today's *Journal* profile. Indeed, for the first time in his marriage, Matthew was genuinely smitten by another woman. He didn't know if she felt the same attraction for him, and he intended to find out soon enough.

"How about lunch?" he said.

"Sure," Laurence said. She clasped her lovely hands together. "You decide."

"Sushi?"

She wrinkled her nose. "I'm not a big fan of raw fish." She gathered her notes together and filed them away in her leather portfolio.

"You just have to know what to pick," he said. "Come on, you'll love it."

Matthew informed his secretary he was going next door for lunch, and a few minutes later they entered the restaurant. A Japanese hostess greeted them with a small bow and led them into the dining area, occupied mostly with Via employees. He waved his greetings to several tables and quietly asked the hostess if she could please seat them in the back. She led them to the rear of the restaurant with its cozy private rooms, screened off with teakwood partitions.

"This is more like it," Matthew said, kicking off his shoes. Laurence slipped off her heels and placed them alongside Matthew's, outside the sliding rice paper door. They sat across from each other in the sunken pit. The hostess handed over menus, then excused herself. The door whispered closed, and they were alone.

Matthew reached over and closed her menu. "How about I order?"

She gave him a doubtful look. "I don't know. I'm not much for exotic surprises."

"Don't worry, I know what I'm doing," he said, and gave her hand a small squeeze.

She looked at him with an uneasy smile, not quite sure how to respond to his forward manner.

"Amazing!" William Harrell said excitedly as Pip retrieved a contact name he had asked it to find in its sample directory. He turned to Peter. "And what did you say ISLE stands for again?"

"Intelligent Speech and Language Environment."

"Right," William said. "Tell me more about the recognition interface."

"It was what really shifted our focus on the whole idea," Peter began.

Byron, John and Rick were seated around the table as well, quiet while Peter described the design.

"We'd already decided on a palm-size form factor, as well as integrating the intelligent agents at the OS level to achieve all the no-brainer synchronization magic we showed you earlier."

Harrell gave an appreciative nod. "An excellent implementation, and notably more useful than our own SoftLink utility."

Peter frowned at the mention of the product Via and ICP had developed together under Matthew Locke's tutelage. Byron urged him to go on.

"Anyway, we wanted more. And when we encountered the ISLE software, the pieces suddenly fell into place."

William nodded again. "I'll grant you that. But do people really want this sort of interface? In tests we conducted at ICP, we found that though users often ask for speech recognition, few actually use it after they get through the gee-whiz stage. Plus, it's very difficult to control, and accuracy tends to be a problem."

Peter agreed on all counts. "However, ours isn't like existing speech-recognition designs," Peter said. "We've figured something

out, then acted accordingly. It was pretty simple, really. See, when people think of speech recognition, they naturally think of dictation. Dictating letters, for instance, orating a book report, or just talking into the computer. But our research revealed that people don't speak the way they write. Which means they don't type the way they speak either. Think about it. You're writing a letter or a memo, and you type a line. You pause. Backspace over some of it, rewrite the sentence. Go back. Look up at what you've written, shift back to the beginning and switch this line for that. It's no wonder speech recognition has so far failed as a viable input means and user interface."

Harrell gave a thoughtful nod. "And you've somehow solved this problem?"

"No," Peter said simply. "We've decided to ignore it. Instead, we're going in a different direction."

"Yet speech and language are integral to your design?"

"Absolutely," Peter said with conviction. "But instead of me telling you all this, why don't we show you instead. Guys?"

The engineers brought out some additional hardware, then turned the table back over to Peter.

He picked up the latest version of their crude little device and turned it on, flashing that same self-confident smile Harrell remembered from the cover of *Newsweek* a few years ago, when Peter Jones was riding at the height of his success. In the back of his mind, William interpreted the expression as a positive sign that Jones was back in the saddle again.

Peter picked up the stylus and pointed it at William. "This is gonna totally wow you."

And for the next two hours, William Harrell was totally wowed.

>     >     >

Greta Locke pulled into Via's parking lot fifteen minutes after her husband had strolled through on his way to lunch next door with Laurence Merrill. Which, Matthew's secretary informed Greta, was where she would find him now.

She went inside the restaurant and scanned the tables in the front room. Conversations suddenly quieted when the diners noticed her. It gave her no small pleasure to know that they all knew who she was. She'd of course participated in all of Via's major functions, often onstage at Matthew's side as he wished the employees season's greetings or congratulated them on a particularly profitable quarter.

Not finding him in the crowd, she remembered the private back rooms, where she and Matthew had dined with some of the other executives and their wives on previous occasions. Halfway across the main floor she was intercepted by the smiling hostess, who asked if she could help her.

"I know my way around," Greta said without slowing down.

She rounded the bend and paused. She considered going down the row until she found them, but then had a better idea. Strolling along the line of closed doors, she observed the shoes set before each room. She spotted Matthew's casual loafers at the end, alongside a pair of not-too-shabby heels. Bally, by the looks of them.

She eased up to the paper partition and listened. Yes, definitely Matthew's voice. Interested by the exchange, she hesitated before going inside.

"Here, try this one."

"Oh no, I don't think so."

"Come on, just a little bite."

"I think I'll stick with the cooked ones."

"These?"

"Mmm, yes. I like those better."

"Here we go."

"Oh, no. You don't have to. I can feed myself."

"Open wide."

"Please, Matthew. Don't."

Which sounded to Greta like the perfect time to slide open the rice paper door and drop in on the party, changing her voice to imitate the woman. *"Please, Matthew. Don't!"*

Her sudden arrival so startled the pair that what happened next struck Greta as almost comically absurd, though none of them would remember it as funny.

Greta watched with astonishment as Matthew inadvertently plunged a bright pink cooked prawn into the young woman's mouth. It appeared he'd been caressing the nape of her neck with his free hand, while she seemed to be pushing him away. Shocked at being caught with his hand on her, Laurence gasped a great intake of breath, which managed to draw the rather large prawn down the wrong pipe.

Her face registered the shocked expression of a choking victim, and she gestured at her own throat with what Greta, despite the urgency of the situation, couldn't help but notice were distinctly gorgeous hands.

Acting fast, Matthew struck the girl sharply on the back and a moment later the prawn flew out with great force, striking him squarely on the chest before falling into his lap.

Seeing that the girl was out of danger, Greta shook her head in disgust as Laurence struggled to extricate herself from the suddenly cramped quarters. Greta pointed her left index finger at her. "Sit. You're not going anywhere till we're through."

Laurence was gasping and shaking. Exasperated, she returned to her cushion and looked up at Greta with plaintive eyes. "Mrs. Locke, this isn't what you think."

"Oh, I think it is, dear. Just shush please, this is between my husband and me, thank you very much."

Matthew was scowling angrily, no sign of guilt on his face. "Close the door, Greta."

Laurence tried again to rise and explain herself, but Greta cut her off. "If you don't shut up and sit down like a good little mistress, I'm going to take that chopstick and poke you in the eye."

Unwilling to test her luck, Laurence sat back and, except for a few gulps of water, didn't open her mouth again until the whole ordeal was over.

A moment later the hostess slid open the door and poked her head in to offer Greta a menu. "Shoo," Greta said, waggling her four-fingered hand at the demure woman.

Matthew asked his wife to lower her voice and sit down. "We were just going over some notes, Greta. This isn't what it looks like."

Greta dropped down onto one of the free cushions. "No, of course not." She opened her bag and fished out the bank form and a pen. She set the withdrawal form on the table, crossed out the number she'd originally filled in, and doubled it.

"This, on the other hand, is exactly what it looks like. Sign it." She slapped the pen down beside Matthew's tray.

Matthew made a face. "This is for a hundred thousand dollars."

"Very good, you can read. And it's going to double again if you don't sign it."

Matthew stared at his wife in disbelief. He'd come here with the intention of feeling out Laurence's attraction to him, and right at the crucial moment Greta appeared, just as he'd placed his hand on the back of the young woman's lovely neck. It didn't look good. With Greta's previous threat of divorce, she could easily construe the situation to seem as though he was actually having an affair, despite the fact that he, unfortunately, wasn't.

Unable to think of a way out, he picked up the pen, signed on the X, and shoved the document back to her side of the table. He crossed his arms and stared at her in stony silence.

Greta collected the form and pen with a triumphant grin. She dropped the things into her purse and snapped it closed. Rising to leave, she suddenly remembered her manners and graced Laurence with a warm smile.

"It was nice to meet you, Ms. whoever-you-are. And oh, here's some free advice: In case you haven't already discovered firsthand, he likes it better when you let him do it himself. Good luck." She giggled and quickly turned and fled, before Matthew could catch her in his lunging grasp.

She swept past the mute diners, positively certain they'd heard every word. She didn't give a damn. At least not at first. But as she climbed into her car and saw Matthew's girlfriend run past in tears, her triumph faltered.

The reality of the situation hit her like a blow to the stomach. How all this time she had been wrong about Matthew. Wrong in her assessment of his obsessive love affair with his work. Because what she had just witnessed made it obscenely clear: Matthew had actually been capable of loving more than only his work.

And he had chosen to share that love not with her, but with another woman.

"Very well," William Harrell said. "Then we have a deal."

The group had gathered in the dining room for lunch. After the meal, the engineers excused themselves, and the three men moved into the living room to talk.

Peter and Byron sat on the sofa across from William. Isle lay on the cushion beside her father. She yawned, and the ICP chair laughed.

"I guess she doesn't realize her name is such a big deal." Byron and Peter smiled, and William considered them with a concerned expression. "Speaking of tired, you guys must be working yourselves to the bone with all the progress you've made. When do you expect to have a final design?"

Byron answered. "The hardware's nearly complete. We've got agreements with suppliers for all the major components. The software's going to take the longest." He looked at Peter. "Six months?"

"Tops," Peter said. "Assuming we get the engineers and support and everything we've talked about."

William assured Peter and Byron they'd get whatever they needed to complete the project as quickly as possible.

Byron was pleased with William's answer; however, there was one last thing Peter wanted to discuss. "What about the strategic alliance with Via?"

"That stays for now," William said. "Listen, consider my position: What you've got is still a ways off. Keep in mind that what we've drawn up here today is more substantial than ICP's current agreement with Via. Our alliance has cost us next to nothing, and both companies are enjoying its success. This is much, much bigger. We're investing hard cash in your baby. A lot of it. I assure you, Peter, we're both shooting for the same thing."

Peter seemed satisfied and nodded his agreement to Byron.

"Then we're set," the older man said.

"Excellent," William Harrell said. He checked his watch. "And I'd better get moving if I'm going to make my flight."

The trio rose and together they strolled to the front door, Isle squirming in Peter's arms. Byron called to Grace that William was leaving, and she came out to say good-bye. She collected Isle from Peter, the men shook hands, and William departed.

"See," Byron joked. "The big guys aren't all so awful after all."

"I like him," Peter said.

"Everything go well?" Grace asked.

"Like a charm," Byron said with a kiss to her cheek. "And we've got a hell of a lot of work cut out for us. Let's hope we don't have any setbacks."

Grace withdrew a Post-it note from her sweater pocket and handed it to Peter. "You got a call while you were talking," she said.

"Thanks, Grace." He was plainly disappointed it wasn't Kate's number written on the Post-it. He didn't recognize the caller.

"I'll call back later," Peter said as he slipped the note in his

pocket. He clapped Byron happily on the shoulder. "Come on, let's go tell the guys the good news."

"My God, Matthew, what happened?" Matthew's secretary said as she rose from her chair. "Laurence came running through in tears, grabbed things from your office, and left without a word. She looked really upset."

"She got sick all of a sudden," Matthew said, still fuming from Greta's unexpected visit and too preoccupied to worry about Laurence at the moment.

"I was about to come get you. Hank Towers just called an emergency executive staff meeting. They're in there now waiting for you."

Matthew looked at her with a puzzled expression. What the hell would warrant an emergency meeting, he wondered as he charged down the corridor to the boardroom. He went inside.

The entire Via executive staff was seated around the table. "What's going on, Hank?"

"Close the door, Matthew," Hank said gravely.

Matthew shut the door and took his seat at the head of the table.

The room was silent as Hank slid a single document in front of him. Picking it up, Matthew noticed everyone else had received a copy as well. A quick scan was all it took to get a reaction out of him.

"Son of a bitch. They're finally going through with it."

Hank nodded, and the tension in the room lightened a little now that their most senior executive had been informed of the news.

"How did we get this?" Matthew asked.

Hank answered him. "It's not supposed to hit the wire until tomorrow; however, one of our developers who also writes for the

PCSoft platform was kind enough to fax a copy to Al," Hank said, indicating Alan Parker, vice president of engineering.

Matthew reread the headline again, aloud this time. "PCSoft and Future Processing announce plans to merge into a single company: FutureSoft."

It was incredible. The two companies already owned each of their respective markets—mainstream software, and the processors to run the software. Together, they would completely dominate all aspects of the desktop and portable computer market, including handhelds. On top of that, it was no secret both companies were making incredible headway in the server business, which was making a dent in the pocketbooks of mini and mainframe computer makers.

"Bastards," Matthew said with a disbelieving shake of his head.

"The biggest deal in our industry's history," Hank added.

Matthew looked around the table at the dispirited faces. Most looked defeated. And he wasn't far behind them.

As the company's head he knew they were waiting for him to say something. He cleared his throat and mustered his best tone of authority.

"The news will obviously have a major impact on our business," Matthew said, knowing it was a gross understatement. "While the At Hand PC Plus is selling well, it has only just started to reach its stride."

"And we have the ICP strategic alliance to thank for that," Hank said for Matthew's benefit. The others nodded appreciatively.

However, Matthew felt no sense of glory for his hand in the alliance. The mention of ICP made him suddenly nervous. He returned to his estimation of Via's position.

"We'll need at least a year's worth of the kind of sales we're seeing right now if we want to capture even a third of the PCSoft-compatible market."

Nods. A few spirited assertions around the table that maybe

they could do it, keep the sales going strong. This was in turn countered by a more realistic prediction, that they were through.

Matthew glanced at Hank, who'd begun tapping his pen on his knee, ignoring the desperate discussion circulating around the table. He looked deep in thought.

Someone joked that at least it couldn't get worse.

"Actually, it could," Alan Parker said, and everyone stared at him. He looked at Towers. "I was going to wait till the shock of this blew over, but we might as well get it out in the open now. All right, Hank?"

Towers nodded but didn't bother to look up. Matthew had seen him like this in the past, at his most intense, quietly working through a multitude of possibilities.

"It's about Peter," Parker said. "There's a rumor going around. A couple of our engineers heard it from their former colleagues who left to join Peter at whatever it is he's up to. They wouldn't give any details, but apparently they've lined up a meeting with an official from ICP. They're meeting today, in fact."

Matthew felt the blood drain from his face. An official from ICP? Was it possible that William Harrell had turned to Jones for inspiration after he, Matthew, had pulled the plug on the final stage of their deal?

Hank Towers leaned forward in his seat. By the look on his face everyone could see that the vice chairman had something to say. The room quieted down, and Matthew held his breath.

"That's it," Hank Towers said calmly, "ICP." He look at Matthew. "Don't you see? It's quite simple."

"I'm not sure I follow, Hank."

"But of course you do, Matthew. Think about it. ICP. We're already in bed with them with our strategic alliance. We're selling more units than ever, and each puts a nice royalty in ICP's pocket. And their take is higher still on the units their own people sell, which as we all know outnumber our sales two to one."

Matthew knew where Hank was going with this, but no one else in the room seemed to make the connection until the co-chairman spelled it out for them. "We invite ICP to buy us."

Matthew burst out laughing, faintly aware of the hysteria mingled in with the eruption.

Hank Towers frowned and scanned the table. "Anyone else think that's so funny?"

Most were still too shocked to respond.

Towers continued. "Imagine it. We've already proven we're more effective as a team. ICP made a grave mistake years ago when it didn't buy PCSoft. Eventually, they went from the number one desktop computer company to just another PCSoft-compatible manufacturer. But we're proprietary. We use the Tangent CPU instead of Future Processing's. And ICP's total business is larger than either of them. In a Via-ICP scenario, we're suddenly playing the same ball game. Huge company, competing standard. We all know we have the better product. With ICP's worldwide force, we could triple our business by this time next year."

It wasn't until the last line of Hank's impassioned discourse that everyone in the room grasped the big picture and what it might mean to each of them personally, where it mattered most—in the wallet. An ICP acquisition would mean greater wealth for all of them, including Matthew Locke.

Yet he was the only one in the room who did not look visibly dazzled by what Hank had proposed.

"Don't you see, Matthew?" Hank said.

"It won't work."

"Of course it will."

"But our culture," Matthew ventured, grasping at straws. "ICP is as big as big business gets. The employees will never go for it."

"Nonsense," Hank said, angered by Matthew's obstinate attitude. "We said the same thing after Peter left, and business kept

right on going. I say on the contrary. When word gets out tomorrow that PCSoft and Future Processing intend to merge, I guarantee our employees will rally. They'll have to. Otherwise, there're going to be a hell of a lot of smart former Via employees looking for jobs next year, because by then this newly created Hard-Soft or whatever the fuck it's called will have run us out of business."

Matthew stood up and stalked over to the window. "And you believe ICP will say yes if we ask them, just like that?" Matthew asked, snapping his fingers to accentuate his point.

"No," Hank said honestly. "I don't believe anything in business happens 'just like that.'" He didn't bother with the finger-snapping part. "But I think there's a good chance of it." He turned to the others. "Am I alone in my assumption?"

The executives voiced various issues and considerations, and someone asked about the Peter Jones and ICP rumor mentioned earlier. Hank turned to Matthew.

"Good point, don't you think, Matthew? I mean, no one misses Peter more than I. However, I doubt you share in the sentiment. Surely this rumor's got you sweating a little."

Actually, a lot. Matthew could hardly take any more of this. Peter Jones. William Harrell and ICP. A PCSoft and Future Processing merger. He'd fucked up royally. Of course he thought what Hank was proposing was brilliant. It was genius. And it had been his idea in the first place. Well, William Harrell's too. But did he believe that William would simply welcome him back into the original deal with open arms? He doubted it. Especially now that this Peter Jones factor had entered the picture. Matthew recalled all too well how interested William had been in Jones, constantly worrying and wondering about what he was up to. And if the rumor was true, he was in fact finding out today, possibly at this very minute.

Matthew turned and faced the room. "I don't think William Harrell will go for it."

Hank glanced from Matthew to the others, trying to gauge their collective frame of mind. He gave an easy shrug. "All right, then. Let's conduct an impromptu vote. All in favor of pursuing the ICP acquisition angle I've put forth, raise your hand."

In two seconds every available hand raised except Matthew's.

Hank Towers nodded his gratitude around the table and looked at Matthew. "You want to make the call or should I?"

Matthew faced Hank with a defiant glint in his eye. "And if I don't go along?"

Hank spread his hands and shrugged, considerate enough not to answer the question aloud. He was obviously outnumbered. If he didn't go along, they would simply call the board together and conduct another vote, just as they had over Peter Jones. And this time Matthew would emerge the loser.

So although Matthew believed the chance of getting William to reconsider a merger was next to impossible, he lifted his hand to indicate aye anyway.

The room burst into applause.

"Good, Matthew," Hank Towers said politely. "Now go land us a deal."

After the restaurant fiasco Greta was not up for the trip to the bank to complete the transaction.

She still couldn't believe Matthew had been keeping a mistress. It caused her to reconsider her own situation with Gregor. To think that her morals had kept her from meeting him face-to-face all these months, while Matthew was banging his young press chief. She'd truly underestimated him, she thought, pouring herself a huge tumbler of wine.

She drifted through the lower floor of the mansion, deciding which things she would immediately take with her, and which would stay. Yes, it was time for a change. A big one. She made a few mental

notes as she wound her way back to the kitchen, refilled her glass, then headed upstairs to her private room and Gregor.

He was of course waiting for her, looking decidedly anxious when she popped open the live view window screen.

"Did you get it, Gret?"

She sipped her wine and nodded her head.

"Excellent. The whole amount?"

"Double," she said. She unfolded the receipt and held it up to the camera.

"I didn't believe you'd do it," he said, and something in his tone made her sit up a little.

"What do you mean by that? Of course I would. And now more than ever. I found out Matthew's been having an affair."

He nodded impatiently. "And the transfer into my account went through no problem?"

His neglect for what she'd said about Matthew surprised her. "Gregor, I'm exhausted. I'll do it first thing in the morning. Didn't you hear what I said about Matthew?"

He looked disappointed. "Tomorrow? Why? There's no problem is there?"

"What difference does one more day make? Did you hear what I said?"

He changed his pitch, as easy as throwing a switch. "Gret, I'm sorry. It's just that I want us to get this over with, that's all. Yeah, I heard. And I'm sorry. Now do you see what an asshole he is? Just like I've been saying, from the very start."

She sipped her wine and let out a tired sigh, unable to disagree.

"Anyway, Gret, I'll show him."

"We, darling."

"I meant to say we. We'll show him."

She changed the subject. "How did it go? Did you pick one out yet?"

He brightened. "Two, actually. A twenty-four-footer and a

thirty-two-footer. Beautiful decks on both, though the smaller one is actually priced higher. Both are in really beautiful shape."

"I can't wait, Gregor."

"Me either," he said.

"And you think you'll finally be able to write? I mean, once we sail off into the proverbial sunset?" She laughed drunkenly at her own joke.

"Oh yeah," he said. "I've got the outline pretty much done, just a few final twists to work out. I can't wait to get out of here and get started."

"And you still won't tell me what it's about?"

He considered her for a moment, then shrugged. "All right, I guess I can say a little about it now that I'm almost ready to start. It's a mystery. Based in Silicon Valley."

"Ooh, that sounds interesting, Gregor. Have you thought of a title?"

He nodded. *"Web of Deception."*

"Very mysterious. I like it." She toasted him with her tumbler as a curious thought crossed her mind. She gave him a mischievous look. "Will I be in it?"

"You bet you *will*, Gret. You're gonna be my heroine."

The cocksure manner of his vow had an arousing effect on her. "I can't wait," she whispered, then leaned into her screen and planted a kiss on his little face.

Matthew Locke charged down the long United terminal, noticing the time as he slowed to pass through the metal detectors.

Upon leaving the boardroom he'd called William Harrell's office in New York. William's secretary kindly informed him that Mr. Harrell was away on business in California, and was expected to return later that evening. He asked her for William's flight number and departure time, thanked her, then raced up the highway for San Francisco International Airport.

He stopped before the departure screens to find out which gate Harrell's flight would be using. He was sweating, and not only from the rigorous activity. On his ride to the airport he'd begun to warm to the possibilities of an ICP takeover of Via. The more he thought about it, the more returning to the deal's original finale appealed to him.

By the time he pulled into the parking garage he decided he'd resort to begging if necessary to convince William to agree. After tomorrow's news of the PCSoft and Future Processing merger hit the wires, an ICP takeover would be Via's only real hope of

staying in business in a meaningful way. And his only hope of
staying on top.

Luck was on his side: The flight was delayed by fifteen min-
utes. He spotted William in the departure gate's waiting area with
his garment bag by his side. He was flipping through a notepad
when Matthew Locke walked up to him.

William Harrell registered total surprise when he looked up.
He rose to his feet and the two men shook hands. Despite Matthew's
double cross, William Harrell remained the quintessential business-
man, professional, courteous—and ever cautious.

He looked at Matthew with curiosity. "Flying to New
York?"

Matthew gave an impatient shake of his head. "We need to
talk." His tone was desperate. He seated himself in the vacant seat
beside William, and the other executive followed suit.

Over the loudspeaker, an attendant announced that the flight
would begin boarding in a few minutes. Matthew shot an anxious
glance at the check-in counter and briefly considered buying a
seat to join William on the flight, if that's what it would take. He
cut to the quick.

"I know you met with Peter Jones today."

William nodded. "Smart man."

Matthew wondered if William had meant him or Jones. He
let it go.

"I'd like you to reconsider, William."

William didn't understand.

"Our deal, as we'd originally conceived it."

"I see," William said. He thought this over for a moment and
shook his head. "I don't think so."

Matthew pressed on. "I do. And I'm sorry for fucking it up,
William. I'm truly sorry."

"Business." Harrell shrugged.

"Good business," Matthew countered. "Look, I don't know what Jones is up to, but it can't compete with what we've already got."

Harrell smiled coolly. "Don't be so sure."

Matthew didn't want to argue. Peter Jones was the least of his problems. And Harrell's as well, he thought, when he remembered the surprising news. He reached into his back pocket and retrieved the photocopy that Hank Towers had given him in the meeting.

"This may change your mind," Matthew said. He unfolded the document and dropped it in William's lap.

The executive turned his unperturbed eyes to the document and picked it up. His brow furrowed as he scanned the first paragraph. He didn't need to read the whole thing to understand why Matthew had chased him down like this. "Where did you get this?"

"One of our developers faxed it over. It's legit."

William shook his head in awe. "So, the bastards are finally going all the way. Well, I can't say I'm totally surprised. But you, Matthew, you've surprised me."

"Think about it, William. An ICP and Via merger is the only way to compete effectively."

William looked unconvinced, and Matthew glanced up anxiously as the gate attendant announced that premier passengers and those who needed assistance were now welcome to board.

"I've got a flight to catch," William said.

"Wait," Matthew said, struggling to maintain a semblance of control. "Listen, let's put aside our prior dealings for the moment and think about our companies." He quickly reiterated his points, the benefits. He expressed the Via executive staff's support.

"And your board of directors?" Harrell said, rising to collect his garment bag.

"Hank Towers phoned them on my way here. The members he reached approved the prospect, which leaves only two votes. They're already outnumbered. It's in the bag."

"Interesting, but I'm sure you can appreciate my position. This is all rather sudden. And I haven't exactly been sitting on my thumbs since your change of heart." He started for the gate.

"Wait," Matthew said for the second time, gripping William's arm in desperation. The executive frowned at the other man's hand and Matthew let go.

"I'm sorry," Matthew said in a strained voice. "I mean, about the deal. About changing my mind when I did. I see now that I made a mistake. Even so, we wouldn't have gone through with it yet anyway. This FutureSoft announcement tomorrow changes everything. William, we can do it. All the way."

William considered the notebook tucked under his arm. He stood like that for a full minute, staring at the closed notebook, thinking over his options while Matthew remained perfectly still at his side, awaiting his response. The gate attendant announced general boarding and William finally looked Matthew in the eye.

He gave a single nod. "Very well," William said. "I'll make the recommendation to my board. I can't promise anything."

Matthew let out a burst of air and grabbed William's hand and shook it furiously. "Thank you, William, thank you. It's the best thing for both of us. You won't be sorry."

William abruptly pulled free and heaved his garment bag onto his shoulder. "We'll see," he said.

Matthew stepped aside as William joined the line to board the aircraft. When he reached the gateway he handed the attendant his ticket and turned once to give Matthew a small wave good-bye.

Peter picked up the handset to call Kate at her studio, as he'd promised Grace he would. But then he remembered the Post-it note she'd slipped him earlier, and decided to stall a little to take care of this call first.

He dialed the number, and a moment later he was greeted by the receptionist at the firm Williams and Williams.

Peter glanced at the note. "David Williams, please."

The attorney promptly came on the line, and Peter introduced himself.

"Thank you for returning my call so quickly, Mr. Jones. I'm representing Ivy Green, who's retained our firm to reclaim her rights to ISLE, which I believe is currently in your possession."

Peter made a disbelieving sound and dropped down on the sofa. "That's an awfully insensitive way of referring to our child."

The man on the other end chuckled. "Oh no, Mr. Jones. I'm sorry for not making myself clear from the start. I'm representing my client's interest in the ISLE software. My apologies."

Peter was relieved. "It's okay. I've been pretty much expecting this call for a while now."

"Good. That will help. But you are correct in the other as well, Mr. Jones."

"The other?"

"Yes, the baby. My partner, Linda, would like a word with you on that matter after you and I are done."

Dropping his head back on the sofa, Peter sat and listened as Mr. Williams presented his case. Fifteen minutes later, the lawyer transferred the call to Ms. Williams, who spent the next forty-five minutes presenting her case, which was a little more complicated. Child custody always was, she informed Peter.

By the time he hung up he was numb. In less than an hour the life he'd managed to somehow get back on track, however shakily, had just derailed. The past year's upsets suddenly seemed trivial by comparison, and never in his life had he felt so utterly hopeless and defeated. Just when he'd finally begun to accept that he'd lost everything he'd ever really cared about, the tables turned once more. On the contrary, he still had plenty more to lose, most of all hope.

He stared with desperate longing at the phone on the table beside him. The only person who could help him pull himself together was Kate, and he needed her now more than ever. But how could he call her, after the lawsuits he'd just been hit with? It would only underscore her reason for leaving him in the first place.

He sat alone in a quiet state of shock and absently wondered if this marked the last of his punishment for his past mistakes, or if he would go on paying forever.

After his jolting turnaround victory at the airport, Matthew began to interpret the reversal as a sort of omen. The mark of a new beginning. A signal to reevaluate his life and make adjustments wherever necessary. Including his marriage.

He wound his way through the mansion in search of his wife. There was so much to tell, so much to celebrate. He found her in the living room, crouched among several cardboard boxes.

She saw him come in but made no effort at civility. He knew she was upset about what had happened at the restaurant, and he couldn't blame her. He had only himself to blame, for so many of their problems. And that was why he needed to talk to her.

"What are you doing?"

"What's it look like I'm doing?" she said without bothering to look at him.

"Packing."

"Bingo."

"Why?"

She blew a strand of hair out of her face and looked at her husband. "Why do people usually pack, Matthew?"

"Are you going somewhere?"

"I am," she said as she poured a quantity of puff balls into an empty cardboard box.

Matthew came over to lend a hand by holding the box's flaps apart. "When?"

"Very soon. And I can do this, thank you." She waited for him to remove his hands from the box before proceeding.

"Greta, I'm sorry."

She stood up and lifted her wineglass, sipped from it while judging the box's dimensions and whether or not it would do.

"It wasn't what you think."

She shot him a warning look, unwilling to get into this conversation.

"Listen, I've got good news," he said, trying a different angle. "We're back on track. I mean the deal. William Harrell's agreed to take it all the way, like we originally planned."

"How nice for you."

"And you, Gret," he said, reaching for her wrists. "You too."

She looked down at his hands and then back at him. "Get your hands off me, Matthew."

He let go, and she went back to adjusting the amount of puff balls in the box. Glancing at the large crystal bowl, she wondered if perhaps she should hire a professional for the job.

"Greta, please. I want you to hear me out. I've done some serious thinking."

"Hooray for you."

"I mean it. There's a lot for us to talk about. What you saw at the restaurant was just bad timing. It's really not what you think."

"Horseshit," Greta said, getting worked up.

"I swear, Gret. She's just my assistant. Or was. She quit this afternoon. My secretary called me in my car to say so. I guess we really upset her."

"We?"

"Well, me. I tried to call her and apologize."

"A lover's quarrel. Poor dears."

"Greta, no. I've never laid a hand on her."

"Really? My stupid eyes, I should get them checked. I thought for sure that was the nape of her neck you were caressing with your hand."

"I mean, you know."

"No, Matthew. I don't know. It's been far too long. And anyway, I don't care who you fuck. It doesn't matter anymore. Now leave me alone." She turned to the large crystal salmon bowl and hefted it an inch off the pedestal, gauging its weight. God, she'd forgotten how heavy it was.

"It does matter, Greta." Matthew was suddenly interested in the beautiful object as he went on with his chatter. "Because it's all over. ICP is going to buy Via, and if everything goes as planned, I'll wind up in the top seat after William Harrell retires. He's pissed off at me, but I think he'll come around. And that means we'll eventually be back in New York. We can live wherever you like. Manhattan. Connecticut. Anywhere you want, Gret. I promise."

She paused and gave him a knowing look. "Ah, now I see. Surely you'll need a wife if you're going to become ICP's big shot. And hey, might as well stick with the one you've already got, save yourself some money that way, cheaper to keep the young thing in an apartment."

His shook his head in frustration. "Greta, don't talk like that. I know you're mad, and you have every right to be. But please, try to hear what I'm saying. I'm sorry for having caused you all this grief. I really am. And I want to try, Gret. I really want to try to make things work."

She went for her glass and then decided against it. He'd already succeeded in upsetting her, but she wouldn't let herself get wound up. She'd had enough drama for one day, and she'd made up her mind. She was leaving, and that was final.

With a bracing breath she hefted the crystal bowl off the pedestal.

"Wait," Matthew said, hopping over to grip the crystal bowl's rim.

The halogen lamp above cast a bright beam into the sparkling object, highlighting its preciousness and vulnerability.

Greta gasped in fright as the bowl wobbled uncertainly and she nearly dropped it. "Let go," she said firmly.

He left his hands where they were and looked at her with an almost wistful expression. "Gret, remember the day you brought this home?"

She considered his squashed thumbs pressed firmly on the other side of the bowl. The piece was too valuable to risk losing, and she set it back down on her side. God forbid she lose it.

Matthew let go as well and knelt down for a closer look. He shook his head in awe. "Look at it, Gret. I mean, really look at it." He focused on one of the engraved salmon, frozen in time.

She stepped back and waited for him to finish with this nonsense. When he kept on rambling about the gracefulness of the salmon's purpose, she finally grew impatient.

"All right, Matthew, that's enough. Yes, they're magnificent. Now please, let me finish." She reached for the bowl.

And he reached too, resuming their tug of war.

"Greta, it's almost over." His voice cracked. "Don't you see? The struggle's finally over. Think back, when you came home with this bowl. To celebrate the first stage of the deal coming together. Our plans coming together. And it's finally going to happen. It's all working out for the good, just like it was supposed to."

"Let go of my bowl," she said anxiously.

"Greta, no. Please. Don't do this. Don't take it. It means everything to me. To us. We can fix it."

"No, damn you. It's mine. And I'm taking it. Let go."

He pulled a little on his side, and she pulled back with equal force. "Where?" Matthew laughed. "Where do you think you're going, Greta?"

"Away," she cried, tugging harder while he tugged back.

"Away where?"

"Mexico. On a yacht. Now let go, Matthew."

He burst out with laughter and leaned his face in to hers. "Like a Carnival Cruise, Gret? For unhappily married women?"

"No, Matthew. With a lover. A young, capable lover."

That got through to him. He tightened his grip on the bowl and pulled harder, his voice taunting. "So you're the one fucking around, then?"

"No. Not yet. But I will be. You can count on it. Now let go." Her fingers were cramping and she could barely hold on any longer. If she released her side he would drop it. "Please, Matthew," she begged, painfully close to letting go.

And this awareness suddenly dredged up a more painful anxiety. That were it not for her missing finger, she might have possessed the strength to hold on a little tighter, a little longer. And this thought gave way to yet another sudden insight, her understanding complete. That were it not for her missing finger, an imperfection so minor to most people, none of this would be happening in the first place.

Tears streamed down her face and she hysterically begged him to please, please let go.

Unfortunately, he did.

What followed lasted only seconds, but to both it felt as though time had slowed to a crawl.

With Matthew's side released the force of Greta's pull drew the enormous crystal bowl into her chest, propelling her backward.

Realizing what his letting go had caused, he dove forward to try and get his hands around the bowl again. His fingers grazed its cool surface and he grappled to get a hold on the object.

As Greta flew into the wall, her face instinctively registered an awareness that she would have to let go of the bowl in order to throw out her hands and break her fall. Her stunned gaze shifted to

her own hands and she couldn't believe what she saw, how almost perfect they were, how strong they held, but by the time she let go, it was too late.

Her head hit first, the center smashing squarely into a framed picture of their wedding day. The glass shattered against her skull, leaving a splatter of blood between their photographed selves. Her shoulders connected next, flattening into the wall with a terrible cracking sound.

Her eyes widened and matched Matthew's own shocked expression as he flew through the air, straight for her. He squeezed his hands together in a last attempt to save the bowl.

It eluded his grasp and landed on the hardwood floor just as Greta's rear hit the ground.

She bounced once, but the bowl didn't.

It shattered, blasting shards of precious glass in every direction. Matthew squeezed his eyes shut as a storm of bits flew into his face. He landed with a crushing smack, crying out in pain as hundreds of sharp points chewed into his chest.

Then, dead silence.

He lay there for what seemed an eternity, afraid to open his eyes, until finally he had the courage to do it. He let out a grateful cry; his vision had escaped the shrapnel.

Then he saw the blood, and he panicked. Glass crunched under his hands and knees and elbows and he struggled to extricate himself from Greta's tangled legs and the bloody bits and shards. Blood gushed from his palms and he tried not to scream.

And then he looked at her, and he did scream. He grabbed the closest cardboard box and tore off a flap, no longer aware of his own pain or bleeding. He tossed the flap over the broken glass between her legs and knelt before her, shouting her name. She didn't respond.

He squeezed her cheeks between his bloody palms and lifted her face. Her eyes were closed and he shouted for her to wake up,

to look at him. He struggled to remember what he'd learned in high school. He clumsily pressed his hands to her chest and tried to make her breathe, put his lips over hers and blew.

He cried in agony and shouted for the housekeeper, not sure whether she was even in residence. He whispered Greta's name over and over as he drew her limp and bloody head against his chest, his own head twisting from side to side in a frenzy as he searched for the phone.

He spotted the cordless handset beside one of the boxes and snatched it up. He promised his Greta that he would fix this, he would fix everything, whispering her name again and again as he dialed.

Waiting for help to come on the line he shook his head sadly and cried at the dazzling array of broken bits that lay beneath them, searching in vain for a larger shard, one that might contain a hopeful fragment of the salmon.

He found none.

Peter stood beneath Hoover Tower on the Stanford campus, exactly in the place where he and Ivy had first met. It was her idea to meet here, to discuss the terms of her cases against him.

Waiting for her to arrive, he considered everything that had happened from the day they'd met until now. He'd gotten over his hurt and anger from being ousted from Via. He missed Kate terribly, but the work with Byron went a long way to helping him keep his mind off losing her. He adored Isle, astonished by how she had entered his life so suddenly and become its center. She was healthy, and so was her mother, the lawyers had told him.

Peter had mixed feelings. He was glad to hear she'd pulled herself together and was well enough to now care for her baby. But it was his baby too, and he didn't want to give her up.

He thought about their night together, searched for any memory of love. Had he felt something for her? He wasn't sure. It seemed so long ago, swept aside by the events that had followed. No, he knew he wasn't in love with Ivy. But he loved his baby, their baby, and the three of them did form a family, even if Ivy might not see it that way. He'd never been a part of a real family, and the thought of his daughter going through life without both parents deeply disturbed him. Would she marry him if he asked her to?

"No lawyers?" Ivy Green said.

He spun around, and was positively stunned by her transformation.

Here was the Ivy he'd first met, youthful and vibrant, her white-blond hair pulled up into a smart bun, complexion perfectly smooth and lightly tanned. She wore loose beige jeans and a purple V-necked sweater. Her blue eyes sparkled with the iridescence of tropical waters.

She smiled and he experienced an unexpected stirring, a connection that somehow attested to the bond between them and their baby. He felt light and uplifted, forgetting for the moment that they were here to discuss serious business. He took a tentative step forward and stretched out his arms.

She took a step back and shook her head. Her smile changed from one of happiness at seeing him to one of being happy to see him looking at her as he was, with attraction and approval in his eyes. With desire. She grinned.

"Amazing, isn't it, what a little time and sunshine can do."

"Sure is," he said, dropping his hands at his side. "You look incredible."

"I feel incredible," she said, clasping her hands casually behind her back.

"Ivy, I'm so sorry. About everything that happened. I mean, how it happened and what you've gone through."

She shrugged. "Listen, I've been in the desert learning how to stop apologizing. Take my advice, don't bother."

He ran a hand through his short hair, gestured for her to sit on the grass.

"No, I've only got a minute."

"Can't we talk a little? There's so much I want to say."

"Um, no. Not now, anyway. This is business, Peter. Maybe in a while, after we settle things between us."

"But I don't want you to be angry forever."

"Poor Peter." She looked sad, but not for herself. "Look, I'm not pissed off anymore. Well, not too pissed. And I'm not sorry, either. What's done is done. I'm definitely not having an easy time of it, but I'm on my way. All I want is to see Isle, and my other ISLE too. I want to see how they've done in your care." She looked at him suspiciously.

"What?"

"Nothing, really. I guess I'm just surprised you didn't bring an army of lawyers with you."

He shook his head. "What about yours?"

"Don't need them for this. They told you what I want." She withdrew a single folded document from her back pocket and handed it to him. "It's all here, simple and to the point."

He eased himself down on the grass and accepted the pen she offered. He scanned the agreement, already familiar with what it spelled out. But he didn't sign it.

Instead, he put the pen down and looked up into her eyes. "What do you feel? I mean, really feel?"

"About this? Excellent."

"No, I mean us. Me."

"You?" She turned her pretty face skyward to ponder the enormous column rising above them. Her expression was softer when she looked at him again. "I'm not sure. But it isn't anger anymore. Honest."

"No, I don't mean that."

"Guilt? Nope. I'm done with that."

He shook his head in frustration. "No, not that either." He looked at her with unconcealed interest, and she finally understood. She blinked rapidly and looked away.

He knew he'd already said enough, but he had to know. "Love?"

Her bright blue eyes glistened.

"Just sign it, Peter."

# PART V

Matthew hadn't slept all night, yet he did not feel tired. If anything, he felt wide awake, ready to roll.

He threw off the covers and rose from his bed. It had become that, his bed, after the freak accident with Greta. But today that event did not trouble him the way it had over the last two months. No, today was his day, and no one could take it away from him.

He strolled unhurriedly downstairs to the kitchen, passing many packing boxes along the way. Even these didn't affect his excited mood today, the most important day of his career. Nearly three years of sweat and frustration had gone into this moment, and it would mark his greatest achievement.

The emerging dawn filled the kitchen with a dull gray light. It looked like rain. He opened the refrigerator and considered making himself a big breakfast, but then decided against it. He had no appetite. Instead, he poured himself a glass of juice and sipped it as he looked out the window and pondered his future.

His presence would be required in both New York and California. He hadn't decided yet which would be his primary residence. Perhaps a high-rise apartment in Manhattan, with a pied-à-terre in San Francisco. The hour-long commute down to Via would be inconsequential, since he'd have his own chauffeured limousine to shuttle him back and forth. His elation was complete. It was still too early to shower and change, so he strolled to his office to run through his speech once more, then checked his E-mail.

Just as he turned on his At Hand PC Plus the telephone rang. He answered before the second ring.

It was William Harrell, who had flown in last night for today's big announcement. Their dealings with each other had been cordial and professional. The men exchanged greetings, and William invited Matthew to join him for an early breakfast before the announcement. The ICP executive named a restaurant near Via.

"Anything I should be concerned about?" Matthew Locke said.

"Just a couple last-minute details to go over," William said, promising to explain everything over breakfast.

They hung up, and Matthew turned off his At Hand. His E-mail could wait.

When she heard the garage door close, Greta Locke climbed out of bed with a groan. She too hadn't slept all night. And like her husband, she was excited, despite her aches and pains.

Her left collarbone had healed nicely, but it still hurt when she arose every morning. The broken bone was the least disagreeable of the injuries she'd sustained in her tug-of-war with Matthew two months before. She'd fractured her skull and suffered a concussion which, the doctors informed her afterward, could have turned into a coma.

Poor Gregor was in a complete panic by the time she'd reached him, two weeks after the accident. Her hospital stay lasted nearly a month, but fortunately her private room allowed her to set up her At Hand and modem to stay in touch with Gregor.

When she finally reconnected with him online he was in a state of shock. He thought she'd dumped him, and it was easy to see why he would think so. The money she'd promised to wire into his account never showed up, and then she'd vanished from World Online. She explained everything, and assured him she would be fine. She detailed the ensuing involvement with the lawyers, the difficult position Matthew had gotten himself into, and the excellent position she was in.

In the one and only conversation that she'd had with Matthew after the accident, she had agreed not to move out until today, when the deal was finally complete. He'd promised to make it worth her while, and the divorce papers would be ready any day now. He'd reactivated her full access to their combined bank accounts, and yesterday she left the local branch with a Coach weekender packed with a hundred thousand in cash and traveler's checks. Half of it would take care of the boat Gregor had picked out. She'd wired him ten grand already to put down on the vessel, and the owner had let him move his things aboard. She would hand over the remaining fifty thousand today, and then they would be on their way to Baja.

She unlocked her bedroom door and made her way downstairs. She'd taken to locking the door every night since she'd returned from the hospital. She didn't really believe Matthew would harm her, but then there were a lot of things about Matthew she hadn't believed. Which was why she'd purchased a handgun as well, just in case. She kept it by her bedside, able to sleep better knowing it was close at hand.

In the kitchen she fixed herself coffee, then headed back

upstairs to shower and change. It was dark outside, and she made a mental note to pack a rain slicker. Her bags were few, all set to go down by the front door. Since she wouldn't be needing her car anymore she'd arranged for a limousine to take her to San Francisco's Marina district, where Gregor was waiting. She was giddy with nervousness. It would be their first face-to-face encounter. She already liked the way he looked, and he swore she was the one for him, but she was nervous just the same.

She had promised to check in with him this morning, before she left, to make sure everything was set. She turned on her At Hand, pleased with the knowledge that after today she would no longer have any use for it.

Gregor was waiting for her, just as he had promised.

"You got the money?" he said.

"Of course, darling. I can't believe it's finally happening," she said.

"Me either," he said, smiling anxiously.

"Are you nervous, too?"

"Oh yeah," he said. "You all set to do what I told you with your computer?"

She hesitated. "Are you sure I have to? I mean, what's the danger?"

"It's just a precaution. We had some pretty intimate talks and peep shows over the wire. But this will ensure there's no trace. No leftover E-mails or pictures of me you might have snapped off, that sort of thing. Trust me, it's best this way, Greta."

"I trust you. You're right. It's just that, well, if it weren't for this silly computer, I wouldn't have ever met you."

"Yeah, but you're about to meet the real thing, and isn't that better?"

"It sure is. I'll do just like you said. Erase the whole thing. I have the little disk to restore it right here."

"Good. When does your car arrive?"

"Half an hour. I'd better do this now so I'm not late."

"And you got my E-mail with the directions to the Marina?"
She nodded.

"Well, I guess that's it then. Okay, Gret. See you in a little bit."

She paused, waited for him to say it, and when he didn't, she did.

"I love you," she said, and smiled for the camera.

"That's my girl," he said, waved good-bye, and vanished from her screen.

My God, she thought, this is really happening. She glanced at the locked Coach bag full of cash and traveler's checks beside the bed, then picked up the floppy disk and inserted it in her computer's disk drive. She restarted the computer and a moment later it asked her if she was sure she wanted to erase the hard disk and reinstall the system software and applications. She clicked the Yes button, then let the At Hand do its thing while she packed her toiletry kit.

It wasn't until she was downstairs and waiting by the front door for the limo that she remembered the directions. She checked her rain slicker pocket, but it was empty. She thought for a moment and tried to recall where she'd put them. Gregor had E-mailed the directions last night, and she'd read them and then—

Dear God, she had printed them, hadn't she? She raced upstairs to her room.

The printer tray was empty, but somehow this didn't come as a surprise. No, she knew it would be empty when she recalled the events of last evening. After opening his E-mail she had signed off and, thrilled this was finally happening, she'd gone into the bathroom to draw herself a hot bath, forgetting to print the directions.

Confirming what she already knew, she checked her computer and the E-mail he'd sent her was gone, erased from her hard disk along with everything else. No traces, just like he had promised.

Her heart thudded in her chest and she forced herself to calm down. She sat on the edge of her bed and tried to think of what to do, how to recover the lost directions.

And then she remembered: Previously read E-mails remained on the World Online system for a few weeks before they were permanently erased. She knew because she would sometimes reread the love letters and poems he'd sent her. She raced downstairs, praying that Matthew had left his At Hand PC Plus home.

Luckily, he had. She turned the computer on and whispered for it to hurry. She launched World Online and a moment later she was back in business. The At Hand announced that she had new mail, and this surprised her—Gregor was the only person she ever E-mailed. She double-clicked the in-box and a moment later she realized her mistake. She'd gotten so used to just turning on her computer and connecting to World Online, that she'd forgotten to change profiles so that it would know it was she, rather than Matthew, logging on this time.

As she moved to close the E-mail box, one of the waiting items caught her eye. When she read the subject heading she nearly fainted.

It read: YOUR WIFE'S CUNT

The message was marked with a little slide icon to indicate it contained a picture.

She stared at the screen in horror. The message was from a someone named "SFScooper," and it took her a moment to recall where she'd seen that name before. She looked around the little office in frustration, and then, as though picturing herself in a dream, she remembered.

It was here, right here. In this office. The first time she'd ever used the computer and gone online. That rude person who had offended her, who had called Matthew a bastard. She swallowed and double-clicked on the message.

The text appeared, a string of profanities and accusations, threats and assurances of revenge.

Much worse was the picture that unfolded beneath the body of the message.

She gaped at a freeze-frame version of herself, captured the instant after she'd unfolded her light blue robe and exposed her most intimate secrets.

"Ladies and gentleman, please find your seats," the announcer's voice boomed through the bustling auditorium.

The hall was already jammed to near capacity with thousands of Via employees dressed casually in T-shirts and jeans or shorts. The front rows were reserved for VIPs and the press. On stage, a bright circle of light shone on the empty podium.

Backstage, William Harrell parted the curtain an inch and peered out at the talkative crowd. Hank Towers squeezed in beside him for a look.

"I've never given a speech to so many people dressed like that," William remarked. He stepped away and rearranged his necktie.

Hank laughed. "You look like you gained twenty pounds," Hank said, making a private joke about what he knew William was hiding beneath his suit.

William grinned. "That crowd is about to witness the world's fastest weight-loss program."

A production assistant asked the two executives to take their places. The show was ready to begin.

The announcer's voice filled the great hall: "Ladies and gentlemen, please welcome Martin Cohen, vice president and general counsel for Via, Incorporated."

Dressed in a dark business suit, Martin Cohen stood before

the podium and greeted the audience. Overhead, the Via logo
splashed onto the projection screen. Cohen customarily opened
the company's quarterly meetings before turning them over to the
company's chief. After some general commentary, he moved to
today's order of business.

"Earlier this year we entered into a strategic-alliance agree-
ment with International Computer Products." ICP's logo materi-
alized alongside Via's on the overhead screen, and Cohen continued.
"Thanks to that alliance, sales of the At Hand PC Plus increased
to record numbers. However, with the recent merger of PCSoft
and Future Processing, which together form the company Future-
Soft, our sales have slowed considerably."

A grumble of concern rippled through the audience.

"We all want to succeed. And what we have to announce to-
day will see to it that we do. Quite possibly beyond our wildest
imaginations—and we all know we've got some pretty wild imagi-
nations here," he quipped, and the audience responded with ner-
vous laughter. "Without further delay, I'd like to turn over the
meeting to the man who helped make our strategic alliance
a reality, William Harrell, chairman of International Computer
Products."

A worrisome murmur filled the huge auditorium as William
strode onto the stage and stopped before the podium. He thanked
Martin Cohen, and then thanked everyone in the audience.

"I have to admit," William began, completely at ease, "I've al-
ways been envious of you sneakers-and-jeans folks out here in
California. I look out there, and I see a sea of beachwear."

There was more nervous laughter, and William knew that
the crowd was thrown off by his presence. Normally Matthew
Locke would be onstage after Martin Cohen opened the quar-
terly meeting. Something suspicious was up today, and this crowd
sensed it.

William quickly pressed on. "And maybe that's part of your

secret," he said, as he casually moved away from the podium to stand at center stage. "Maybe the environment you have out here is what makes it possible for you to invent brilliant products like the At Hand PC Plus."

On the overhead screen an older photo of the original At Hand team appeared, with a younger Peter Jones kneeling in the center of the group, proudly holding up an original At Hand PC. The audience applauded with pride and appreciation for their company's legendary founder and product team.

William continued. "The fact is, I've always been jealous of Via and the At Hand. Jealous that we, the big guns, hadn't invented something as spectacular. And it makes me uncomfortable." He yanked at his tie, surprising the audience. It was all part of his prank, which he hoped would ease the initial shock of what he was going to announce.

A striptease song piped in through the loudspeakers, and the audience watched with wonder as William shrugged off his business jacket and began unbuttoning his dress shirt.

"In fact, it makes me really hot under the collar." He unzipped his trousers and shoved them to the floor, revealing faded jeans. "Itching to just let myself go, get in touch with my more creative side."

He tore off his dress shirt and flung it aside, then raised his arms to offer a full view of his spanking new Via T-shirt with its colorful roadway-and-horizon logo.

The audience broke into applause and cheers as William sauntered back to the podium. "Now, dressed like this, you'd think I could probably dream up some of the amazing products you folks are famous for, right?"

"Right," a chorus of voices shouted, playing along.

He shook his head. "Wrong. And that's what makes Via so special. Its people. You. You are Via."

The audience quieted down at the somber tone in his voice.

"Which is why today I'd like to help you continue to be the special company you are. The extraordinary people you are. So you can keep on building the amazing products you build."

He took a deep breath and revealed the deal. "Today, I am excited and proud to announce a very special marriage—the merger of Via and ICP."

While he'd expected a certain level of surprise from the crowd, nothing prepared him for the mayhem that exploded throughout the audience.

Acting fast, he raised his palms to try to calm the crowd down. "Wait, please." He took a step closer to the outraged congregation and begged for quiet. "Let me explain. There's more."

A pen flew over his head, and several floppy disks whizzed straight for him.

The crowd rose to its feet in angry protest as William lifted his arms to protect himself from the onslaught of shouts and pro-jectiles flying at him.

As the limousine pulled away from the Lockes' front gate Greta spotted Matthew's car racing up the hill. She absently wondered what he was doing back so soon before her mind returned to her own troubles.

She was in shock. Seeing herself like that, so vulgarly exposed, had absolutely devastated her. She'd just stared at the screen, trying to understand and piece it all together. Small fragments drifted through her mind, but she was too stunned to fathom the whole pic-ture just yet. Operating like an automaton, she'd proceeded to sign off from Matthew's account, then back on with her own. She found Gregor's directions to the Marina, printed them out, and left the whole mess just as she'd found it. It did not occur to her yet that Matthew would see it.

She'd walked out of her husband's office in a daze, unsure what to do next. The limousine arrived, and her first reaction was to send it away. There was no way she could go now. But as she sat on the bottom step and struggled to understand, it occurred to her that if the one photo existed, then it was likely that there were more.

This SFScooper, who might or might not in fact be Gregor, might have further intentions to exploit her picture in ways she didn't want to consider. She had no idea who SFScooper really was or why he had chosen to surprise her husband with the photos. But she had to find out. Her own uncertain future depended on it. My God, she thought, if photos like that were so easy to send around, God only knew where else they might appear. She'd calmly asked the driver to wait while she carried her bag of money upstairs to her room and retrieved a few things.

She looked at the black Coach bag at her feet, hefted it to gauge if it was heavy enough. It felt right. And so did her plan. Whatever Gregor's part in this was, she would find out. Her mind raced with vengeful fury, but she refused to let herself fully face the fact yet that the man she'd come to believe was her lover had lied.

Turning onto Bay Street, the driver informed her they were coming up on the Marina. The forty-five-minute ride had gone by in a flash. It had started to rain, and she was grateful for it. Her slicker made it easier to conceal what she was hiding in her pocket.

The chauffeur turned into the parking lot alongside the San Francisco Yacht Club, and before climbing out she asked the driver to leave and come back for her in a half hour. She handed him a hundred-dollar bill, and he promised to return.

She carried the Coach bag in one hand, while the other she kept in her raincoat pocket, ready. She had memorized the boat

slip number, and as she neared it Gregor—or whoever he really was—emerged with a big smile on his face that faltered as she got closer. He warned her to watch her step on the slippery dock. She put on a smile and declined his offer to take the bag, assuring him she could manage. She climbed aboard the boat, noticing his suspicious expression.

"You're nervous," he said.

She nodded. He was older than she had expected, or than he'd said. She guessed maybe thirty-six. It was interesting how she'd thought she'd gotten a clear picture of him on the computer screen. But it had been so small, so grainy.

"Me too," he said. "I can't believe you're here."

"Me either," she said seriously.

He was a little heavier than she thought, and his tan did not hide mildly pockmarked cheeks. His eyes were yellowish, a little bloodshot, and when he came closer she smelled alcohol on his breath. Or maybe it was seeping from his pores. Either way, it made her feel nauseous.

"You look fantastic," he said, reaching out a hand to her.

"You don't," she said with a nervous laugh, like she'd made a joke.

"But where are your bags?"

"I'm traveling light today, Gregor. Or whatever your name is."

He looked at her funny, and she could see that somehow he knew he'd been caught. Still, he tried to recover. "What do you mean?"

"Fuck what I mean. What do you want?"

"Greta."

"Yes, Greta," she said sarcastically. "And you are?"

"Look, it doesn't have to be this way." He wiped the back of his hand across his wet brow. "Let's go down below, talk."

"You first," she said.

He glanced at the bag.

"Oh no," she said, "not until I'm through with you. Move it."

He bristled. "Hey, don't talk to me like that, Greta."

She drew out the small handgun in her left hand, careful to keep it low.

He lost the tough guy act and looked up with terrified eyes. "Let's not do anything stupid."

"Too late. You already did. And now we're going to do a little undoing. Let's go." She waved the gun, her hand nearly steady.

He turned and climbed down the steps into the main cabin.

Keeping the muzzle pointed at him she followed, glancing around quickly to find what she was looking for. There it was, on the counter that he'd set up like a desk.

"All right, a couple things," she said. "First, turn that thing on." She waved the gun at his At Hand PC Plus.

"What for?"

She let out an exasperated sigh and grabbed one of the pillows from the bench seat. She held it against the gun.

"I don't have a silencer, but I've seen it done like this in the movies, and I'm willing to try it. Now, turn the fucking thing on. And take off your clothes."

His tan face was pale as he followed her orders. When he was down to his briefs she started questioning him.

"Who are you?"

"Just a writer."

"Who is this Mr. Cooper? Is that your name?"

"Cooper?"

"Yes, Cooper. SFScooper."

"No. It's my profile."

"What does it mean?"

"San Francisco Scooper."

"Am I missing something?"

"From when I worked at the *San Francisco Examiner*. You know, scoop. Scooper. As in a reporter getting a scoop."

"I see. How stupid."

He made an angry face, formed a profanity.

"Ah, ah. No more potty mouth. I already saw what you sent my husband."

His not-so-great-in-person face registered understanding, how she'd figured him out. His shoulders slumped as he turned to check on the At Hand PC Plus. His ass was flabby, and the sight of him held none of the virtual attraction she'd previously felt. Or thought she'd felt. That first, tantalizing photo he'd sent was obviously a fake. Of course the fact that he was a liar and probably a thief helped make him less attractive too.

"What's your real name?"

"Joshua."

"All of it."

"Ellis. Joshua Ellis."

She thought for a moment. "Why do I vaguely know your name?"

"Because your husband fucked me. He was going to hire me to coauthor his autobiography, but then he changed his mind. So I was getting back at him."

"Through me."

"Hey, I lost my job because of it."

"Doesn't sound like you much cared for it anyway, budding novelist that you are."

"That part's true, at least."

"Good for you. But your memory of me, at least whatever you have left of it, we're going to erase."

"I was only kidding. You're not really in the book."

"I'm not talking about the book," she said. She smirked when he cupped his hands over his privates. "So shy all of a sudden. Well, let's get this over with."

He looked at her, not knowing what to expect next.

"Shoot yourself," she said calmly.

"Greta, wait." His voice cracked.

"I don't mean with the gun, you idiot. With your camera. Full frontal, with your face please. Give me a few. And grab yourself in a couple of them."

He spent the next five minutes pleading with her not to make him do it. She showed him that the gun was loaded and the safety was off. Her red hair had been blown wild by the wind on deck, and he didn't need further convincing. He took four photos in all, and she asked him to put them on a disk for her.

"I only have Zips," he said.

"I'm easy. And while you're at it you'd better bring out all your backups too."

He did as he was told, withdrawing a pile of Zip disks. He handed them to her, along with the one containing his new pictures.

"Good. Now, stand over there."

She waved the gun and he begged her not to shoot. She kept the muzzle pointed at him while she quickly checked the fore and aft windows to see if anyone outside would hear.

She came forward with the pistol extended in her left hand, while in her right she held the pillow.

He raised his hands protectively and started to cry as a stream of urine rained all over the freshly shampooed cabin rug.

She shook her head disapprovingly. "That's gonna cost you," she said.

She pressed the gun into the pillow and fired three times, astonished by how quickly and quietly the whole ugly affair terminated.

"Ladies and gentlemen, please," William Harrell shouted to the enraged audience. "Please take your seats."

It was no use. They were out of control, screaming at him with shaking fists. There was no way to get through to them. He started back to the podium and shouted for the production assistant to kill the houselights.

The entire theater went pitch black and suddenly the noise was cut in half. A second later a spotlight snapped on and focused on the curtains at center stage. The crowd instantly quieted as the curtains parted.

Out strolled Peter Jones.

The crowd went wild, but this time with cheers and applause and whistles, a wave of excitement that carried on for a full five minutes, with Peter unable to do anything but stand there and smile. It was the greatest welcome he'd ever received, and he told them so when they calmed down enough to let him speak.

His voice was shaky with emotion, and the audience remained absolutely silent as he explained everything. "Today I've

become the first new employee of Via as a subsidiary of ICP, and I've got to admit, I never thought I'd wind up working in this company." There was quick laughter punctuated with random boos.

"When I left Via," he continued, "I found a few new friends, and we started working on a new kind of handheld computer, unlike anything ever invented. A few months ago we were contacted by William Harrell, who was interested in what we'd developed. We decided to let him have a look, and he loved it," Peter said. "ICP then became a silent partner in our product, which I'll show you in a moment. When the boards of directors at Via and ICP decided to merge, William asked if I'd like to come back to put the Via label on our new invention. We haggled over a few small details, but ultimately I decided it was the right thing to do."

He drew his palms together and smiled with evident pride. "And now, I'd like to show you Via's newest product, the In Hand PC."

He reached into his back pocket and withdrew the wallet-size, leather-clad device. The crowd rose to its feet and cheered, and a minute later Peter began a demonstration of the device using a bigger, less-refined version. His actions were displayed on two huge overhead screens. He promised the final In Hand PC would look like the smooth wallet-size device he'd first held up.

He pressed the side of the In Hand and spoke: "Pip, create E-mail."

The In Hand said: *"To whom?"*

The crowd gasped and then instantly quieted.

"To William."

*"William Harrell or William Shakespeare?"* the In Hand said.

"William Harrell," Peter said.

On the large screen, the audience watched as the In Hand filled in the To, From, and Date fields. It asked Peter to say the subject of the E-mail. "The deal," he said, then proceeded to write a short message on the unit's screen, congratulating William on

today's announcement. The audience marveled at the device's accuracy. There wasn't a single interpretation error, no "there" for "their" nor "cat" for "cap."

Peter withdrew a small lid from his back pocket and turned it around to reveal a tiny keyboard. He snapped it onto the unit and finished his message by tapping out his thanks. "This is for all those holdouts who insist they want a keyboard," he said. "Or a wireless digital phone," he added, and the audience went nuts when he punched in the phone number of a local pizza shop. A moment later a voice came on the line and asked him what kind of pizza he wanted. "Sorry, wrong number," he said, and hung up to riotous laughter.

"As you can see, there's a slot for an optional wireless modem and phone card." He pressed the Listen button. "Pip, please send now." The device dialed up the Net and fired off the E-mail message.

*"Message sent,"* the In Hand said. The crowd loved it, and Peter proceeded to show off more of the device's features, including its bantam Web browser, note taker, contact and schedule program, and voice recorder capability.

He signaled backstage, and a table was rolled out bearing At Hand PCs and an assortment of PCSoft-compatible clones. He pointed out a small optional infrared box that attached to the desktop computers to wirelessly beam information between it and the In Hand. And finally, he told the audience that he had saved the best for last.

"First, all of the In Hand's functionality will be available in the next version of the At Hand, so fans of our existing devices can enjoy all of the In Hand PC's same advanced features. Second, ICP will give every In Hand buyer a free year of access to its Net service, which is the largest in the world." He paused, pulled the In Hand PC model from his back pocket once more, and snatched out three crisp hundreds from its side flap. He held up the cash for

everyone to see. "And third, we're gonna sell this little wonder for just three hundred bucks."

The crowd rose to its feet and gave Peter a five-minute standing ovation, during which he waved for Byron, Ivy Green, and Isle to join him onstage. He introduced the trio, and held up the baby Isle so the camera could get a nice close-up of her adorable, bewildered face. Peter then turned the stage back over to William Harrell, who was greeted this time with warm cheers.

For the next half hour he flashed charts and projections and schedules, as well as the company's new organizational chart, which showed him as the company's acting chief executive officer. Peter Jones once again held the position of chairman of the board.

William Harrell concluded by reporting that Matthew Locke had chosen to resign, for personal reasons.

Greta climbed back into the limousine and calmly asked the chauffeur to drive her to the Golden Gate Bridge.

Pulling away from the lot, she looked back at the man formerly known as Gregor as he reemerged from below deck.

She'd asked him why he'd used such a silly name, and he said it was the name of the protagonist in Kafka's "Metamorphosis."

She admitted she wasn't much of a reader, then remarked that his little blackmail scheme hadn't quite transformed him the way he'd imagined. She asked what he'd planned to do with her if she hadn't caught him.

He showed her the dinghy on deck, and said he'd intended to play along with the farce until they'd reached Mexico's Baja coast. At which point he would be free, and she would be cast overboard in the little rubber raft—close enough to shore, and with provisions, of course.

He stood now on the deck, shaking his fist at her and flinging handfuls of Monopoly money and discarded gloves in the air. She'd

of course left the real thing at home, and as for the hundred or so pairs of gloves, she wouldn't be needing those anymore. At least she had him to thank for that, for helping her overcome her fear of showing her hands as they were. She got to her knees and moved closer to the limo's back window to give him a special good-bye. She turned her hand around and waggled her four fingers, then folded down all but the middle one, which she held up until she could no longer see him.

She turned around and settled back into the seat, looking at his destroyed At Hand PC Plus on the seat beside her. She'd shot it twice, to be sure he would never have access to his dirty pictures again, and she'd fired a third bullet through his stack of backup Zip disks. She'd meant to leave the whole mess for him to remember her by, but then he got wise and stupidly blurted out that he knew ways to extract the information from even the most damaged disks.

She pointed out there were still a few bullets left, and he backed off when she collected the computer and disks and departed. She doubted she would hear from him again.

As they approached the Golden Gate Bridge the chauffeur asked if they were going to Sausalito. Just the bridge, she said mysteriously as the driver started over it.

Upon reaching the mid span she asked the driver to pull over. He said he couldn't, that it was illegal to stop on the bridge.

She drew out the gun and asked again, and the car came to a smooth stop in the right lane, facing the city. It was the side where almost all jumpers chose to leave the world, giving the city one last look at them before the end, she supposed. She didn't share in the same sentiment—she would have actually preferred the other side, facing the Pacific Ocean; however, she wanted to just get it over with, so the city side would have to do.

Traffic started to clog behind the limo, and cars horns honked noisily. She climbed out with the At Hand PC Plus and the backup

Zip disk, checking her slicker pocket to make sure she still had the disk containing Gregor's nude photos.

She walked over to the rail and leaned out, ignoring a jogger who shouted to watch where she was going. She withdrew the gun and a young man on a mountain bike suddenly screeched to a stop and begged the woman with the crazily blowing red hair to put the gun down, that no matter how bad things seemed it would be all right, everything would be all right.

Greta turned to the rider and calmly agreed, that everything would be fine, then leaned out over the rail and flung the bulleted At Hand PC Plus and Zip disks over the side. The handgun followed right behind them.

She brushed her hands together, climbed back into the limousine, and asked the stunned driver to take her home.

And saying so finally brought the tears she'd kept at bay through the entire insane ordeal. She lay across the soft limo seat and cried the whole way back.

Not because of the make-believe Gregor and her unrealized flight of fantasy. But because it was really what she wanted, to just be home, regardless of how wrong it felt.

Matthew Locke sat at the breakfast table with his head in his hands. It was over. His work. His career. His marriage. He'd lost it all.

He rubbed his wet face and nose on his sleeve and made a retching noise when he looked at the vulgar color-printed picture of his wife, wearing a wanton grin and little else. The sender promised there were more where this one came from, and threatened to distribute them freely over the Net if he didn't pull out of his autobiography book deal at once. Which after today didn't matter anymore anyway. That, along with everything else he'd worked for, was history. He looked at the first draft of the completed manuscript lying on the table and thought of all the talk that had gone into it. Beside it were two documents. One was his "package," the other the lawsuit.

Three hours ago he'd been on top of the world. He should have known something was up when he spotted Peter Jones's Z3 in the parking lot of the restaurant where William had asked to meet him. He hadn't immediately connected the two. It wasn't until he went inside that he saw them sitting together, along with Hank

Towers, and an older man who looked remotely familiar. Matthew didn't catch the older man's name as he excused himself and said their business didn't concern him.

Hank Towers invited Matthew to sit down, and he felt Peter Jones's eyes on him, but he refused to look at anyone but Hank. There was obviously some mistake, and he said as much.

Towers addressed him calmly and with sympathy. "We've got a couple of changes in today's program, Matthew."

Matthew balked with indignation and demanded to know what was going on. Diners at nearby tables could not help but stare. Many of them were Via employees, which Hank graciously pointed out, asking Matthew not to make things more difficult than they already were.

Matthew went on sputtering questions without waiting for answers. He pointed an accusing finger at William and threatened revenge. Eventually he ran out of breath.

Hank extracted two documents from his jacket. He placed the first one in front of Matthew, who blinked when he saw the word "severance." He scanned the page quickly, shaking his head at the part about taking only a fraction of his granted stock options. Hank indicated the big X at the bottom, and asked him to sign it.

"I won't be driven out!" Matthew shouted.

Hank said he had no choice. The board had voted, and the deal was done. Before Matthew could protest again, Hank produced the second document. This one was the kicker, and it totally floored him.

He sat there for what felt like a very long time, and eventually Hank asked that he try to pull himself together.

Matthew lifted his head and finally looked at Peter, who stared back with no emotion in his eyes. How, Matthew wondered, could he just sit there like that? His voice was a disbelieving rasp when he finally addressed the younger man.

"Why? Why didn't you just go along with me back when I first started thinking in this direction? It would have been the same, the same outcome. Why, Peter?"

Peter shook his head. "Sorry, Matthew. But it was never that simple. . . ."

But it could be now, Matthew thought, sitting at the breakfast table and staring at his severance package agreement letter—and the second document they'd handed him, asserting he'd sexually harassed Laurence Merrill.

He was not a crying man, and he didn't cry now. The wetness around his eyes had come from sweat rather than tears. He was sweating all over, his palms especially, coating the gold band he held in one closed fist.

He was completely spent, used up. Alone. There was no one for him now, he thought. He'd lost his wife, too. Poor Greta. He'd destroyed her that night of the accident, on the yacht. He squeezed his fist tighter around Greta's wedding band. He'd furtively rescued it from the vessel's shifting deck in the middle of the chaos, and had kept it hidden in his briefcase ever since.

Greta. She was the only person who'd ever truly adored him, and he'd driven her away, into whatever it was she'd found to replace him, online sex and pictures.

His dream had become a nightmare. He wondered how to do it, which way was best. He was sure he had a gun somewhere in the house. Maybe Greta had left some pills in the cabinet upstairs. Another option was the damn car in the garage. He could do that, or maybe drive it off the highway. He folded his arms and lowered his head, considered his options.

Sometime later he awoke to the sound of the doorbell. "Leave me alone!" he screamed, certain the press had heard the news and

was now scaling the gate in hopes of snapping off some pictures of the stunned ex-everything.

But it wasn't the press, his housekeeper Dolores informed him.

He leaped up from his chair, sending it sprawling. As Matthew rushed down the foyer his resolve finally broke and the tears streamed down his face.

He shot back the dead bolt and swung open the door for his sobbing, soaking wet Greta.

She stood helplessly before him and he reached out and grabbed her left wrist and drew her back inside, fumbling with her hand and the moistened gold band until it was firmly seated around her middle finger.

He kicked the door shut and they fell into each other's arms. They remained like that for a very long time.

## >CHAPTER 24

Peter sat on the rug with his legs crossed, Isle in a bundle beside him. Together they listened to Kate's soothing voice mingling with the quiet rain outside.

Ivy strolled into the room, humming softly to the music. "She asleep?"

"Not quite," Peter said. "I think she's sort of wired. She's had a busy day. You too."

"You three," Ivy said, ruffling his hair.

Peter stood up. "Thanks for letting her stay here tonight. I'll bring her over tomorrow afternoon, if that's cool."

"Sure. That was the agreement."

"Thanks."

He'd offered to marry her, but she had declined. It wasn't what either of them wanted, and they both knew it. In the out-of-court settlement, Peter had agreed to child support payments, and Ivy had granted him liberal visitation rights.

For the rights to her ISLE software ICP paid Ivy two million dollars, plus royalties.

They hugged, and she saw herself out.

Peter returned to Isle and she stirred. He took her in his arms. "You miss Grandma Gracie and Grandpa Byron already?" he said, pretending she understood every word. He kissed her forehead. "Me too."

Byron and Grace had left a few hours earlier to return to Maine. They would be back in a few weeks to choose a vacation home in the area, where they would reside for however long Byron chose to stay on with the project.

Peter's own home suddenly felt like it used to, before Isle. Quiet and empty. Yet at the same time it was more full of life than ever. But this, he could not help but think, was only temporary.

The next song started, and he picked up the remote to bump up the volume a few notches. Kate's lovely voice made him feel both happy and sad. He put his finger in Isle's hand and she squeezed it.

"When you're a little older," he whispered, "I'm going to teach you how to sing just like that."

"And who's going to teach you?" Kate's voice said from behind.

He spun around.

"Kate," he said with unrestrained shock.

"I let myself in," Kate said, twirling a key on her finger. She was dressed in a raincoat and carried a large bag over one shoulder. Her smile was tentative.

She dropped the bag on the floor and made her way into the room, shrugging out of her wet coat. He rose with Isle in his hands.

"I can't believe it's you." His voice was trembling.

She bent with her hands on her knees and smiled brightly at Isle.

"Look at you, little girl. What a pretty baby you are." She looked up at Peter. "Come on, what kind of welcome is that? I thought you'd be happy to see me."

"Are you kidding? I am, I am." He touched her arm. "I just can't believe you're really here. I mean, it's been forever."

She smiled, but he couldn't read her expression.

"Congratulations," she said, drawing out a copy of the *San Francisco Examiner.* "And to you too," she said, waving the front page of the business section at Isle. Beneath the headline was a photo of Peter with Isle in his arms, flanked by Byron and Ivy.

"Back to Via," Kate remarked. "Sure surprised me."

"Me too, more than you can imagine."

Kate held out her hands. "May I?"

"Yes, of course." He gently placed Isle in her arms. "Be careful, you have to support her head." He moved Kate's hand so that her palm cradled Isle's head. "That's right." He left his hand in place for a moment before letting her hold Isle by herself. He watched with pride and satisfaction as she gently rocked the baby in her arms. His throat tightened.

Kate moved over to the sofa and sat down, humming softly to the baby in her lap. She glanced up at Peter.

"So, is it true?"

"Is what true?" Peter said, seating himself beside her.

She scanned the body of the news story. "Ah, here it is. Quote: 'I'm not going to be working like I used to. There are more important things in my life now.' End quote."

"Totally," he said.

"What about Ivy?"

He explained the arrangement they'd made and her deal with ICP.

"Good for her," Kate said. "She's sure earned it."

Peter agreed, and he sat there quiet for a while, unsure how to say what he wanted to say. Finally he just came right out with it.

"What about us, Kate? You. I mean, do you think I deserve you? Is there any way I can earn you back?"

She smiled tenderly and took his hand in hers and gently

placed it beneath Isle's head, the way he'd shown her. They sat without another word for a long time, adjusting to the feeling of being so close again after so long apart.

"I'm so scared, Kate."

"Of what?"

He struggled to find his voice, and she settled a reassuring hand on the back of his neck.

"This. The future." He inhaled a deep breath and looked her in the eye. "Remember when you came to take me to Maine? How you told me that when you create something great, no one can ever take it away? How it only gets better and better?"

She nodded with a smile, massaging his neck encouragingly.

"That's what scares me."

"But you've done it, Peter. You're back."

He shook his head in frustration. "No, I mean us. We had something great, but it went away. I want it back, but I'm afraid you don't."

"But I do, Peter. I do."

He closed his eyes and touched his forehead to hers, drew her closer.

"Say it for me again," he whispered. "But this time, make it a vow."

"I do," Kate said emphatically. "I do!"

They kissed.